Spiralling
solo

I0721240

Armour

MICHELLE DENNIS EVANS

Spiralling Solo
© Michelle Dennis Evans 2025

Published by Armour Books
P. O. Box 492, Corinda QLD 4075

Cover Images: Nixprint | Baby B, Etsy;
cove703, K for Kreative | Creative Fabrica
Spirals: rarinlada | Creative Fabrica
Cover and Interior Design and Typeset by Beckon Creative

ISBN: 978-1-923533-07-3

 A catalogue record for this
book is available from the
National Library of Australia

This book is a work of fiction set in Australia and any resemblance to persons, living or dead, or places, events or locales is purely coincidental. The characters are productions of the author's imagination and used fictitiously.

Note: 16+ Young Adult Reading Material. Australian spelling and grammar conventions are used throughout this book.

All rights reserved. No part of this publication may be reproduced, stored in, or introduced into a retrieval system, or transmitted, in any form, or by any means (electronic, mechanical, photocopying, recording or otherwise) without the prior written permission of the publisher.

Spiralling solo

MICHELLE DENNIS EVANS

Contents

Chapter One

ᏚTEPHANIE

A knock at the door
Two police officers
Standing tall
Blurting news
Devastating news
News that should
have brought closure.
But instead
brought more confusion.
She'd loved him
He'd loved her
He'd led her down paths
she'd never taken.
It got messy

It had to end.
Past tense
Past life.
And now
in her arms
the remnant.
A fatherless burden
she'll carry forever.

$\mathscr{S}$TEPHANIE

THE CLANG ECHOED DOWN the driveway.

'She's not happy.' Gravel crunched under Steph's feet as she pushed the stroller towards the apartment. 'You know how I can tell? She only bangs the dishes when she's not happy.'

'You talking to me?'

Steph checked her surroundings. *I must look an absolute idiot talking to myself.* This mum business had so many disadvantages.

'Yo, in here.' The male voice drew her attention to the window of the apartment next-door.

'Oh, no. I was just talking to …' She pointed to the pram. She'd become one of those crazy mums, talking to the air, hoping her daughter was listening. Whatever. It beat letting the voices in her head take over.

'I'm your new neighbour.' He gave her the thumbs up.

'Welcome.' Steph nodded and rushed past. The neighbouring apartment had a revolving door. Tenants came and went more often than the moon orbited the earth. Meet-and-greet could wait. Lola needed a nappy change.

Steph pushed her door open wide enough to fit the stroller through. 'Hi.'

Tabbie glanced up from the sink. 'Steph—'

'I know, I know, it's my turn. Leave it. I'll get to it.'

Tabbie raised her eyebrows and continued scrubbing a plate.

'We needed milk, and Lola needed to get her crankies out.' Steph pulled the baby from the stroller. 'Thought I'd pop out and let you have a sleep-in. Did she wake you? She was impossible, super grumpy. I expected you'd head straight to the pool. I was going to clean up once I settled Lola down.' *Well, I kind of intended to get it done at some stage today.*

'Don't worry. I'm not finished.' Tabbie dried her hands. 'You're welcome to take over.'

'I'll just change Lola's nappy first.' Steph swung Lola onto her other hip and took her into the bedroom.

Chapter Two

TABBIE

TABBIE RETURNED TO THE SINK. Steph's idea of getting it done happened when no crockery or cutlery was left in the cupboard. *Yep, it's time to move back home.*

'I said I'll finish out there,' Steph called.

Tabbie shrugged, finished the dishes, then wiped the benches spotless.

'Really, I said—' Steph reappeared.

'I've left the bin for you.' Tabbie attempted to sweeten her voice as she threw the cloth into the sink.

'Okay. Can you please take her? She won't let me put her down.' Steph passed Lola to Tabbie.

Lola whined and wriggled and watched her mum heading for the bathroom. Tabbie could usually calm her down, but today the whinging escalated into a scream. 'Shh. Shh.' She rubbed Lola's back. 'Steph, is she hungry?'

'She doesn't give me much of a break at the moment.' Steph raced back, chased by the echo of the toilet flushing.

'True, and I'm not her favourite aunty today.' Tabbie handed Lola back, thankful she wasn't a mother yet. 'You'll be right, if I go for a swim?'

'Of course.' Steph paused. 'Hey, did you wash her bottle?'

Tabbie shook her head. Steph rushed to the kitchen.

'Steph!'

'How did I forget that?' Tears formed in Steph's eyes. 'Sorry, Lola.'

'Here, I'll get her a bottle before I go.'

'Sorry.'

'It's okay.' Tabbie smiled to push away the niggly annoyance. After prepping the bottle, Tabbie pulled her shoes on and grabbed her backpack. She jogged out, heading for the pool but, as she got there, she wanted to keep running. Wanted to push herself faster, further. She needed to get fitter. She stopped when her chest burned, and checked her surroundings, heaving in air. *Optimum fitness is the new black, isn't it?* That was her motivation, but she didn't feel motivated.

She grabbed her water bottle from her backpack, drank half, then threw her backpack over her shoulders along with her negative thoughts. She retraced her steps. Danny. He took up ninety-five percent of her thought time. His words replayed in her mind: *It'll only be a year.*

She'd fallen a sweet long-distance relationship with him, sending and receiving regular sweet emails. But. That. Stopped.

Abruptly.

Had he even read her last messages? He'd said they were moving to a remote village, but it'd been months since she'd heard from him. Five, to be exact. Steph told her to give up, but he continued to invade her thoughts. Her heart hurt. A dull ache that all the running in the world wasn't going to soothe.

Soon she'd be smack-bang back into domestic life. *Steph's helper. Lola's other mother.* She wanted to be an aunty, not the other mother.

Would moving home mean she could revert to her old resolve and stop focusing on boys? *And let go of Danny?* Maybe it was time to focus on herself for a while. But wasn't life meant to be about others?

Tabbie stopped and contemplated the tall eucalyptus trees, in awe of their greatness. It was time to look to the future. She breathed in the fresh summer air. Just as the leaves would soon fall with autumn, change was imminent.

School. She needed to increase her average. Since pouring all her energy into helping Steph or lost in a fantasy thinking about Danny, she'd barely passed.

Tabbie wanted to live again. She headed home. Steph's home. Her best friend. The elegant and sophisticated friend who was all the things Tabbie had thought she wanted to be until Steph's life derailed. Lately, their friendship seemed confused.

The gravel rolled under her feet as she reached their outdated apartment block. The sun threw dark shadows as it peeked through the lone tree at the end of the driveway. When she opened the flimsy screen door, another flake of paint fell from the doorframe.

'Hi, honey. I'm home,' Tabbie called her regular greeting. 'Steph?' Silence.

Tabbie closed the door quietly and checked Steph's room. Lola slept in the cot. She heard the pipes rattle and the water flow in the shower.

Steph hadn't finished the kitchen. *Urgh!* The bin overflowed. Her parents were right. She should never have stayed this long.

Tabbie went to her room, closed the door and threw her backpack onto her bed. At her feet lay the tattered email she'd printed off. Danny's last words to her. She scrunched it into a ball and threw it in the bin. She'd already read it a trillion times. She needed a shower. Hopefully, Steph wouldn't take too long.

Half an hour later with her hair wrapped in a towel, Tabbie returned to her room and retrieved the scrunched paper ball from the bin. The stench from the kitchen followed her. 'Steph, the rubbish,' she called in a soft voice, hoping not to wake Lola.

'Onto it,' Steph whispered.

Doesn't sound like it. Tabbie lay on her bed. She needed to read Danny's last email one more time before closing that chapter of her life.

Hey Tabbie, I wish I was writing to tell you we're on our way home, but it's kind of the opposite. Mum and Dad accepted an invitation to move to another village and want me to stay with them. It's remote. Really remote, and we won't have much access to the outside world.

The cool thing is we've had heaps of breakthroughs with the programs we've been running here. That's why they want us to move into the village where the needs are greater.

I talked to Mum and Dad about coming home and going to boarding school, but they reckon I'm a good influence on the kids because I sit down and do my schoolwork with them. There aren't many kids my age still at school here. Most of the families need them to leave school and work.

Anyway, you know I love you and think of you often.

Love, Danny. x

That and then months of silence. *Where is he?*

Stupid. She'd been certain he was her forever man, who'd return so they could live happily ever after.

Stupid. She squeezed the paper back into a ball and threw it across her room. It had been fun to have some independence, but she'd had enough of babysitting. And it wasn't only Lola. She'd been pretty much babysitting Steph as well. Her best friend was only ever one bad decision away from slipping back into her old ways.

Her thoughts jumped to Danny in Uganda as she picked up the rubbish, carrying it to the outside bin. She'd put it down to experience. Teen romances rarely went further. Her heart pinched in her chest.

'Looks like I won't get anything done again today.' Steph bounced Lola on her hip as Tabbie returned.

'I thought she was asleep.'

'Yep, from out of it to screaming in seconds.'

Lola sobbed and hiccupped. Tabbie shrugged and sat on the lounge. She knew being a mum was tough on Steph. But was she helping or hindering Steph by staying? She'd moved in to help—babysitting to give her time out and distracting her through her alcohol cravings. Well, except for that time when she came home blind drunk. Steph relied on her too much. Yes, it was time to go home. Steph would be okay. She'd have to be.

Spiralling Solo

Chapter Three

$\mathcal{S}$TEPHANIE

STEPH LOOKED INTO LOLA'S deep brown eyes—the eyes that reminded her every day of Jason, her first love. Though her heart didn't feel as shattered as it had a year ago, a dull ache often returned. Lola would never meet her father. She sat on the floor and brushed fine wisps of dark blonde hair out of Lola's eyes. 'You know, some days I still expect Jason to come knocking on the door.'

'Woah, where'd that thought come from?' Tabbie slid off the couch to sit with them. 'Didn't the police say he was definitely in that inferno?'

'Yeah. It's just… every time I look at Lola, I see him in her eyes. And I guess because I didn't go and identify him, there's a possibility…' Stephanie blinked away the image of the police officer delivering the bad news just a month ago.

'Maybe you should have gone to see for yourself. For closure.' Tabbie grabbed the remote control and flicked through the channels.

Steph shivered at the thought of Jason's charred body. No, she'd rather remember him alive. Even though it ended so ugly. She hated that she'd given in to him so easily. He'd filled the fridge with cheap bubbly, organised her fake ID, pushed her into taking drugs. But she hadn't said no. She'd been the one to open the fridge when he wasn't around. She'd been the one who drank to numb herself.

They'd had good times. Lots of them. But the memories that hurt her most, that continued to plague her, were how he'd pushed and shoved her in those last months, and the final incident on the stairs. Her insides hurt just thinking about it.

Lola reached out to Tabbie.

'Finally.' Steph stretched and sat up straight.

'Oh, now you want me.' Tabbie tickled Lola. 'You must be giving your mummy strong muscles, making her carry you around so much.'

Steph shrugged and glanced at her flabby arms and legs. She hated her out-of-condition mummy body compared to her taut dancing physique. She'd dreamed of becoming a professional dancer, but now there were too many bad memories of dancing and Jason tangled together. He'd only called her once after she'd left rehab to tell her someone had shot him, but he'd survived. How did she get mixed up with that kind of crowd?

Stephanie watched Lola with Tabbie. Lola was a survivor too. She was a mini-Jason. A knot formed in her stomach as his accusations replayed in her head. *Who've you been with behind my back?*

'Steph.' Tabbie interrupted her thoughts. 'You know how Mum said it's time for me to move home?'

'Yeah.'

'Well...' Tabbie bounced Lola on her knee. 'With Year Twelve being so intense… it might be a good idea. For both of us. You can come with me.'

'Of course.' Steph shook her head. 'Yes, I agree. It's best for you. But Tabbie, I can't.' Lola cried and reached out for her. 'That didn't last long.' Steph stood and took Lola. 'I put your family through so much when I was living there. I couldn't put them through more. Having you here has been great, but you need to go home. I get it.'

'I don't want to leave you paying my half of the rent. Perhaps you could get another flatmate or ask Jason's parents for support. Maybe he had life insurance.'

'Don't worry. I'll be fine.' There might be some bonuses living alone, without Tabbie watching her every move. She could relax a little. Start dating again. But paying rent on her own was going to prove difficult.

'I'll still be nearby. It's not like we won't chat every day or anything.'

Stephanie walked down the hallway, Lola still whinging. *Happy thoughts. Smile. Don't let Tabbie see any sign of worry.*

'I mean, the bus ride is only twenty minutes. In an emergency, Mum could drive me here in ten minutes. We'll still hang out heaps.'

'Are you trying to talk yourself into it being okay?' Steph turned. 'Or don't you think I'll cope without you?'

'I'd love to stay here. But I'm torn. I want to be sure you'll be okay.' Tabbie stood and moved towards her. 'But …'

'What's your biggest but?' Steph blinked away the threatening tears and forced a smile before brushing past Tabbie. *Maybe she's right. Maybe I won't cope on my own.*

'I have one year left of school. I need to do well to get into uni.' Tabbie's voice seemed strained.

'Right. So move home, get great results and be the big career woman you've dreamed of. I've put up with all your lovesickness for the past year. Either find him and jump his bones or get over him.'

Tabbie fake-laughed. Pink crept into her cheeks. 'If only he still wanted me, it might be an option.' She swiped away tears with the back of her hand.

'I knew you wanted to jump him.'

'Stop it.' Tabbie's cheeks turned fire-engine red. 'You also know I'm going to wait until I'm married.'

'Yeah, yeah, I know. Miss Goody-Two-Shoes Christian, no sex before marriage. I'm sure he'll come back eventually. But stop wasting your time on him. You might be missing Mr Right while you're waiting for Mr Silent.' Steph grabbed a tissue from the box and handed it to Tabbie.

'But —'

'Until you see him and can't keep your hands off him.'

'Stop!' Tabbie's eyes widened. 'I'm meant to be getting over him.'

'You will…' Steph took a deep breath. 'So, when are you moving out?'

'School starts in a few weeks, so I guess sometime before then.' Tabbie grabbed her house keys. 'I'm heading over to and see Mum and Dad now.'

'No worries. See you when you get back.'

Tabbie dipped her chin. 'You'd tell me if you weren't okay with this?'

'Seriously. I'm fine. Lola and I will be fine. Now go!' Steph heard the clunk of the washing machine finishing and rushed towards it, pushing away the unease squeezing her chest.

Chapter Four

TABBIE

TABBIE REPLAYED THE CONVERSATION she'd just had. Steph had seen her as Miss Goody-Two-Shoes for years. Tabbie's cheeks heated. She'd be lying if she said she'd never dreamed of sharing a bed with Danny. Marrying him. Starting a family with him. She shook her head. It was time to get over Danny and move on. She needed to set her mind on studying to pick up her average, or no university would even look at her.

The Danny she thought she knew would never leave her hanging in limbo without an explanation. But did she really know him? Her church friends had encouraged her to spend time getting to know him when he came back. That would imply she didn't really know him. Would Danny in the flesh be different to their online conversations?

Leaving the path, she turned towards her parents' front door, sick of replaying the same stories in her mind. She needed to change her mental mini-movies.

'Hello, love.' Her mother wrapped her in a warm hug. 'I wasn't expecting you.'

'Sorry I didn't call first.' Tabbie dropped her backpack on the floor.

'No need to call. You know that.'

'I told Steph I'm moving home.'

'Great. I'm so glad you've let her know. Will she move here with you?' Her mother headed to the kitchen.

'Well… no.' Tabbie followed and filled a glass with cold water.

'I see.' Mum wiped the benches. 'How's she going to afford the apartment on her own?'

'I don't know.'

'I'll have a chat with her to see if I can convince her to come here. I don't understand why she's against the idea.'

'You know Steph. She doesn't want to burden you.' Tabbie poured herself another glass of water. 'There's something I was hoping to talk to you about.'

'Hmm?' Her mother stopped wiping and looked at her.

'I want to go to uni.'

'Yes. That's always been the plan, hasn't it?' Mum raised her eyebrows.

'My results last year weren't high enough to get in. I might have left it too late.'

'Perhaps a meeting with the school?' Mum set the jug to boil and walked towards the door. 'Could you make us a cuppa, please, love?'

No, I don't want a meeting. Self-discipline and focus. That's what I need. She jiggled the tea bags and breathed in the familiar scent until the water was dark. If she studied every afternoon, hopefully she'd be able to get through.

Tabbie's father cleared his throat as he walked in.

'Would you like a cuppa, Dad?' Tabbie pulled another mug off the shelf.

'That would be great.' He wrapped his arms around her in a hug. 'Your mother tells me you have big plans.'

 Spiralling Solo

'Yeah, hopefully.' She leaned towards him, enjoying the security his hugs had always given her. 'I'm scared I've left it too late, but I want to go to uni…' *Now I don't have Danny to think about.*

'I'm thrilled you've made this decision.' He passed her a bundle of papers.

'What's all this?'

'Information about a few universities. I had a feeling you hadn't looked into them.'

She flicked through the huge pile. *Has he collected something from every uni and college in the country?*

'Your mother mentioned Steph is going to have a go on her own. It's well past time for you to move home, but I'm concerned about her.'

'She said she'd be fine.' Tabbie wanted to believe her. Plus their friendship could do with some space. 'Am I doing the wrong thing?'

'No, you're absolutely doing the right thing.' Mum came back into the room. 'Love, it was never meant to be permanent. You've spent a whole year keeping her on the straight and narrow, and look where it's got you.'

'Your mother's right. Your grades have suffered because of your kindness. Steph knows we're here for her. The plan was for you to only be there until Lola was born.'

Her parents had a point, but letting Stephanie make more mistakes twisted her stomach into a knot. She'd made so many already.

'When should we pick up your things?' Dad asked.

'In the next few days.' She handed her father a mug filled with tea.

'How about this weekend?'

Tabbie nodded. *Bittersweet.* The word that came to mind as a warm sense of calm settled in her. She didn't want Steph to stuff up again. She didn't want to 'get over' Danny. But home was warm and comfortable and safe. She went upstairs to prepare her bedroom for her return. When she finished, she lay on the floor and dreamed. Just one more time, then she'd let him go.

In her small, shabby room back at Steph's, Tabbie straightened out the scrunched-up ball of paper to read it one last time. Recognising her habit, she ripped it into shreds and threw it in the bin. *Habit broken*. She'd loved hearing about Danny's missionary adventures and yearned to be on the mission field herself, with or without him. But first she needed to clear her mind and get some useful qualifications.

She opened a notebook to get her thoughts out of her mind and onto paper.

> Sweet oh so sweet,
> Perhaps too innocent,
> Perhaps too naïve,
> Why didn't our time start earlier?
> Why did it end before it began?
> The joy of emails now ripped and thrown away,
> The dreams of marriage dumped like a wave in a cyclone.

Tears slipped over her lashes. But it felt good. She dropped the notebook on her bed and began to pack her belongings into a box.

It was just a new chapter in her life. It wasn't like she was joining the army or anything. She'd still be close if ever Steph needed her. But her father's concerned voice played on repeat in her mind.

$\mathcal{S}$TEPHANIE

The next day, Stephanie's insides churned like a wild ocean. *What if I'm not okay?* She had to think of Lola now too, not just herself. *What if I completely stuff up again because Tabbie isn't here?*

Tabbie had taken off for a run. It seemed like she ran or swam every time Lola was cranky. Maybe the whole thing about university was just an excuse. Maybe Tabbie just wanted to get away. Maybe Tabbie was sick of sharing a house with a baby.

Steph watched the shadows grow long through the window. Oh, how she wished Tabbie would return to break the monotony of playing with the baby. It was going to be lonely without her around.

As familiar scuffing footsteps grew louder, Steph jumped to her feet and threw Lola onto her hip. She opened the door to greet Tabbie. 'Do you have to move back home?'

'You said you were okay with it.' Tabbie wiped the sweat from her brow with her forearm.

'You're right. Momentary lapse. I can't wait to have the bedroom to myself again. And I'm sure Lola will want some more room to play soon.'

'Yeah, you'll love it. And you won't miss me returning all sweaty after running.' Tabbie sniffed her armpit and laughed. 'Yep, I need a shower.'

Steph tried to push out something that resembled a laugh, but it came out all wrong and sounded like a groan.

'Are you okay?' Tabbie looked back as she reached the bathroom.

'Sure.' *I'll be fine. Eventually.*

'Okay. I need that shower. Let's chat later.'

'Sure.' *But what's there to talk about? Tabbie's moving out. End of story.*

The pipes knocked as they always did from the hot water in the shower. Stephanie slid Lola into her highchair and fed her some mashed pumpkin. Lola grabbed the spoon and flung the pumpkin onto the wall and floor. Then she put her fingers into the bowl and smeared the pumpkin through her hair. 'Oh, Lola! Now you need a bath, baby girl.' Stephanie left Lola strapped in the highchair and wiped up the mess. 'Are you finished in there?' she called to Tabbie.

The bathroom door creaked as it swung open. 'Yep, all done.'

Steph grabbed Lola and sat her on the bathroom floor while she ran the shower to fill the baby bath. 'I know you've outgrown it, but until you like showers this is all we have.'

'Were you talking to me?' Tabbie returned to the bathroom with her hair wrapped in a towel.

'No. Just telling Lola a bathtub would be handy, that's all.'

'You know the offer is open for you both to move in with us.'

Stephanie's heart thudded in her chest. *No, I can't. I'll be fine.* She could look after Lola without Tabbie's help. Couldn't she?

'Mum and Dad would love having you and Lola around.' Tabbie's voice had that too-confident-to-be-honest feel about it.

'You know I can't. Not after what I put them through.' *I can't turn back now. I have to keep moving forward in life.*

'Can't or won't?' Tabbie raised her eyebrows, turned and walked away.

Ouch. Tabbie always knew how to twist her words and make her double-guess her decisions. Trouble was, most of the time Tabbie ended up being right.

Steph sighed.

Chapter Five

STEPHANIE

STEPHANIE FELT THE WEIGHT fall on her shoulders with each box Tabbie piled against the wall. Tom and Francine knocked on the door before Steph had finished her coffee.

'Hi,' Steph greeted them. 'Tabbie's been awake for hours, throwing boxes around.'

'I guess you're always up early now with Lola,' Francine said. 'Now, where is that precious little girl of yours?'

'She's playing on the floor in my bedroom. It's a little crowded out here.'

'Let me get these out of your way.' Tom picked up a box and carried it outside. Francine headed for Steph's bedroom.

'I didn't realise I'd accumulated so much stuff here.' Tabbie burst from her room with a huge smile until she saw Steph's face. 'I could stay.'

'No. You need to go home. We'll miss you, but we'll be fine.'

'Is there anything you need?' Francine called, as she began cooing to Lola.

Money. Car. Licence. Job. Nanny. A father for Lola. 'No. I'll be fine.'

Tom returned for another box.

Francine came out of the bedroom. 'I'll be back to play soon,' she said to Lola. 'Let me help.' She heaved a box into her arms before following Tom.

A grizzly cry escaped Steph's bedroom. It hadn't even been a minute since Francine left, and Lola had somehow got herself stuck under the bed. Once Steph had settled her down, she sat on the floor to watch her play.

'I think we've got it all.' Tabbie threw her backpack over her shoulder. 'Ring or text if you need anything. I'll leave my keys on the bench.'

'You don't have to give them to me now.'

'I know, but I won't come over unless you're here, so I may as well leave them.'

'Yeah, I guess.' Stephanie bit her lip, willed the tears to dry up and searched for a happy thought.

'Lola, make sure you look after your mummy, okay?' Tabbie scooped the baby up and carried her to the now-bare second bedroom. 'Look at all this room for you to play.'

Steph followed, busying herself by pushing the cot into the room. 'I don't know how Lola will go in here all by herself.'

'If she doesn't like it, move her back in with you and turn this into a playroom.' Tabbie took Lola to the window and pointed at the birds in the tree. 'Try putting the cot here, so she can watch the birds and the trees.'

Stephanie looked out the window. 'More like fence and concrete.'

'That too. Maybe I could find some nice window stickers or something.'

Steph rushed back to her bedroom to pick up her buzzing mobile phone, swallowing the lump in her throat. She didn't even have money to make her daughter's room pretty.

Tabbie hovered in her peripheral view. Stephanie tapped her phone.

'It'll take a bit of time, but we'll all get used to this.' Tabbie bounced Lola on her hip.

'Yeah. I've got a text I have to reply to.' Stephanie let her hair fall over her eyes. She'd love freedom like Tabbie had. 'Have your parents already left?'

'Yeah, they texted from the front to say goodbye. They didn't want to leave the loaded ute on the driveway for too long. We'll be back for the desk. Call me if you need anything, okay?'

'Okay. See ya.' Steph bit her lip. She didn't want Tabbie to leave. *I won't survive on my own.* Her phone vibrated. Acting like it was an incoming call, she pulled it to her ear. 'Hi.' Stephanie gave Tabbie a wave before turning away.

The front door closed and Steph escaped her bedroom. Tabbie had gone. Her phone buzzed again. Another text from her sister. She'd deal with that when she had a clear mind.

At least she'd avoided an over-emotional teary goodbye. She was on the cusp of the rest of her life. A chill ran down her spine. *Tabbie's gone.*

*T*ABBIE

Tabbie rubbed her toes over the shiny drain at the pool where she'd tripped a couple of years ago. One of her many dumb moments, and she'd managed to do it right in front of a hot guy. *Danny.* She shook her head to stop thinking about him.

She stretched her ankle forwards and backwards. It finally felt strong again. More than a year had passed since she'd had any klutzy falls. Quitting dance and sticking with non-competitive swimming and running for exercise had been one of the best decisions she'd made. She jumped in, letting the water cool her skin and mind as she set off on her regular swim.

With each stroke, she thought about the last twelve months. Living with Steph had tested their friendship but, looking back, she was glad she'd been supportive. Sure, Stephanie had fallen off the rails a few times, but nothing like she'd done in the past.

With ten laps done, she dried off, pulled her clothes on and checked the time. She rushed outside to find the bus pulling into the bus stop. She ran to catch it. As she reached the bus, she glanced through the window. *Danny?*

No way.

She walked closer. The hair. The eyes.

The guy stared back at her and then stuck his tongue out in a creepy way. *Stupid.* The lookalike would have been in his mid-twenties. *Idiot.* No way was she going on that bus now. She shook her head to get rid of the image and took the path towards home. Was she going crazy? Seeing Danny in strangers? She was meant to be getting over him.

After a year of freedom, what was it going to be like having Mum and Dad constantly checking up on her? At least starting the year without a boyfriend meant one less distraction. She missed her friends at youth group. If it wasn't for the regular weekly text, she was sure they'd have forgotten her by now.

Surrendering control over to God was something she'd stopped doing. Perhaps it was time to try again. What had Priscilla said? Something about not striving and allowing what was meant to be, be.

A guy jogging towards her grabbed her attention. She let her gaze follow. *Seriously.* She had to stop checking out every guy with dark curly hair. If only Danny hadn't been so sweet and kind with such ridiculous good looks. And those biceps. *No. Stop.* The ocean had caused a rift between them, and she had to let the relationship slip away like low tide.

 Spiralling Solo

Everyone had warned her long-distance relationships rarely lasted, but she'd hoped what she'd had with Danny would be counted amongst the rarities. She pulled her air-dried hair into a ponytail as she took the last turn before home.

'Hey.' Tabbie pushed open the front door.

'Hello, love,' her mum said. 'I was about to send out the search party.'

'Sorry. I walked from the pool.'

'Why didn't you ring and ask me to pick you up?'

'It's okay. I felt like a walk.' And there she was, back in the hands of the parentals, questioning her whereabouts, and wanting to know her every move. Goodbye, Danny. Goodbye, freedom and independence. Hello new opportunities and house rules.

Chapter Six

TABBIE

TABBIE STRETCHED AWAY her sleepiness as a stream of sunlight drenched her with sweat. It had been months since she'd had a solid sleep-in. Bonus number one to living at home.

'Are you ready to go and pick up your books?' Mum knocked on her door.

'Huh?'

'It's after ten, love.'

'Hang on, why are we getting them? Aren't they online? I'd rather go for a swim.'

'You went for one yesterday.' Mum pushed the door open. 'Studies show it's easier to learn from paper than screens.'

'I know, I know. You've told me a million times.' Tabbie kicked off the damp sheet and sat up. 'It's hot already. I'd love to get a few laps in. Do you have time to pick me up from the pool in an hour or so?'

'Alright. Then we can get the books.' Mum checked her watch. 'How about I drive you to the pool in fifteen minutes?'

'Sounds great.' She watched her mother leave, then pulled her swimmers on. Another bonus of living at home—a chauffeur.

Tabbie threw her towel over a plastic chair and pencil-dived into the indoor pool. Towards the end of every lap, she glanced to the side, imagining what it would be like if Danny appeared. *Stop it!* It's never going to happen. Out of breath, she squeezed out her hair to find her mother had returned and was sitting on the chair, holding her towel.

'Let's go grab those books.'

Tabbie nodded and climbed out, letting her thoughts about Danny dry up.

An hour later, as she unpacked the heavy parcel of books her laptop dinged. She lunged towards her computer on the floor to see who the email was from.

Danny. The familiar sender address blinked at her in bold. She fumbled to click 'open.'

> Hi Tabbie.
>
> Been offline.
> Just wanted to—

Tabbie stared at her laptop screen. *Just wanted to what?* How did an email get cut off halfway through? She replied straight away.

> Hey. How are you? T x

Silence. *Where is he? What happened? Why did he do that? Has he met another girl?* She wanted to get over him, but what if…

'Are you settling back okay, love?' Her mother appeared in her doorway.

'Fine.' She couldn't shake the email from her mind. 'But I'm not sure how Steph will go. She looked like she was about to cry when I left.'

'Why didn't you tell me? I thought she seemed quiet. Let's invite her over for dinner.'

'Sure. I'll ask her when Dad takes me to get the desk later.'

A long continuous rap on the front door interrupted their chat. 'Only me!' Stephanie called out.

Tabbie scrambled off her bed to follow Mum downstairs.

'It's never only you,' Mum said. 'It's gorgeous you and your delicious little Lola.' Mum pulled Lola out of the stroller. The baby cooed and giggled.

'We were planning to invite you for dinner, so now that you're here, would you like to stay?' Tabbie plonked onto the couch beside Stephanie.

'Are you sure?'

'You're like one of the family. You know you're welcome any time.' Mum sat on the floor with Lola. 'And there's room here if you ever want to move back in.'

Tabbie watched darkness creep into Stephanie's eyes. It had only been one night since she'd moved out, and Steph was already looking for company. 'Is everything okay at the apartment?'

'It was more fun until you —'

'You said you were okay with me leaving. Why didn't you say something?'

'I'm just having a pity party. I'll be fine in a few days. Must be hormones or something.'

'Steph, if you need anything at any time, we're here for you,'

Mum said.

'Yeah, I know.' Steph tightened her ponytail. 'Look, Francine, Lola's nearly crawling.' They all turned to watch the baby pulling herself forward on her elbows.

'You're such a clever girl!' Mum clapped. 'Gosh, we'll have to childproof the house again.'

'Hasn't been any babies here for a while.' Tabbie's father hung his keys on the wall rack as he arrived home. 'When are you moving back, Steph?'

'Ah, no. Not me. I'm just visiting.'

Dad raised his eyebrows. 'Just so you know the offer still stands. Now, please excuse me. I have a few things to do before dinner.'

'I'd love to watch Lola and play boo all day, but I must go and put dinner on or there won't be any.' Mum stood, smoothing her skirt before heading to the kitchen. Steph slid off the couch and pulled Lola back from trying to follow.

Living with a baby for the past six months had slammed the door on any romantic ideas Tabbie might have had of becoming a nanny or rushing into having children herself. 'I got an email from Danny today.'

'Finally! What did he have to say for himself?'

Tabbie focused on Lola as tears prickled in her eyes.

'Well?'

'Nothing other than he'd been offline.' Tabbie shrugged and blinked. 'It was like he hit send before he'd finished the email.'

'What if he's been busy? As in met-someone-busy. She might have walked in on him.'

'That did cross my mind.' *Like a thousand times.* Reality slammed her feet back on the ground.

'Maybe, but don't jump to conclusions.' Stephanie stood and pulled Lola to her hip.

'Why are you saying that now, after telling me to move on for so long?'

'I don't know the guy. But I still think you shouldn't waste time pining over him.' Steph shrugged. 'Thanks for the dinner invite, but I'd rather get home before dark.'

'We can give you a lift,' Dad offered as he returned. 'We need to pop over and grab that desk anyway.'

'You don't have a baby-seat for the car.'

Dad frowned. 'Oh, yeah. Shows how out of touch I am.'

'The next bus leaves in twenty, so I'd better pack up.' Steph strapped Lola into the stroller.

'See you Saturday. We'll come for that desk.' Dad held the door open.

'Sure, thanks, Tom. See ya, Francine.'

A flock of birds flew through the trees. Ah, the sounds of home were sweet music to Tabbie's soul. 'Wish you could stay.'

'It's okay. I wouldn't mind some quiet time tonight anyway.' Steph led the way to the bus stop.

'You'll have plenty of that with me gone.' A nervous twinge pulled in Tabbie's stomach. *What if Steph isn't okay?*

'About Danny—I reckon you should wait till you hear from him again. Don't jump to conclusions.' Stephanie unclipped Lola, slung the nappy bag over her shoulder and folded up the stroller ready to catch the bus.

Tabbie waited until Steph and Lola were on the bus. *Why did she have to say that about Danny?* All she'd done was light another spark of confusion, like the bright sunlight before dusk.

     Spiralling Solo

Chapter Seven

$\mathcal{S}$TEPHANIE

STEPHANIE'S HEART TWISTED with envy as a pull of anxiety surged through her. Climbing onto a crowded bus with Lola while clutching a stroller was not her idea of fun. If only her mother was half as supportive as Tabbie's, life would be so different.

The small baggage bay was already filled with other strollers and bags. Steph had no choice but to stand in the aisle. She grabbed a handle to steady herself as the bus pulled back out onto the road. At each stop, she pulled Lola a little closer, breathed in, and shuffled from side to side as other passengers moved around her.

Watching families on the bus took her thoughts back to her mother, and how she'd told her to abort the baby. One text she'd received still hurt. *Consider yourself no longer a daughter of mine.* Since that, they'd hardly communicated. Steph vowed she'd never return to Toowoomba. She'd fantasise sometimes when she saw happy families, wishing she had the same. But reality always crashed through the dreams and left her relying on Tabbie.

Her phone rang in her pocket. She wedged the stroller against a seat with her hip, lifted Lola a little higher on the other hip and reached for the phone. Her sister's name flashed on the screen. April was the only thing she missed about Toowoomba. But a conversation with April could wait until she was off the bus. Steph didn't have the energy or know-how to deal with her. She slid the phone back into her pocket as the bus turned a corner, sending the stroller into the person in front of her.

'Sorry,' she said.

The person groaned without turning around. Lola grizzled and kicked.

'Not far now.' Steph clung to her baby, bouncing her gently on her hip. By the time the bus pulled up at their stop, Lola was screaming. Steph pushed past other passengers to get off as quickly as she could.

Wolf whistles swirled through the air as she shook the stroller to unfold it. She slid the nappy bag off her shoulder and felt the hem of her skirt high on her thigh. She straightened and pushed down her skirt. After all she'd been through, it would take more than a wolf whistle to bring colour to her face.

On the short walk home, her phone chirped with a text message.

Hey Steph, just noticed baby wipes on the couch. Why don't you come over for dinner tomorrow night?

Nights are hard,

Steph replied to Tabbie as Lola screamed again.

I'll have to buy a car seat so I can get a lift sometimes.

For sure. C U soon. xoxox.

Where she'd get the money for a baby seat, she didn't know. Her dreams of sitting her driver's test and buying a small car slipped through a drain of lack. Stephanie felt eyes boring into her as she unlocked her front door. Spinning around to check her surroundings, she pulled in a sharp breath.

A guy with scraggy orange hair was stomping out a cigarette butt in the garden. 'Hey beautiful.' He let a puff of smoke shoot to the sky. 'You look young to be pushing a baby around.'

'Yeah, guess I do.' Stephanie continued to her door.

'Is she your baby sister?'

'No.' That voice. She'd heard it before.

'Are you the babysitter?' He stepped closer.

'No. She's mine.'

Lola threw her plush toy elephant to the ground. A frown creased her little forehead. Stephanie pushed the stroller back and forth.

'Where's her dad?' The man picked up the elephant and handed it to Lola, but she pushed it away.

'He died.' Stephanie clenched her teeth as the words swelled and echoed around her.

'Gee, that's sad. I'm Warren. Hi, bubba. Say hi to Uncle Wazza.' He plonked the elephant into her lap.

'I've got to go. See ya.' Steph shoved the key into the lock and opened her door.

'I might see you around then. I've just moved next door.'

'Sure.' She locked the door behind her as a shiver ran down her spine. Then she remembered. The guy from the window. *Warren.*

'Dinner time, Lola.' An over-friendly guy next door could make life interesting, but was she looking for interesting right now?

Lola grizzled. Steph pulled her out of the stroller to her hip, then scanned the fridge for food. She'd have to settle for a stale piece of pizza. She took a bite. Gross. Maybe it would be better reheated. She turned the oven on.

'Right, let's get your bottle.' Steph filled a bottle with formula and settled Lola down in her cot. Ten minutes later, she sat in front of the TV and bit into the not-hot-right-through horribly stale piece of pizza.

Still hungry, she stared into her almost-bare fridge. At least the rent had been paid for the week. She'd just have to live on two-minute noodles until her parenting pension hit her account next week. There wouldn't be much left over now Tabbie wasn't paying half the rent. The cost of nappies, wipes, and formula would pretty much take the rest of it. Perhaps dinner at the Morays' a couple of times a week would be a good idea.

She pulled her phone out to message Tabbie and remembered the missed call from April. 'Hi, sis, can't talk long. I don't have much credit left.'

'Can I come and live with you for a while?'

'April, you can't keep asking me. I've told you it's best to stay at home until you're older.'

'But you left and you're okay.'

'I was fifteen when I moved in with the Morays. You're only thirteen.'

'But I could stay with you and help with Lola. I could apply for a scholarship and go to school at Hill Top. I've already looked into it.'

'I can't help you, April.' Stephanie looked around her apartment with one sofa and a tiny table with a folded napkin under one leg to stop it from rocking. 'Have you tried Dad? Maybe you can stay with him for a while.'

'No way! I can't stand Liv. She's only twenty and treats me like she's my mother.'

'She must be thirty at least.' Stephanie tried to calculate her age. Liv's boys were four and six. She might still be in her twenties. She still hadn't met the woman her father was obsessed with. 'Look, I don't have any answers for you. Our family sucks.'

'You've got that right. Mum's going clubbing again tonight.' April's voice wavered. 'I'll talk to you tomorrow.'

Their mother seemed to care even less about April than she had Stephanie. Had she even noticed April still had eating issues? Steph bit her lip to stop crying. It was useless. Tears toppled over her lashes until she fell asleep on the couch.

Chapter Eight

TABBIE

> Hi Danny!

TABBIE TYPED, then swung from side to side in her swivel chair. If Danny had already moved on with another girl, was there any point in even emailing? She hit delete and started again.

> Hey hot stuff,

she typed, and then backspaced. Too flirty, too… urgh. Maybe a simple *hello* would be better.

> Hello Danny, I really miss our chats. I know it must be hard over there. If you are near a computer, please reply.

How should she sign off? *Love from Tabbie?* That sounded too formal. She backspaced.

After reading through the email one more time, Tabbie leaned back in her chair and clicked send. She closed her eyes and prayed Danny would respond with something… anything. She groaned at her lack of discipline, but she missed him.

When she opened her eyes, his reply flashed in her inbox.

The words shouted at her from the computer screen. *Time to move on.* She didn't need to read between the lines. He'd said it.

Time. To. Move. On.

She clutched her stomach, cradling the virtual punch until her vision blurred through pools of tears. 'No,' she whispered to the screen.

He didn't miss her. She wished she hadn't wasted the email. Why hadn't she just asked if he'd met someone else or if they were over? She flicked away the tears and typed as quickly as she could to catch him before he shut off. But it was useless. She second-guessed every word she typed and ended up deleting the email.

What did people do when they weren't ready to let go? She'd been trying for weeks. How was she meant to simply get over him? Another spear jabbed her heart as she closed her laptop and lay on her bed. Tears soaked her pillow. She curled into a ball.

People changed, but it was usually because of drugs or trauma. There was no way Danny would be taking drugs or doing anything weird while he was with his missionary parents. *What had changed?*

She rolled over, comforted by the heavy blanket. Sleep enveloped her as dark lonely dreams swept through her mind.

Stephanie woke to an irritating *tap, tap, tap*. She blinked. *Tap, tap, tap*.

The TV flashed with ads in front of her and sunlight speared dust particles suspended in the air. She lifted her head off the couch. Lola gabbled happily to herself on the other side of the wall.

Another *tap, tap, tap* sounded at her front door. 'Hello?' a male voice called.

'Hang on.' Stephanie fingered her hair into a ponytail. Through the frosted glass, she saw the outline of her neighbour with a raised a hand to knock again. She unlocked the wooden door but left the flimsy screen door closed.

'Hi.' He held up a cup.

'You want flour? Are you baking? I'm sorry, but I don't have any.' She stepped back to swing the door closed.

'Ha ha, not flour. I'm out of sugar and need a coffee.' His willowy smile and beard hid his age, but the slight crow's feet suggested he was a few years older than her.

'I can't help you there either.' Stephanie stretched, trying to wake herself up. Out of the corner of her eye, she noticed a couple of sugar sachets on the kitchen bench. 'Oh, hang on, Wa—'

'Warren. I know—not many Warrens around. I'm bringing the name back.' He puffed out his chest. 'But please call me Wazza. Is that all you've got? I don't want to take your last sugar.'

'It's okay, I don't use it,' she lied. But sugar was one thing she knew she could go without. One less cost.

'Sweet enough already, eh?'

Steph bit the side of her mouth to stop the giggle wanting to escape. Why did she find his lame line amusing? 'Yeah, something like that.'

Lola grabbed her attention. 'Mum, mum.'

'Right, well, I've got to go.' Stephanie went to shut the door.

'Oh, I'd love to say hi to your little princess again. May I?'

'Wait here. I'll bring her out.' Stephanie left the screen door closed between them. She picked up Lola and a sticky dampness oozed up the baby's back and leaked all over Steph's arm. 'How about another time, Warr… Wazza. I've got to give her a bath.'

'I could help run the water.'

'Bye. See you round.'

'Just let me know where the towels are, and I could get one ready.'

''Nother time!' Stephanie called as she took Lola to the bathroom. 'Sheeez. Why the persistence?' Lola watched her turn the taps on.

'And short,' Steph said as the water splashed from the shower into the plastic tub. 'Been a while since I met a guy I looked down at. Been a while since I met a guy full stop. What do you reckon, Lola? It might be nice having a friend next door now with Tabbie gone. She loved to keep me away from guys. A male friend might be just what I need.'

Her mobile phone buzzed with a text message.

'That will have to wait until I've got you cleaned up and dressed,' she told Lola. Ten minutes later, she picked up her phone to read a message from Tabbie.

Waiting for the bus. I'll be there soon to hang out. Dad's got the car seat thing sorted. He'll come by and pick us up for dinner if that's still ok. C U in half. T

Stephanie smoothed down the clothes she'd slept in. *Free dinner. Yes.* A thankful warmth ran through her until she looked at the mess in the kitchen and the pile of unfolded washing in the lounge. 'Oh, boy. So much to do, not enough time. Bubba, it's back to your cot for a few minutes. Don't want Tabbie to thinking I'm not coping.'

Steph jumped into the shower, dressed, then washed the dishes. She gathered the bundles of clean and dirty laundry and threw it into a pile on the other side of her bed.

Tabbie arrived just as she finished wiping down the benches. 'The place looks great, Steph. I knew you'd be fine without me.'

'Yeah, well, it's only been a couple of days.' Stephanie rubbed her eyes.

'I bet you've been up for hours. As much as I love baby Lola, it sure is nice to sleep in a little without her morning call for a bottle.'

'Actually, she slept in this morning.' Stephanie smiled. 'The new guy from next door—'

'Did you find out anything about him? Does he live on his own?'

'Not sure. Anyway, he came over asking for sugar this morning.'

'Doing some baking, was he?'

Stephanie shook her head. 'Another caffeine addict. He needed it for his coffee. He's super friendly though. It'll be nice having a friend here.'

'Just be careful,' Tabbie warned, dipping her chin.

'Of course I will.'

'Yoo-hoo,' Warren called from outside.

'I think that's him,' Steph whispered.

'Talking about me, were you?' Warren said when Steph opened the door.

Has he been listening to our conversation? Stephanie unlocked the flyscreen door and Warren walked through.

'And you are?' He extended his hand to shake Tabbie's.

'Tabbie.' Tabbie ignored his hand. 'I noticed you'd moved in.'

'Oh yes. Hard to miss in these apartments—'

'And we were just about to leave.' She squinted at Stephanie. 'We need to go now, or we'll be late.'

'You—' Steph tilted her head.

'Yes, you grab the stroller. I'll grab Lola.' Tabbie's glare had heat like flames.

'I'll see you again soon.' Warren backed towards the door.

Stephanie watched him leave, then turned to Tabbie. 'What was that all about? You didn't have to be so rude.'

'He's a creep, Steph,' Tabbie whispered. 'I can't believe you let him in here. I had to think quick to get rid of him. Let's go for a walk so he doesn't come back wondering why we haven't left. Come on.'

'Let me get a bottle ready first.'

Tabbie gave Steph that same look she'd given her when she'd taken off and left Tabbie to babysit one-week-old Lola. A look that yelled, IRRESPONSIBLE! But she'd needed to escape and numb herself from the new responsibility. She'd gone looking for entertainment and found a group of boys at the local supermarket who'd responded to her flirting. She led them to the bottle shop, where they'd bought her a bottle of bubbly. After downing the bottle, she was ready to take on the best-looking… although by that time, they all seemed to be the best-looking boys she'd ever seen, so she took all four of them home. It'd been late and she'd expected Tabbie and Lola would be asleep. She'd tripped through the doorway and found Tabbie rocking a red-faced, bawling Lola.

Steph had sobered instantly as Lola's screams cut through the alcohol. She glanced back to see the group of boys running away. Tabbie had given her the death stare. 'You're a mother. You can't go running off getting drunk and expect me to look after your baby! Get a grip, Stephanie. You didn't touch a drink your whole pregnancy. Don't do this to yourself.' Even though she'd felt sober, her body heaved and threw up everything until only bile was left. She'd cried herself to sleep and woke the next day vowing to never do it again.

Steph followed Tabbie out the door, wanting to remind her how responsible she'd been after that event. But she said nothing. Despite everything, she still craved a drink when fear and anxiety set in.

Chapter Nine

TABBIE

WHAT WAS STEPH THINKING, *inviting that creepy neighbour inside?* She could feel it—Steph was on the verge of stuffing things up again. Tabbie clenched her teeth to stop her guilt rising. 'It's a nice day to go to the park.'

'Isn't your dad coming over soon?' Stephanie caught up with her.

'After lunch at the earliest. We've got at least three hours to kill.'

'Alright.' Stephanie stopped. 'We should go back for her blankie.'

'We'll be right.' Tabbie didn't want to return and risk running into Warren again, despite the chill of an unusually cool breeze. 'Come on, let's go.'

'You're being a little forceful today.'

'I wear forceful well, don't you think?' Tabbie threw the words over her shoulder.

'You wear sweet and lovely better.' Steph took Lola from Tabbie and buckled her into the stroller.

Tabbie poked her tongue at her friend, hoping to lighten the mood. Stephanie laughed and tripped over a crack in the path. Tabbie caught her arm just before she fell, but lost her balance. They both ended up on the grass beside the path unscathed.

Lola giggled from the stroller. Tabbie's shoulders relaxed. It was good to laugh with Steph again.

'Did you get your stuff for school?' Stephanie asked after they'd dusted themselves off and walked to a picnic table in the park.

'Yep. The only thing I need now is my desk.' Tabbie planned her next words carefully. 'So… Warren seemed kind of familiar, walking in like that.'

'I told you I'd met him.' Stephanie kept her eyes forward.

'It seemed like you'd been hanging out, for him to walk straight in like that.'

'Yeah, it did seem that way, I guess. But that's the first time he's come inside. All the apartments are the same. Maybe that's why it seemed familiar to him. I've only spoken to him a couple of times.'

'Hmm. What if…' There were too many what-ifs going through Tabbie's mind. 'I don't trust him.'

'You only just met the guy. Give him a chance. You know, innocent until proven guilty. Isn't that the saying?' Steph hit the pedestrian crossing button with more force than needed.

'Sorry. I just got an icky feeling when he turned up.' *More like a strong, gut-churning feeling.*

'I need to make some new friends. I can't rely on only you. It could be perfect timing that Warren moved in next door.'

A shudder ran down the back of Tabbie's neck. But she'd thought Danny was a total dweeb when they'd first met, and she'd been proven wrong. Maybe her gut feelings weren't the best thing to trust. Her phone rang. She glanced at it. *Shelly.* 'Shelly, you're back? Oh, my goodness, you've been gone forever!'

'I know.' Shelly let out a long sigh. 'It was a pretty hard choice but, someone had to do it.'

'Oh, stop it!'

Spiralling Solo

Shelly's laugh boomed through the phone. 'You have to do it sometime.'

'What? Go on a cruise?' Tabbie asked.

'Yes, or even just go overseas. I'll tell you all about it tonight. That's what I was ringing about—to make sure you're coming.'

'Wouldn't miss it for anything.' Tabbie felt caught up in Shelly's excitement.

'Awesome!' Shelly said. 'Would you like a lift?'

'Thanks. That'd be great. I'll be at my parents' house. See you soon.' Tabbie ended the call.

'Does that mean dinner is off?' Steph asked.

'No, of course not. Why don't you come with me? We can eat early, then go. I can get Mum to drive us and meet Shelly there.'

'Look, let's forget about dinner tonight. I don't want to make you late.'

'Are you sure?' Tabbie asked.

'Of course I am. I wouldn't have said it if I wasn't.' Steph's gaze was fixed on the trees. Composed. Expressionless.

'Then, let's do dinner tomorrow night instead. I'll let Mum know.' Tabbie grabbed her phone and texted the change of plans.

The next hour was filled with magpies warbling, and silence. *What's going on in Steph's mind? Am I doing the wrong thing, going to youth group with Shelly?* Another call came through. *Mum.*

'Hey, love, I need help with a few things here for the afternoon tea I've got coming up. Does it spoil your plans if I come and get you now?'

'Should be okay. I'll check with Steph. Hang on.' Tabbie put her phone down. 'It's Mum, she needs help with something. Want to come with me?'

'No, it's cool. I was hoping to spend some time looking for a job.' Steph turned away.

'Okay Mum, we'll be back out the front of Steph's in around thirty minutes. Oh, what about my desk?'

'Sorry, not today Dad's busy. We'll make arrangements to pick it up another day.'

$\mathcal{S}$TEPHANIE

The conversation may as well have been on speaker. Steph glanced at Tabbie when she'd hung up. 'I get to look at your desk for a few more days?'

'Sorry. Is that okay?'

'Yeah.' *What's the point in saying anything else?* All she wanted was a drink with some fizz from a bottle that went pop. Anything to numb the loneliness falling on her like crushed autumn leaves.

Half an hour later, she plastered a smile on her face and waved goodbye to Francine and Tabbie from the kerb.

'Hi, Stephanie. Beautiful day, isn't it?' Warren was on the path near her front door.

'Hey. Don't you have anything better to do than hang around my front door?'

'Not today. In fact, you've made my day by turning up in time for lunch. I'm hungry and hate eating alone.'

She pointed to the stroller. 'Lola's sleeping, I should get her inside.' But his offer was enticing. She was hungry, and her kitchen was bare. As she unlocked her door, she glanced back to check his features, trying to work out his age. Possibly twenty, maybe a few years older.

'If it's easier with your little one, I can come to yours.' He pointed to her door.

'I'm really sorry, my fridge is empty. I need to go shopping.' But not until her payment arrived.

'No, no. I wasn't inviting myself to eat your food. I've got a hot chook. Do you eat chicken?'

'Yeah.' She salivated.

'Great. I'll bring it over.'

Why hadn't she put more effort into getting a job? Then at least she'd have something in the fridge. She smiled as she transferred

Lola into her cot. A new friend. Someone who knew she had a baby, but knew nothing of her past. She closed the bedroom door. Hopefully Lola would sleep a while so she could enjoy getting to know Wazza.

Chapter Ten

STEPHANIE

'Is she in bed already?' Wazza dumped the chicken on the table.

'Yeah, she was fast asleep.'

'We could wake her.'

Stephanie laughed. 'Why would I want to do that? I look forward to these moments of quiet in my day.'

'She's such a sweet little thing. Maybe I can hang around till she wakes up.' He opened the plastic bag, letting the scent of warm chicken fill the room. Steph pulled some stale bread out of the fridge, then grabbed two plates and set them beside the chicken.

'Do you have anything to drink?' Wazza asked. 'I should have brought something with me.'

'Only water or coffee.'

'Coffee sounds great.'

'But I'm out of sugar. Sorry.'

'I'll try it without.' He smiled.

There was something kind of cute about his smile that intrigued her. She put the jug on to boil. He wasn't pin-up guy kind of attractive. He was pretty much the complete opposite of Jason. She recalled Tabbie telling her to look at the heart. Maybe she should just get to know this guy and not think about his looks so much.

Steph carried two cups of black coffee to the table. 'I'm out of milk as well. Sorry.'

'I'll try anything once.' Warren grinned and winked a cringeworthy wink. He made her a sandwich. Well, chunks of chicken between dry, stale bread. At least it was food.

'So where did you move here from?' Steph asked.

'Huh?'

'You said you'd only just moved here. Are you new to Sydney or just this area?'

'Oh, yeah. The girlfriend and I split.'

'Is that a good thing?'

'Yeah. We were only together because of the kid.'

Her eyes opened wide. She put the pieces together as she blinked her eyes back to their usual state, hoping her reaction wasn't obvious. 'Girl or boy?'

'Girl. Bit older than yours. I left just after her first birthday.'

'What's her name?'

'Mindi.'

'Do you have any other kids?'

Warren laughed and puffed his chest out. 'Why? Do I look like a baby-making machine?'

'Just making conversation.' She was struggling to read his responses. The last thing she wanted to do was get into a conversation about the past. Her past. She looked across the table to her new friend. Ungroomed chin stubble and scruffy hair full of product. 'So...' *What's a safe conversation topic?* 'Are you working at the moment?'

'Yeah, at the local bottle shop.'

Bingo. She smiled, raising her eyebrows.

'That's why I moved here. So I can walk rather than spending half the day on public transport.'

'You're carless?'

'It's not too bad. Means I can have a few drinks and not worry about getting pulled over. One less hassle.'

She bit her lip at the mention of alcohol.

'When do you reckon Lola will wake up?'

'She's only been asleep for an hour. Hopefully she'll stay there for another hour.'

'Do you mind if I come back then? Kind of fills the hole my ex has left taking my little one. Seeing others, I mean.' He pushed his chair back, scraping it against the floor.

'Sure.'

'Right. Later then.' He went to the door, gave her a wave and a wink, then left.

Steph put the dishes in the sink. They could wait. She stared at the chicken, wanting more, but packed it into the fridge for dinner. Maybe she could stretch it to last a few days.

Wazza returned an hour later wearing black pants and a polo shirt with the *Thirsty Horse* emblem on the pocket. Her mouth resembled that horse. 'What time do you start work?' She could almost smell the bubbles pouring from a bottle.

'I've got an hour or so to hang around. Is Lola awake yet?' He glanced around the room.

'Still fast asleep. I just checked in on her.'

His smile dropped and he turned as if to leave but stopped. 'I haven't got anything else to do. I may as well sit here and watch the telly with you.'

Steph relaxed with the unexpected comfort of sitting on the couch with someone and not talking. He hadn't asked anything about her past. The longer they sat there, the further he leaned towards her. So close his arm brushed against her. Without turning from the TV he stretched, then let his arm rest on the couch behind her. She looked at him, raising her eyebrows.

Spiralling Solo

'Just more comfortable, you know, with my arm up.'

Stephanie laughed. 'You have the lamest come-on lines.'

'Do you think I'm coming on to you?'

'Well?'

'Well, what?' He slid closer, letting his arm relax around her shoulders. 'Are you saying you'd like that? You're okay with my arm here?'

'Do I get a choice?'

'Of course you do. What do you think I am?'

'I'm trying to work you out.'

'I finish work at eight tonight. If Lola sleeps all day, does she party at night?'

'Sometimes, but not usually.'

'Is it okay if I come round after work?'

'I guess.' She chewed the inside of her mouth, wondering if she should ask him to bring a bottle of bubbly back.

'Great. I'd better be off. Can I bring you back something to drink?'

'Yes, please.' She took a breath trying not to sound so desperate. 'A bottle of bubbly would be fantastic.'

'Expensive taste, hey?'

'Not really. Any wine with bubbles is fine.'

'I'm really enjoying getting to know you, Stephanie from next door.' He stood in front of her, leaned down and pecked her on the lips.

She blinked. A chill ran through her. He didn't turn back as he left. When did they go from hello to kissing? Had she flirted too much? Was hoping he could supply a drink now and then skewing her behaviour? Steph pushed the thought out of her mind. Loads of people kissed each other hello and goodbye. He probably meant nothing by it. It would be okay. He seemed okay.

Still unsure if she was building a mountain out of a split-second kiss, she jumped in the shower and washed her hair. As she dried off, Lola cried out. She attended to the stinky nappy and then blow-dried her hair and applied a little make-up ready for her new friend to arrive with the bottle of bubbly.

A moment of guilt lingered. All the AA meetings she'd gone to while she was pregnant. All the counselling she'd had at rehab. A twinge of knowing she was about to make a bad choice hit her. If it meant numbing the past while getting to know Wazza better, it would be okay. *Right? There's no need for guilt. Really.* She was just having a little fun.

Chapter Eleven

While Shelly drove to youth group, Tabbie filled the silence with details about moving home.

'How's Stephanie with the change?' Shelly asked.

'She seems okay, but I'm not sure if I've made the right decision.'

'I reckon you have. You need to focus on Year Twelve, and Steph has to live her own life.' Shelly glanced at Tabbie then back to the road as she turned into the church car park.

'You're starting to sound like Dad.' Tabbie unclipped her seat belt. 'There's something else.'

'What?' Shelly turned off the engine, looked in the rearview mirror and pushed her curls into place.

'Danny and I are over.' The words spilled out and she wished she'd held them in.

'No way!' Shelly reached over to hug her. 'Are you okay?'

'Yeah.' Tabbie bit her lip.

'What happened?'

'Well, I didn't hear from him, and then he said not to email. I think he's met someone over there.' Tabbie swallowed over and over to keep tears from falling.

Shelly's big cow-like eyes mirrored her sadness. 'Wow. I really thought you two would last. I know I said to not get too hung up, but…'

Tabbie forced a smile. Part of her wanted Shelly to tell her she was wrong, tell her Danny would never do that. Their conversation ended when someone knocked on the car door.

Tabbie sighed as Shelly left the car and disappeared into the swell of people near the church doors. She hadn't even asked her about the cruise holiday. Hanging back, she pulled out her phone to avoid talking to anyone until she knew her tears had dried up. She released a breath slowly. Why had she let her mouth run away on her like that? She sent a text message to Stephanie.

> Wish you were here with me tonight. Maybe next week.
> Love T. xox

Shoving her phone back into her pocket, she joined the crowd enthralled with Shelly's stories of Fiji, Lifou, and Vanuatu. Tabbie welcomed the darkness in the auditorium after hang time. She knew her emotions were like a levee about to break. The distraction of singing was just what she needed.

'I hear we're heading to the beach tomorrow. Who's in?' Shelly asked after the service. 'Being away on holiday was great, but I sure missed hanging out with everyone.'

'A day at the beach sounds great,' Tabbie said. 'Can I grab a lift with you?'

'Sure.'

Hopefully tomorrow she wouldn't be so emotional and she'd have a chance to chat with Shelly in the car. Tabbie thought back to the past few months and how Stephanie seemed to need her every time she'd planned to go to the beach with the youth group. Would some crazy crisis come up and stop her again this time? She checked her phone but the battery had died. She shouldn't think about Steph like that. A wave of guilt hit her. Maybe she should invite Steph and Lola to join them tomorrow.

$\mathcal{S}$TEPHANIE

Lola rubbed her eyes and fell asleep on Steph's lap. Steph got that Warren was missing his daughter, but keeping Lola awake just so he could see her was stupid. He said he finished work at eight, and it was now half past. He'd have to wait for another time.

She transferred Lola into the cot then, knowing the drone of the vacuum never woke her, Steph cleaned the floors. She glanced at the time. Nine-fifteen and he still wasn't there. She sat to watch TV, and yawned, remembering Tabbie had sent a text earlier that night. She replied. xxx

She had no intention of going to youth group with Tabbie, but that conversation could wait. She dropped the phone on the couch and let her head relax against the cushion.

A loud thump sounded at the door. *What's that?* Steph blinked away the darkness and looked for Lola. She was fast asleep in her cot. She checked the time—after ten. Another thump sounded. She spun. *The front door.*

'Oh, has Lola fallen asleep?' Wazza reeked of cigarettes and alcohol.

'Hours ago,' Steph whispered. 'Come in. But can you not make so much noise?'

He clanged a six pack of beer and a bottle of wine onto the kitchen bench. 'You got any stubby holders?' He called, like she was in another room.

'Ssh! Sleeping baby.'

'She'll be right. Have you got any wine glasses?'

'No, and I don't have a stubby holder either.' Steph pulled a short tumbler out and let her senses go wild as he popped the cork.

A slight shiver ran down her spine as she took her first sip. She rolled the liquid over her tongue, backwards and forwards before letting it slide down her throat. Warren drank his beer nearly as quickly as she finished her first glass.

'Gee, you downed that fast.' He put his empty bottle on the bench with a clunk.

Steph chewed the side of her cheek as she poured another drink and handed Warren another beer. The warm, familiar haze surrounded her.

'Hey, is there any of that chicken left?' Warren pulled the fridge open.

'Yeah, still a little there.' Stephanie topped up her tumbler for the third time as Warren stripped the chicken bare. He wiped his hands on the kitchen cloth then slipped his arm around her waist. She giggled at his touch. He pulled her in so their bodies melded together. He leaned in and kissed her with a sloppy open mouth, pushing his tongue against hers. She responded, accepting the attention. She needed this. An escape from her reality.

Warren stepped back, filled her glass and opened another beer for himself. 'Cheers.' He clinked the bottle against her glass.

'Cheers.' She laughed and finished the last of the wine.

He locked her front door, flicked the light off and led her to her bedroom. In a blurry haze, she welcomed his closeness.

Chapter Twelve

$\mathcal{S}$TEPHANIE

'SEE YOU LATER.' Warren pulled his clothes on and left her room.

She heard him open Lola's door on the way out. 'Goodbye, little one.'

Stephanie closed her eyes. She needed more sleep and let herself drift off again. The front door slammed and Steph sat upright.

'Mum, mum,' Lola called between sobs.

'What's up, baby?' Her head throbbed. Her stomach churned.

She made her way into the next room. Lola was wide awake, with the sheet and blanket scrunched and jumbled at her feet. Blinking her stinging eyes, Stephanie pulled Lola out of the cot and cuddled her. She tried to recall exactly what happened last night. Had Warren woken Lola as he said goodbye? Or did she kick the bedding off herself?

Stephanie held Lola up and checked her over to see if she needed a nappy change or if her clothes were poking into her. The nappy was full and smelly like it was every morning, but that didn't usually cause her to scream. Steph cradled Lola close until her heart stopped racing.

She replayed the night. How could she drop her guard and let Warren in like that? What if he was dangerous? He seemed okay but… No, he wasn't dangerous. He'd been gentle with her last night. A chill ran down her spine. Hadn't he? She couldn't remember.

She needed to be alone for a while. Alone with Lola. Rushing to the front door, she locked it and slid the security chain in place.

Lola clung to her as she warmed a bottle. Then she returned to her bed, holding Lola as she sucked on the bottle. Steph let her eyes close again and sleep took over.

TABBIE

The sun woke Tabbie. After a year without blinding morning light, it was taking some getting used to. She needed blackout curtains. She reached for her phone and turned it on.

Steph had replied to her text last night with xxx.

She scrolled up, to re-read the message she'd sent before her phone battery died. That was Steph's way of saying *no thanks.* She'd leave it for a bit and chat to her later. She really wanted to go to the beach today. Steph could wait.

When Shelly picked her up, it took one question. 'What really happened with Danny?'

Tabbie blurted the full story. She swiped at the stream of tears with the back of her hand. 'I just don't get it.'

'Hmm. I wonder what's really going on over there. I'm sure there's—'

'It's probably like Steph reckons. He's met someone else.' Tabbie swallowed, blinking back more tears.

'Doesn't really make sense, though. He was besotted with you.'

'Something's changed.' Tabbie thought about the ridiculous number of emails Danny had sent declaring his love. 'Something in his tone was different in the last few messages. I didn't think much of it at the time, but when I read back through them, I can see the change.'

'Maybe it's just that he's moving around and doesn't have time. Try not to jump to conclusions. Wait till he emails again. Then you'll know more.'

Just wait and see? Sit in limbo? Unknowing? Tabbie's chest tightened. She didn't want to talk about it anymore. She parked the hope Shelly had given her at the back of her mind for later.

STEPHANIE

Stephanie went to move her arm but couldn't. She wiped sweat from her forehead with her free hand, and grabbed her phone. *Eleven.* How had they both slept so long? Again, she replayed what she could remember from the previous night in her mind. Her memory was sketchy.

She needed to avoid Warren for a bit. A shiver ran down her spine. *Dinner at the Morays' house.* Yes, that's what she'd do. Go and spend the rest of the day there and work out where Warren fitted into her life. Where had her brain been last night?

She eased her dead arm from under her daughter. Stretching it to get the blood moving again, she noticed a shadow outside. *Warren?* A shudder raced down her spine. Did he spend all his spare time hanging around outside her home?

She checked everything was locked up, ducking at windows. If he was outside, she didn't want him seeing her. Footsteps approached her door, but she ignored them and popped Lola in her cot with some toys before stepping into the shower.

As she shut the water off and wrapped a towel around her, knocking rattled her front door. She turned on her hairdryer, drowning out all the noises. Except Lola. She put the hairdryer down and she soothed her baby.

Stones crunched and the sound of shoes scuffing the driveway faded into the distance. If it was Warren, she hoped she could get away before he returned.

Stephanie turned the TV on to Lola's favourite program, leaving the volume low. The sight of empty bottles on the bench made her head pound even more. She'd throw them in the outside bin on the way to the Morays. After she dressed and fastened Lola in the stroller, she flicked the TV off and headed out to catch the bus.

Tabbie

Tabbie returned from the beach and, out of habit, checked her emails. Nothing. She slammed her laptop closed. She had to stop checking. Her phone buzzed with a text message.

Is the dinner invite open for tonight? Steph x

Yes!

Great. See you soon.

Tabbie dropped her phone on her bed and headed downstairs. 'Hey, Mum. Steph's coming for dinner. Do you want me to help you cook?'

'Thanks for the offer, love. I've already prepped a roast. There will be plenty. Maybe you can help me serve it up.' Mum flicked on the kettle. 'Would you like a cuppa?'

'Sure.' Tabbie pulled out two cups.

'Are you still brooding over Danny?'

'Probably. And I'm a bit worried about Steph.'

'It'll be okay, love. Things always work out for the best.'

Tabbie blinked to stop herself from eye-rolling her mother. Just as she handed her mum the cup of tea, a knock sounded at the front door. Stephanie was there, leaning on the stroller.

'You okay?' Tabbie asked, noticing dark circles under Steph's eyes.

'Yeah, just had a strange sleep last night.' She looked away.

'Come in. Come in.' Tabbie took the nappy bag from Stephanie's shoulder and held the door open. 'Did Lola keep you up?'

'No. Yeah. Kind of.' Steph pushed her fingers through her hair.

'Why don't you stay here tonight? We can help with Lola,' Mum suggested.

'But all of her stuff's at home.'

'What's in here?' Tabbie unzipped the nappy bag and shuffled through the contents. 'You usually carry enough to last a week.'

'Usually, but I didn't repack it this morning. I don't think there's enough nappies or formula.' Stephanie flopped onto the couch.

'Well, why don't I come over and stay with you?' Tabbie pushed the bag aside and unclipped the stroller straps, pulling Lola to her hip.

'But you've just moved your bed back here.'

'And I miss you already.' Tabbie smiled.

'How are you going getting over, you know who?'

Tabbie shrugged. *How did the conversation turn around? Is Danny written all over my face?*

'Are you still emailing him?'

'No. I don't want to talk about it.' Tabbie tickled Lola and smiled as the baby giggled. 'So, is it okay if I come and stay the night? She's grown since I moved out.'

'If you want to.'

'Yep, I do.' Getting out of the house without her laptop would be good. Maybe it would break the addiction of checking emails so often. Her phone buzzed with a text message.

Heading home from Grandma's in the morning!
I know… bout time, right? Let's hang. J xx

Tabbie sighed and threw her phone down.

'What's up?' Stephanie asked.

'Nothing really. That was Jaya. I'll reply later.'

Her mother appeared. 'Don't leave it too long. You know how annoying it is when you send a text and don't get a reply.'

'Mum, that's what phone calls are for.' Tabbie forced her eyes not to roll. She reached for the phone and hit reply, knowing her mother would keep pestering her until she did. The joys of living at home again.

For the rest of the afternoon, Tabbie entertained Steph with romcom movies. After dinner she packed her pyjamas and a change of clothes, then went to check her email account. Then remembering her resolve, she stopped herself. Tomorrow would be soon enough to check again.

Chapter Thirteen

'I can't believe you bought a car seat for Lola.' Steph opened the car door. 'It's not like we're going to be driving around with you all the time.'

'Just one small thing we can do to help.' Tom smiled.

'You know he thinks of Lola like a granddaughter.' Tabbie waved her father off. 'Plus, I think he's hoping Peter and Phoebe will start a family as soon as they're married.'

'Have they set a date?' Stephanie asked.

'Not yet but while we're on the subject, are you over your crush? Or do you still have a thing for him?'

'What are you talking about?' *My secret.* She'd thought she'd hidden it from Tabbie.

'Well, you did, didn't you? Remember when you visited over the school holidays? I came home and you were talking to Peter. You were so awkward. Your face turned redder than an overripe strawberry.'

'What?' Stephanie dropped the nappy bag inside her front door, then went to tuck Lola into her cot. She didn't want to talk about the past. She just wanted to move forward.

Tabbie raised her eyebrows when Steph emerged from Lola's room.

'Alright, alright. Your brother is hot. But I knew he'd never go for someone like me.'

'Someone like you? My beautiful, sophisticated, and elegant best friend? Who wouldn't go for someone like you?'

'Peter, that's who.' She sank into the cushions on the couch.

'We were still kids to him. Plus, I guess he just saw you as my best friend. Anyway, he's taken, and you deserve someone just as good or better than my brother.'

'Who'd want me now that I'm a single mother? That's enough baggage to turn anyone away.' *Wazza*. Her shoulders shuddered a little. He hadn't been turned off. In fact the complete opposite.

'Is that getting to you at the moment? Being a single mum?' Tabbie joined Steph on the couch. 'What if you go back to the young mums support group we visited?'

'They were all fake storytellers plus half of them lived with their boyfriends. It was meant to be for young single mums. I'm not going back.' Stephanie flicked the TV on. 'What did Jaya want?'

'Ha. Nice change of subject.' Tabbie grabbed the remote from Steph and silenced the TV. 'I thought the girls in the support group seemed nice.'

Steph rolled her eyes.

'What about trying playgroup? What if I come with you before school goes back? I've got one week of freedom left.'

'Back to school. Such a burden. You'll be so tied down.' Just a *day* of freedom would be good. 'I'm not interested in trying any group thing.' She wanted to start fresh and not have to tell people about her past. 'Jaya?'

'She gets back tomorrow.' Tabbie tucked a wisp of hair behind her ear.

'So will you be back to being her guardian angel, dropping everything when she calls?'

'Steph! You two could be friends again, if you'd be kind to each other.'

'Too much water under that bridge.'

'Bridges are for crossing over.' Tabbie took a deep breath as Steph shook her head. 'How's the job search going?'

'It's pointless. I haven't found daycare for Lola. Who's going to give me a job with a kid on my hip?'

'Have you checked out the childcare centre down the road?'

Steph shook her head.

'You can always leave Lola with me to go for interviews. You don't have to take her with you.'

'That's if there's any jobs going that I'm qualified for.' She'd looked in windows of nearby shops, but no one was advertising except the *Tiger's Eye*, and there was no way she was going back there.

'If anything comes up, call us. Mum or I could look after Lola.'

'Okay, but can we drop it for now?' Steph grabbed the TV remote and flicked the volume back on.

The rustle of a plastic bag outside drew her attention to the front door. Warren's outline appeared through the frosted glass. Steph jumped up, desperate to ask if he'd heard Lola screaming before he'd left. But she couldn't say anything with Tabbie sitting there.

Right now, she had to get rid of him. Quickly. As she opened the door, he held a bottle of bubbly up in the air like a trophy. She shook her head, but he didn't take the hint. 'How ya going?' Alcohol fumes reached her.

'Hi, Warren. Tabbie's here.' She turned and hoped she cast a look of apology to Tabbie.

Tabbie's eyes bulged.

'Wazza, remember.' Warren stepped through the doorway. 'You girls wanna drink?

'Ah… no thanks. Tabbie's staying the night. I'll see you another time.' She stepped forward, pushing him backwards out the door.

'But…'

'See you round.' Stephanie closed the door, muffling Warren's disgruntled voice.

'What was that about?'

'Just the friendly neighbour thing, I guess.' Steph locked the door and avoided looking directly at Tabbie.

'I think I'm missing part of the picture. What's been going on?'

'Nothing.'

'So he knows your drink of choice?'

'Coincidence?' *Is there any point in trying to hide it? Tabbie knows.* 'Yeah, well… Um, he ah… brought lunch over yesterday, then popped back in after work.'

'Popped back in?'

Stephanie combed her fingers through her hair. 'Seriously? What's the problem with me making new friends?'

'You tell me. If he's your new friend and there isn't an issue, why didn't you invite him in?'

'I didn't think you'd want him here.'

'Steph, what if—'

'Shh. You know how thin these walls are,' Steph whispered. 'He's okay. He's not a murderer or anything. He's just split with his girlfriend, and he's missing his one-year-old. Like me, he's ready to make new friends.'

'You've only just met the guy. How do you know he's really okay?' Tabbie frowned at her.

Is he okay? Steph had tried to ignore the uneasy feeling all day. She had no idea how she could make Tabbie trust the guy when she didn't. She pulled at her fingernails. 'He seems okay.'

'Well, I'm glad you sent him away. I want it to be just us tonight.'

'Why the sudden exclusivity?' Stephanie slipped the chain lock in place on the door and returned to the couch.

'Best friends need it sometimes.' Tabbie curled her legs under her. 'About that wine he was holding—'

'Yeah, how about that?' Stephanie reached for the remote control again. 'So why just us? Is there something you wanted to talk about here that you couldn't say at home?' She fingered the remote looking for a distraction. Her mouth watered at the thought of the bubbles in the bottle. Maybe she could wait until Tabbie went to sleep, then slip next door.

'You've been drinking again, haven't you?'

Heat crept up her neck. 'Look, it was just a few. No big deal.' Stephanie jumped off the couch and filled the jug. 'Want a cuppa?'

'Steph.'

'Tabbie, you're not the one trying to live this life.'

'I know that. But you are. And you know you can't stop if you have one.'

'Thank you, Miss Alcohol Cop.'

'Maybe it's a good thing I'm here tonight. But I won't be tomorrow night. What will you do then?'

'Gee, one week at home and you're already sounding like your mother.' Where did Tabbie get off trying to control her? She had no idea how hard it was to be a single parent. At least Wazza had an idea. 'If you've got such an issue with me, call your dad and go home.'

'No. I'm staying the night.'

Shame. Steph hoped Tabbie wanted an out.

'And don't even think about going out after I go to sleep.'

'As if.' *How can Tabbie read me so well?*

Tabbie looked to the ceiling then back at her. 'He's next door. And you're predictable.'

'Keep your voice down.' Stephanie glanced over her shoulder. 'I don't feel like dealing with Lola again tonight.'

'That's one of the reasons I'm here, remember? To look after her if she wakes up and to allow you to have a good sleep. But now I'm starting to wonder if something else kept you awake last night.'

'Are you like this with Jaya?'

'Only when she's being stupid.'

'So you're calling me stupid. I wish you stuffed up sometimes.' Stephanie poured boiling water into two cups and threw tea bags into them.

'What do you mean? I stuff up all the time.'

'Yeah, right. Name the last time.'

*T*ABBIE

'Pining over a boy who no longer seems interested. That's a stuff-up.' Tabbie clenched her teeth. The plan was to keep the conversation on Steph, not draw attention to herself.

'But it's not like his communication has been great. No real stuff-up there.'

'Have you looked to see what jobs are available?'

'Now who's changing the subject? Why do you find it easier to point out my faults than talk about yourself?'

'See, another thing I keep stuffing up.' *Selfish, self-centred.* Tabbie could find a whole lot about herself not to like if she looked. Why had Danny even noticed her in the first place? *Urgh.* She needed to keep her mind off Danny. 'What I meant was, do you really want to find work or would you rather be a full-time mum?'

'I realised when you moved out, that the single parent pension doesn't cover rent plus food. I don't want to ask Jason's parents for help. So I either move somewhere cheaper or get a job. But what if I can't find either?'

'Maybe we should have an early night. Things never seem as hard after a good night's sleep.'

'See, you're always right.' Stephanie yawned. 'You always know what to do and never stuff up the way I do.'

Tabbie shook her head. She reached for the book in her bag. 'Bed-time. We can chat in the morning. And don't get up for Lola. I'll hear her.'

  Spiralling Solo

'What are you going to do?' Steph yawned again. 'You never go to bed this early.'

'I've got this book to read. An early start for English.' Tabbie mentally prepared for an all-nighter.

Chapter Fourteen

$\mathcal{S}$TEPHANIE

SLEEP. WHY WOULDN'T IT come immediately the one night she had a babysitter? She stared at the ceiling, visualising the bottle in Wazza's hand. The sliver of light under her door disappeared with the click of the switch. Steph waited until she could hear Tabbie's deep sleepy breaths and tiptoed out to get a drink of water.

'Hey, you okay?'

Steph jumped at Tabbie's voice. 'Yeah, just thirsty.' She retreated to her bed and urged sleep to come but her mind was wide awake. An hour must have passed, so she padded out again. All she could hear was the hum of the fridge and Tabbie's deep breaths. She glided towards the front door and slipped the chain lock off without making a sound.

'Where are you going?'

Steph spun around. Her heart thumped in her ears. 'Just checking. The door. You know. The chain.' She reattached the chain, shuffled back to her room and plonked herself into bed. Hopefully it was too dark for Tabbie to notice she was fully dressed.

Steph counted to a hundred forwards then backwards while listening to Tabbie toss and turn on the couch. Her taste buds screamed at her, knowing the wine sat in the fridge next door.

Light. The room was light again. Sun shone through the window and Steph tried to remember when she'd fallen asleep. She rolled out of bed, yawned, and found Tabbie in the kitchen holding Lola.

'Tell me, has drinking with Warren become a daily thing? I've only been gone a week and—'

'Good morning to you too.' Steph pulled a mug from the cupboard and flicked the jug on. 'Someone comes to my door holding drinks and you jump to conclusions. I need a shower. You right with Lola?'

Tabbie nodded.

Steph tried to let the water bury her secrets in the drain. How long would she be able to keep it from Tabbie? She didn't need to know everything. Steph had only slept with Wazza once in a drunken moment. It wasn't like there was any commitment or anything. She could easily give him the flick. Except for the fact he could buy drinks.

'What are we up to today?' Tabbie had brewed two cups of instant coffee and was stirring a sachet of sugar into each.

'Have you forgotten already? I don't have sugar anymore. Need to lose this baby weight.'

'Sorry. Do you want me to make another?'

Stephanie glanced at the coffee jar. It would hardly last until her next payment. 'No, it's okay. I'll drink this one. So… what time were you planning to be off? I was thinking of checking out the local childcare centres.'

'I could come with you.' Tabbie took her coffee and sat at the small table.

'Mum, mum.' Lola threw her elephant on the floor and began to cry.

'I'd rather go by myself.' Steph hoisted Lola onto her hip. 'You've been so helpful, but since you moved out, I realised I relied on you too much. I need to stand on my own feet.'

'That's great, Steph.' Tabbie took another sip of coffee. 'But what about getting a job?'

'If I get an interview, then I'll ask for help.'

'The drinking thing.'

'I know I can't have alcohol.' As usual, Tabbie was right. Tabbie was always right. *I can't afford to have even one drink.* It wasn't something like the flu that she'd get over. It would always be too hard to stop. Steph put Lola on the floor with her squeaky elephant. She had to look after her daughter and stop being selfish.

'If he comes around again with the bottle and you can't say no, call me.'

'Yeah, okay.' Steph opened and shut cupboard doors in the kitchen then sat down. Coffee would have to do for breakfast.

'I'm serious, Steph. Let me be your lifeline.' Tabbie had moved to stand beside her. 'Promise.'

'Okay, okay.' She would. She'd call Tabbie. She would.

Wazza knocked on Stephanie's door soon after Tabbie left. 'Will your protector be staying often?'

'Protector? You mean Tabbie?'

'I thought she'd moved out.' Wazza scratched his product-filled hair.

'She did. School's about to go back and…' Steph let her voice trail off. Maybe she should hold back a bit.

'I got the message loud and clear to take off last night.' He moved inside a little further. 'But it's a new day. And I still have your bottle of bubbly. Should I bring it round now or after work tonight?' He winked.

Stephanie looked to the ceiling, shaking her head, cringing at his flirting and insinuations. She glanced back at him. His work shirt was crushed and only half tucked in. 'Are you on your way to work now?' She could taste the bubbles as she imagined them hitting her tongue.

'In an hour or so. Got the afternoon shift today.'

'Okay, maybe leave it with me.' *What am I doing? I need to call Tabbie.*

'Sure. I'll go grab it. And I'll see what I can do about getting another for tonight.' He had the look Jason often had. The same look the guys in the clubs had when she danced.

No. Not tonight. 'I'm pretty tired. Stayed up talking way too late. I think I'll have an early night.' Lola called out to her. 'I'd better deal with Lola. She needs a nap.'

'Need help with that?' Wazza crouched down to tickle Lola and she leaned back.

'Mumma.' Lola pushed his hand away.

'She'll warm to me.'

Lola's cries escalated.

'Thanks, but I've got it.'

'Righto. Leave your light on if you change your mind about tonight.' He winked again and left.

Steph picked Lola up and let her snuggle into her shoulder. As she was putting her into the cot, a knock sounded at the door and she jumped. *Wazza.* 'Enjoy!' He handed her the bottle and winked. 'Might see you later.'

'Thanks.' Hopefully Lola wouldn't start crying again.

He strode down the driveway, glancing at her over his shoulder twice, then waved. No, she wasn't attracted to him, nor did she want him to visit again after work. Closing her door, she held the bottle up to the light.

Call me. Tabbie's voice echoed in her mind. Steph shook her head. She'd get back on track tomorrow.

Pop! Mist burst from the mouth of the bottle. She grabbed her phone and tapped Tabbie's name. It rang.

And rang.

Tabbie's voicemail message played and she ended the call. Tabbie would call her back soon. She always did.

Steph took a swig. She was meant to be checking out the childcare centre, but that could wait until Lola awoke. Right now, she needed an escape. With Tabbie gone, loneliness shadowed her. Wazza didn't fill the gap. He just wanted sex. Her entire body shuddered at the thought. She wished she could be content with Lola and life.

Just one glass. Then she'd go for that walk to see which centres would be best for Lola. It would only take one glass. One calming glass. *Just one.* She reached for a tumbler and splashed the effervescent liquid into it.

Chapter Fifteen

TABBIE

TABBIE'S MIND CLEARED little by little as one foot fell in front of the other. With the sun about to slip off its highest point, and virtually no shadows on the ground, she took a long sip of water and flicked sweat from her brow. She breathed the earthy scent of forest before turning towards home. Her phone buzzed in her pocket. A missed call from Steph. She'd call when she got home.

Then she noticed a text.

I'm back! When can we hang? J x

Tabbie stopped in the shade of a tree and hit reply.

Come over. I have no other plans this arv.
Would love to see you. ☺

Cool, on my way. Be there in 20. x

Tabbie rushed home, ran a cool shower then tidied her room. She heard the front door at the same time as she glanced at her computer. A new email.

'Jaya's here, love,' her mother called.

Had it been twenty minutes already? The pull to know what the email said was greater than the pull to see the friend she hadn't seen for weeks.

'Be down in a minute,' she yelled as she clicked her mouse pad. The computer screen flashed then started automatic updates. 'Argh!' She slammed the laptop closed.

Jaya appeared in the doorway. 'Whoa. What's up?'

'Sorry.' Tabbie pointed. 'My computer. Stupid thing.'

Before thinking, she told Jaya everything about moving home and what had happened with Danny and how she'd thought she'd seen an email but then her computer restarted itself.

'And I thought my life was messed up.' Jaya laughed. 'Sorry. I shouldn't be laughing.'

'Hmm. Your life isn't messed up, but your parents do kind of fit into that category.' Tabbie forced a smile. Jaya's parents were B-grade movie kind of messed up.

'Welcome to the messed-up club.'

'Gee, thanks.' Tabbie decided to change the subject. 'Tell me about your holidays.'

'I was so bored. Nothing much happens out in the boondocks. The only entertainment is watching the grass grow.'

'All you sent was pics of food.'

'I know. All Gran's cooking. Look at the size of me.' She turned side on and pulled her clothes tight around her stomach. 'See, all I did was eat and watch the grass grow.'

'Jaya, you're the same size you were before Christmas.'

'Am not! I've had to buy new clothes. Gran force-fed me.'

'The pavs and lemon meringue pies you texted was to prove you've been force-fed?' Tabbie laughed. It felt good to laugh. She looked at her computer and shook her head. 'Let's go to the park.'

They headed to the park under beaming rays of summer sunshine. 'Man, it's hot today.' Jaya steered them toward a shady tree.

'Sorry, what did you say?' Tabbie's mind had flicked back to the email waiting at home. She should have asked Jaya to wait for her and rebooted her laptop to read it.

'Are you even listening to me?' Jaya put her hands on her hips.

'No, it's fine. I need to get Danny out of my mind. Quick, distract me.'

'Let's go.' Jaya linked her arm through Tabbie's and guided her back home. 'You need to find out what the email said. *Now.*'

Her computer had rebooted and the new email sat there in bold, begging for her attention.

> Sorry I haven't emailed. It's really dangerous here at the moment. Time to move on. Please stop emailing. D.

'What did he say?' Jaya sat on Tabbie's bed and pulled out a nail file.

'Um.' *Time to move* on. She knew that. He'd already told her. Why did she think he'd change his mind? What an idiot. *Stop emailing.* It was loud and clear.

'Not good?'

Tabbie shook her head. Why did she keep going back to being hopeful? She needed to listen to Steph's advice and give up. 'I'm so stupid!' *So naïve. What a mess.* She'd moved back home in pure selfishness. Steph wasn't ready to be on her own. She'd been gone for a blink in time and Steph had already started drinking again—not to mention whatever was happening with the neighbour.

'Well, I guess that's that then.' Jaya read the message over her shoulder.

Tabbie brushed away tears. Perhaps she should move back in with Stephanie. But now she was home, her parents had been firm and told her to stay until the end of the year.

Danny's words played in her mind. *Time to move on… stop emailing.* It would have been clearer if he'd said, "we're over", but something in her wanted to believe she'd read it wrong. She bit her lip as more tears spilled over her lashes and onto the keyboard. She shut the computer and pushed away any hope until her heart ached so much she sobbed.

Chapter Sixteen

$\mathcal{S}$TEPHANIE

STEPHANIE POURED THE LAST DROP into her glass, lifting it to her lips at the same time as Lola grizzled for her bottle. 'Hang on, hang on.' She put the glass down and grabbed the formula out of the pantry.

The powder spilled on the bench as she scooped it out. Holding the bottle over the formula can, she scooped again to fill it, this time with success. *Next, water*. She picked up the boiled kettle and filled the bottle until it overflowed, spilling blobs of formula into the sink.

Take three. Formula and water into the bottle. *Success*. She shook it, but somehow, the contents trickled out all over her hand. Lola's cries vibrated off the walls. 'I'm going as fast as I can. Just stop crying!'

Steph sucked a little to check the temperature. *Too hot*. She pulled the freezer open and sat the bottle on the shelf.

Lola squealed in protest, her chubby cheeks flushed. She pulled her daughter into her arms and squeezed her a little too hard. A sob erupted from Steph's core. Her best friend's voice echoed in her ears. *You need to start making good decisions.* Tabbie had lectured her over and over when they'd first moved in together.

'I'm so sorry, Lola.' Tears ran rivers down her cheeks. 'You deserve so much better for a mother. Mum was right. Maybe I should have handed you over for adoption. Maybe I still should.'

She opened the freezer, checked the bottle, and held Lola close while she drank the milky liquid. When the bottle was empty, she placed Lola on the floor amongst her toys, then lay beside her, letting the alcohol knock her out.

Lola's whine punctuated the air, waking her. Steph blinked. Stretched. Lola poked a finger in her eye. Stephanie laughed and pushed her daughter's hand away. She stood up and scooped her baby into her arms, kissing her soft cheeks.

'As Tabbie says, "Tomorrow is always fresh and new with endless possibilities and a chance to make right choices." I promise I'll try harder tomorrow, little possum.'

Warren was definitely not welcome tonight. She left the lights off as night came and chain-locked the front door. An early night would do her good.

$\mathcal{T}$ABBIE

'Thanks for hanging out today.' Tabbie walked Jaya to the bus stop.

'Even if you were miserable company.' Jaya bumped her shoulder against Tabbie's. 'It's about time I repaid all the times you've stood by me in my misery.'

Tabbie kicked a stone. 'Are you staying with your mum?'

'Yep. It sucks, but it's the way it is. Can't wait to move out. Maybe I should move in with Steph for a while.'

'You two would end up murdering each other!'

'Or learn to get on.' Jaya winked.

'Maybe it's best to just try the getting on part to start with.'

'You're probably right.'

'What about boarding at school?'

'Sounds like a simple solution, but we don't have enough money. Mum reckons Dad's hidden it. Dad reckons Mum spent it. Thankfully they aren't blaming me.'

'So they're being mature then?' Tabbie raised her eyebrows.

'Ha! I'm out of there as soon as I finish school.'

'You'll stay in Sydney though, won't you?' A feather drifted between them as birds flocked to the trees.

'I need to get away.' Jaya shook her head and led the way to the bus stop. 'I'm going to get a part-time job and save to go to Europe next year. You know, take a gap year.'

'Wow. And you're only telling me this now?'

'I thought I'd mentioned it to you.'

Tabbie shrugged. *Have I been so self-centred I didn't notice?* She needed to start putting others first.

'No biggie. It's months away. Like…' Jaya lifted her hand to inspect her fingernails. 'I won't be leaving before school is out. I want to get into uni. Then I'll defer.'

'Maybe I should join you. I haven't got anything else pending.' Tabbie forced a smile.

'Here's my bus. But yes, come with me. Let's do it together. It'll be so much fun!'

Tabbie felt lost as Jaya climbed onto the bus. For the past year she'd been busy looking after Steph and Lola and messaging Danny. But now? She lacked motivation. All she'd done last night was stare at the pages while listening to Steph's movements. The sun disappeared and she walked home.

The next morning, Stephanie woke with the familiar dark blanket smothering her. She had to get the empty bottle out of her kitchen. As she opened her front door, a slip of paper was on the doorstep.

> *I saw the lights out so I didn't knock. See you tonight. Luv Wazza.*

Luv Wazza? She'd let him into her bed in a drunken moment and now he's signed a note with *luv?* There was no chemistry between them. No love. Just soul-destroying lust. Steph checked Warren wasn't outside, then dumped the empty bottle in the bin and almost ran back inside. Lola sat in front of the TV giggling, mirroring facial expressions.

'How could I have been so stupid to drink that whole bottle? Thank God you're okay.'

Steph had no one to blame but herself. It was stupid and she had to own it. *Stupid. Irresponsible. Selfish.* She thought she had some self-control. Maybe she should go back to AA. But who took a kid to AA? But neglecting Lola and getting drunk wasn't ideal either. She couldn't rely on Tabbie, and no one else cared enough.

Who could she turn to?

No one.

A chill ran down her spine as she thought of the day ahead with only Lola to keep her company. In a few hours Lola would have a nap, and she'd be completely alone. A bottle of bubbly would fix it. Take the loneliness away. Just for today.

No. She had to stop even thinking about a drink. It never fixed anything. It only ever silenced the pain until she sobered up. Plus, there was no way she was about to ask Warren to get her another bottle. *Wazza.* It was a lose-lose situation.

She needed to not drink. She needed to keep away from Wazza. She flicked through TV channels to find a mind-numbing morning advertorial.

Chapter Seventeen

TABBIE

TABBIE LAY ON HER BED and studied the ceiling after another long sleep in. A whole year of school to get through before freedom could begin. Maybe travelling overseas with Jaya was a good option. Although it would only be fun if Jaya promised not to drink, and that was unlikely.

Picking up her grades from last year wasn't going to be easy. Getting into university was what she wanted, wasn't it? Working with orphans in Africa sounded much more worthwhile than getting good grades. Helping people in developing countries seemed far more significant than uni and a career here in Australia.

If only Danny…

No. He hadn't invited her. She wasn't welcome where he was.

If she studied first, then she'd have something to offer a missionary organisation. But she wanted to work with Danny.

Her chest tightened. Tears welled, spilling down her cheeks. Why did her thoughts continue to return to him? She wanted to change the world but did she want to do it on her own? Together, they could have made an impact. *Would* have made an impact.

She donned her runners, packed her towel and swimmers into her backpack, and jogged to the aquatic centre. Once in the pool, she swam lap after lap, tears hidden by the splashes as she pulled her arms through the water. For the past year, girls at school questioned whether Danny was real. Now they'd all laugh at her.

She'd been so involved looking after Steph she'd hardly done anything other than turn up to classes. Would anyone even care about her boyfriend dumping her? Tabbie turned at the end of the lane and slowed her strokes as her heart flipped with the thought of Danny. Why did he keep penetrating her thoughts?

She knew why.

There was so much to like about him. And he was where she wanted to be—on the ground, helping people.

Now she was single. In Australia. And he didn't want her.

If she achieved reasonable grades this year, she could get into a social work course majoring in child health and safety. Her passion was children, wasn't it?

She pulled herself out of the pool, unsure of everything.

$\mathcal{S}$TEPHANIE

Stephanie stared at the TV as ads blended with shows. It was easier to let Lola sleep through lunch than look after her. The only thing that would lighten her heaviness was a drink. A fizzy alcoholic drink. She clenched her jaw.

Steph dragged herself into the kitchen and prepared a bottle. Scooping Lola up gently, she managed to place her in the stroller without waking her, then headed out. Maybe it was time to visit the childcare centre. If she could book Lola in for a few days a week, she'd be able to get a job.

As she turned out onto the path, Lola woke, kicking her legs, whining. Steph gave her the bottle, but she threw it onto the path. 'Here.' Stephanie pushed it back into her hands.

Lola threw the bottle down again, still whining.

'Lola!' Stephanie picked up the bottle and put it in the bag. She continued to push forward, hoping Lola would settle before they arrived at the childcare centre. She passed a billboard with bright advertising. A new vodka premix. Steph's mouth watered. Lola's whining escalated to screaming. Stopping, she bent over to check on Lola. 'What's up?'

Lola kicked her feet.

'Oh…' The stench hit Steph. 'Your nappy.'

She looked up and down the street. It was still another block to the childcare centre, and Lola's screams were embarrassing. Steph pushed the stroller behind a bus shelter. Lola tried to roll over as soon as Steph undid the straps. She was too big to change in the stroller. Lola continued attempting to escape as Steph wrestled the clean nappy on. Tabbie's voice echoed in her head. *You can do this.*

She fastened the nappy, but Lola's crying continued. Steph picked Lola up to console her as tears welled and a lump caught in her throat. Every time she went to put Lola back into the stroller, Lola arched her back and kicked her legs, her face red and blotchy.

'I give up. I'm taking you home.' Steph held Lola on her hip as she pushed the stroller with her other hand. The childcare centre would have to wait.

She wasn't motivated to do anything for the rest of the day other than flick through the TV channels. As the news started, Lola rubbed her eyes. She muted the TV and put her to bed for the night.

With hunger pangs too strong to ignore, she opened the pantry and found a few rice crackers. She sat in front of the news, then the current affairs show, then a reality renovation show.

Thud, thud, thud.

Steph jumped.

Thud, thud, thud. Steph froze. She took a breath when she realised it was Warren's outline in the shadow. She let him in.

'Glad you're still awake tonight.' He held a bottle of bubbly out. 'Grab some glasses. Let's make a toast.'

'What for?' Stephanie pulled two tumblers from her cupboard without thinking.

'I am a single man. And I owe no money.' Wazza popped the cork and overfilled the first glass before filling the second.

'I thought you already told me you were single.' The scent of the bubbly hit Steph's nose. She leaned towards it. Self-control fled as she gripped the glass.

'I signed the divorce papers today.'

'You were married?'

'Yeah, the Vegas deal. Stupid, I know. But we were… you know, half-tanked, and at the time thought we'd be together forever. But we both knew as soon as we got home that it wasn't going to work. So here I am, twenty-one, back on the market and ready to become your knight in shining armour.'

Steph picked up the glass in front of her, clinked it to Warren's, and drank. 'The only thing is…' She took a sip. 'I don't need any knights or shining armour.'

She watched his grin change to an expression she hadn't seen before. Was it disappointment or frustration?

'I have a best friend.' Steph almost squeaked the words. A best friend who, up until now, had stopped her from doing anything dumb.

If Tabbie knew Steph had a drink in her hands right now, what would she do? Would she move back in? As Steph poured a little more of the bubbling liquid down her throat, she knew the answer.

Wazza shrugged then looked around. 'Are you hiding that little one from me?'

'Lola?' Steph clung to her glass and drank again. 'She's sleeping.'

'I've been hanging out to play with her for days. Does she sleep all day every day?'

         Spiralling Solo

'Well, no. But she's asleep now. I hate waking her once she's down.' Stephanie glanced towards the closed bedroom door.

'My little one used to be awake nearly all the time. Hardly slept.'

Stephanie took the last sip. 'Lola seems happier in a routine. If she goes to sleep late or doesn't sleep well through the day, she's horrible through the night.'

'She's different to my daughter. She was our entertainment. Are you sure we can't wake her up?'

'I'd rather not.' Steph put her glass in the sink. 'What else were you so excited to celebrate? The news?'

'What news?' Warren asked.

'Something about owing money?' Stephanie cringed at her words as they came out.

'Oh, it was just some alleged charges. They have no proof. I'm clean. Noth'n else to prove.' Warren draped his arm around her waist. 'So, while the night is young… what do you say to going out for a while?'

Her body tingled. Was it his touch or the rush of alcohol?

You need to be responsible.

What was that? Steph looked around. No one else was in the room but she was sure she'd heard a deep voice, deeper than Warren's. 'Did you hear that?'

'What?'

'A voice?'

'What kind of voice?' Warren laughed. Too loud.

'Shh. You might wake Lola.' Steph moved back from Warren and avoided eye contact.

'So what do you say? Let's head out for a bit.'

'I can't. Lola's sleeping.' Steph clenched her fists again.

'Exactly.' He looked up and down her body. A look of hunger sent a shudder down her spine. 'She's sleeping. You said sleeps well. The routine thing. She'll be fine. Cheap drinks down at the local tonight. We'll be just down the road.'

Steph cast her eyes to the ceiling. *Help!* She couldn't do this on her own. Could it have been God's voice she'd just heard? *If you really are out there, God, now would be a good time to help me.* She couldn't do it. She needed another drink. She reached for the bottle but somehow she bumped it. It tipped over and smashed into the sink with a clatter.

'What are you doing?' Warren grabbed the bottle before all the contents ran down the drain.

'You know what?' Steph pulled at her fingernails. 'I'm only seventeen. Not legal drinking age.'

'Man, are you serious? You fooled me. I thought you'd be at least nineteen.' He splashed more wine into his glass. 'Don't have to be eighteen to have a baby, I guess.' Warren drained his glass and collected his six-pack of beer. 'Guess I'll catch you later then? Just leave your door unlocked. I'll let myself in.'

Stephanie let him press his lips against hers before he left. She looked at the smashed glass in the sink, then to Warren's tumbler with millimetres of wine in the bottom. The door bumped as it closed, pulling her attention away from the wine.

She had to find a way to control herself. The thought sounded ridiculous in her mind.

Help!

She left the kitchen, showered, and got changed. Before she lost control again, she grabbed the bottle and dropped it into the sink like it was on fire. To be sure, she upended the bottle and watched until the last drop ran down the drain. Memories of drunken episodes could stay there too. She walked away. Cleaning up right now was too much. She'd deal with it in the morning.

She punched her pillow to fluff it up. *Wazza.* His reason for wanting to celebrate bugged her. She'd had it with messy relationships. Jason had turned her off them for life. All she wanted was to keep everything simple.

Prickly heat ran up her spine. Warren told her to leave her door unlocked. *No way.* She jumped out of bed and locked the door, making sure the chain was firmly in place.

A nervous churning in her stomach pushed her to check her windows. She returned to the kitchen, and the smell of alcohol assaulted her. She squirted some detergent, then ran the tap to wash it away. The smell was still there, on her hand. She lathered it with more detergent and scrubbed to remove any residue. How could she be so stupid?

Stupid. She doubled back to the front door to make sure it was locked and the chain secure before returning to bed.

Unsure whether she'd fallen asleep, Steph was startled by the sound of keys jingling then a slam of a door. *Warren.* Thank goodness he'd gone to his own apartment.

Now wide awake, Steph jumped up to check on Lola without turning on any lights. Thankfully, she was fast asleep. She returned to her bed and relaxed. Within minutes sleep claimed her again.

Chapter Eighteen

TABBIE

TABBIE STOOD ON THE EDGE of the group, distracted by the buzz in the room. Snippets of holiday stories swirled around her.

'Hey, Tabbie, we're off to the beach again tomorrow. Probably play volleyball. Are you in?' Shelly was sorting everyone into cars and pick-up points.

Tabbie nodded. Belting the volleyball would release some of her frustration.

'Yeah, let's have a comp. Girls versus boys.' Priscilla readjusted the curls in her ponytail.

'Sounds great.' Shelly glanced at Tabbie. 'Make sure you strap that ankle.'

'I'll remember.' The pain of the previous sprains shot through Tabbie's legs at the thought. The last thing she wanted was to roll her ankle and be on crutches again. It was almost habit now to strap it before doing anything physical. Dr Frank's voice resounded in her ears, advising her to take care so no permanent damage ensued.

A warm tingle moved through her chest as she remembered Danny carrying her onto the beach. Trust the thought of ankle injuries to bring back memories. If only those strong arms could embrace her now.

The next day, Tabbie, Shelly, and Priscilla had to weave their way through the crowded beach. Everyone seemed to have the same idea while the weather was good. They found their friends, dumped their towels, and joined the volleyball game.

With a firmly strapped ankle, Tabbie jumped, ran and dived for the ball. She high-fived her teammates and cheered when they scored the winning point. Sweaty and red-faced, they all ran to the water, splashing each other until they had cooled off.

Later, as they sat on their towels, Tabbie asked one of Danny's friends if he'd heard from him. He hadn't. Tabbie smiled with gratitude.

Shelly's car was loaded with people and sandy towels as they drove home, dropping girls off on the way until it was just Tabbie left in the car.

'Have you ever thought about being one of our leaders? I think you'd be great.'

Tabbie shrugged. 'You think?'

Shelly nodded. 'You're a natural leader. Will you?'

'I guess so.' Maybe she should have said she'd pray about it first. It might be a good distraction, but would she have enough time?

On the first day back at school, Tabbie dawdled along the path looking for Jaya.

'It sucks!' Jaya slapped her locker before opening it. 'You've had so much fun, and I've been stuck with Granny.'

'You could have come back and stayed with me. Why didn't you say yes when I invited you to the beach?' *What's changed since we hung out?*

'Gran refused to drive me anywhere.'

'Why don't you stay here next holidays?' Tabbie unloaded some books into her locker. She hoped that didn't sound like an invitation for Jaya to move in with them. It was one thing to live with Steph, but Jaya was another level.

'If only.'

'You're seventeen. Don't you get a choice where you spend the holidays?'

'I do, and my choice was to spend some time with Gran while Mum and Dad made their marriage breakup final and signed the divorce papers. Dad's latest Miss Floozy has moved in with him. There's no way I'd stay with them. She hovers, acting all I'm-your-best-friend. And Mum, well, she's drunk or sleeping most of the time. But she's the closest to school, so it's more convenient to stay with her.'

'That's tough. It'll be great if you do hang around here next holidays. I've missed having you round.'

'Crap! You gave up on me when you moved in with Stephanie. You barely said *boo* to me all last year. Now you've moved back home, you come to me all caring and stuff.'

Tabbie's jaw dropped. 'Jaya—' *But last week?*

'Don't... J-a-y-a me. You weren't there for me when I needed you.'

'Why are you bringing this up now? Why didn't you say something last—'

'Don't think I'm going to be here for you now you and Steph've had a falling out.'

'Jaya! There hasn't been any falling out between Steph and me. And seriously, all you needed me for was hold on to your hair while you spewed from drinking too much and to get you home in one piece.' Tabbie took a deep breath to calm herself. 'I'd had enough. That's why we didn't hang out much last year.' She wanted to pull the words back as soon as she'd said them.

'So you dumped me because of my hair?' Jaya slung her bag onto her shoulder. 'You could've talked to me about all that at the time.'

'I tried. You wouldn't listen.'

'Well, off you go in your happy little world. I don't need you anyway.'

Tabbie watched Jaya shove a couple of girls as she pushed through the congested corridor. *What's eating her? Why didn't she listen instead of being nasty?* Tabbie closed her locker and followed in Jaya's wake. They were in the same homeroom.

Did everyone else think the same as Jaya? Tabbie's life last year had revolved around being Steph's live-in carer and cleaner. She'd been to AA meetings as Steph's support person, and her grades had suffered because of the late night debriefs. She'd taken time off school to make sure Steph got to her pregnancy check-ups, not to mention when Lola was born. She hadn't been involved with anything at school, including her friends. Now she had to face the consequences.

Tabbie knew the separation between Jaya's parents had been ugly, and she should have been there for her. But Jaya seemed fine the other day. Maybe coming back to school triggered how she'd felt last year.

What was Shelly thinking, asking her to be a leader at youth group? She was such a terrible friend. How could she lead other kids? She'd have to let Shelly know she wasn't the right person for the job.

Chapter Nineteen

STEPHANIE KNEW SHE'D PUT it off long enough. She needed to visit the childcare centre. Her eyes stung from lack of sleep. For the past week, every little noise outside had woken her. She kept waiting for Warren to knock, but he hadn't.

With a well-stocked nappy bag hanging on the stroller and Lola happily buckled in, Steph double-checked she'd locked the door before throwing her keys into her bag.

Two uniformed policemen walked straight towards her. She clenched the stroller to stop her hands from shaking. The memory from only a few months ago flashed in her mind. She took a step back, then reminded herself she was no longer running from the law.

'Morning ma'am. We have a warrant to search your apartment. Won't take long. Could you open up for us please.'

'W… w… warrant? What for?'

'Just routine. If you aren't hiding anything, we'll be in and out in a few minutes and you can be on your way.'

She slipped her hand into the nappy bag. But before she could find her keys, it slid off the stroller and the contents spilled onto the pavement. She bent over to collect everything and found herself at eye level with a gun in its pouch on the officer's hip.

Images of BJ and his gun flashed in her mind. The gun he told her he'd use if she didn't shut up. Jason had been shot. Had BJ shot him? She shook her head. She didn't know.

Stephanie shuddered and glanced up. One of the officers crouched down in front of her. His stale musty cigarette breath turned her stomach.

'I'm sorry, but we don't have all day.' He helped toss the nappies, wipes and clothes into her bag. 'Now, did you find the house keys?'

She nodded and hung the bag on the stroller as she unlocked the door. Tobacco-breath police officer handed her the warrant before walking inside. Lola whinged, grabbing Stephanie's attention. She rolled the stroller backward and forward to settle her. Would she always be on the police watchlist because of Jason?

Tobacco-breath's partner returned. 'Warren Hale… a friend of yours?'

'Warren from next door?' She realised she didn't even know his last name. *Stupid, stupid, stupid.*

'That's the one. Are you aware he's moved out?'

She shook her head and tried to breathe as her chest tightened.

'Looks like he's done a runner. We were told he spent quite a bit of time with you. Are you sure he didn't say anything to you about moving?'

She shook her head again.

'Or where he was going?' Tobacco-breath swung the door open, leaving the apartment.

'No. Nothing.' *What if they don't believe me?*

'Did Warren mention his daughter to you?' Tobacco-breath asked.

'Yeah. He really misses her.'

'Your assistance to locate him would be very helpful,' the partner said.

'Have you met his daughter?' Tobacco-breath scratched his chin.

'No.' Steph pulled at her fingernails.

'Do you know when he last saw his daughter?'

Stephanie shook her head. 'A couple of weeks ago, I think. He mentioned his divorce and clearance recently. But that was the last time I saw him. I don't know him well. He's only lived here a couple of weeks.'

Tobacco-breath's partner looked at her with distrust as he wrote in a notepad. 'Well, it seems he's abducted his daughter. Would you know anything about that?'

'What?' Stephanie recalled the time Lola screamed and the front door closed. *Stupid, stupid, stupid!* Lola's whinging escalated. She unclipped the stroller harness and lifted her up, showering her with kisses. 'I haven't seen Warren for a couple of days. I don't even have his phone number or any way to contact him.'

'If he comes back, be cautious. We believe he may be dangerous. Make sure you call us if you see or hear from him.' Tobacco-breath's partner handed her a card. 'That's my number. Call me direct if he returns.'

Stephanie cuddled Lola as the officers walked away. 'What was I thinking, Lola? Thank God we're okay.'

Chapter Twenty

Tabbie

Tabbie opened her school diary and checked she'd entered all the important dates for each class. Every teacher seemed to think their subject was the most important. Why couldn't the teachers work together and spread assessments out evenly?

She had a maths assessment due on Steph's birthday. If she'd stayed at Steph's she'd end up with results like last year. Not high enough to get into uni. And based on what Jaya had said, she obviously hadn't done very well keeping up with her friends either.

Tabbie put her diary away and called Shelly. 'I don't think I'm the right person to be a leader.'

'Why not?' Shelly's voice squeaked, like she was choking.

'I'm too selfish.'

'You? Selfish? Tell me, what happened to give you that impression?'

'I've been thinking about last year and something one of my friends said—' She stopped mid-sentence. 'I wasn't there for her.'

Jaya's attitude didn't make sense, but the more Tabbie thought about it, the more she could see how self-centred she'd become.

'Maybe you're being a little hard on yourself.'

'No, I'm not. You're too kind to me.'

'I think God's grace is all you need.'

Tabbie realised she should have known Shelly would pull out the God card, something she couldn't argue with.

'You should call Priscilla and make a time to talk. She really helped me a couple of years ago.'

'Really? I thought you had your stuff sorted?'

'Yeah, it might seem that way. Priscilla was radically changed a couple of years ago when she started following Jesus. She seemed to understand the Bible the first time she looked at it. She gets God's grace in a way I'm still trying to understand.'

'But I understand grace.' Tabbie recalled messages she'd heard preached about grace during church.

'You know, we're all on a journey. We all make mistakes. And from what you've said, you're a work-in-progress like the rest of us. Maybe you simply missed some signs a friend needed you, because you were busy looking after another friend. From my point of view, you were just doing the best you could.'

Could Shelly be right? Was she really being too hard on herself for letting Jaya down? 'Alright, I'll call Priscilla. Thanks for listening.'

'Hey, anytime. And… would you be able to come in early this Friday to help us set up?'

'Okay.' She ended the call and rang Priscilla without putting the phone down.

STEPHANIE

Steph lay in bed, watching tree shadows dance on her wall with the slight breeze in the night air. Her nerves were on high alert. She jumped with every little noise and wished she had a fan to cool the stuffy room. She never felt safe at night with the windows open. Since the police had visited, she'd been a nervous wreck.

Alcohol would settle her nerves, but she had none. She could ring Tabbie, but she'd be at her youth group. The only thing left to do was watch TV. She got up, lay on the couch, and flicked through channels.

The wind picked up outside, rattling the windows. A draft swept under her door and she tucked her feet under a cushion. Before she could get comfortable, an electrical lightshow filled the sky and thunder rumbled through her apartment, vibrating anything loose.

Stephanie stood to unplug the TV just as the room went dark. Lola's high-pitched scream startled her. She rushed to pick her up. Her stomach grumbled in time with the thunder as she rocked Lola. She hadn't eaten a full meal all day. Her cupboard was bare. She'd spent the last of her money on formula and nappies. When Lola was heavy on her shoulder, she lay her back down in the cot.

The emptiness in her stomach took her thoughts back to her sister. April hadn't called for a few days. Was she eating? Stephanie couldn't imagine inflicting hunger pains like this on herself if she had a choice. With the worst of the storm blown over, she sat on the couch and called April.

'The doctor says I'm clinically depressed.' April's voice lifted as if she was happy with her new title.

'I reckon I was clinically depressed that year I spent in Toowoomba.' Stephanie hugged her legs. 'Maybe it's the town.'

'So help me get out.'

'Your only choice is to go and live with Dad. Mum isn't going to move.'

'Maybe foster parents would care more.'

'Maybe, maybe not. The grass isn't always greener.'

'What makes you say that?'

'Sometimes you have to enjoy where you're at rather than wish you were somewhere else.'

'Is that what you're doing? Enjoying living by yourself as a single mum with no support?'

Stephanie burst into tears. 'No. Not at all.'

'Well, why don't you move up here for a while? We can be miserable together. Or I could come down there, and we could be happy together.'

'That's not the answer, April. I don't have enough money.' Steph mopped her tears on her sleeve. 'I'll learn to enjoy this life. It's an attitude, you know, a decision.' It was going to take time.

'What about—' April's words cut off as Steph's phone ran out of charge.

She dropped it on the couch beside her, wishing she could move her sister down. But right now, she couldn't even afford milk or coffee. And now that the power was out, she couldn't even make herself a black tea. She found a glass in the sink, rinsed it and filled it with water.

TABBIE

Tabbie used the blackout to pray that Steph would be safe during the storms of life. When the cracks of thunder distracted her, she put her earbuds in and turned on some music to dull the rumbling. *Argh!* Her mind kept wandering back to Danny. She found a match and lit candles until her room glowed.

Perhaps she was better off using the time to start one of her thousand school assignments. She opened a book and skimmed the words while she tried to work out when she'd become such a horrible person. She phoned Steph, but the call went straight through to voicemail.

Tabbie awoke to bright sunshine. She reached for her phone. Steph had texted.

Good. Steph's okay. *She didn't need me after all.*

Over the next few days, Tabbie let her life flow to the rhythm of school and homework. On Thursday afternoon, she spread her textbooks out on her bed as the thud of a car door closing punctuated the air.

Priscilla. She'd forgotten about their coffee date. She left her books and ran downstairs.

'So tell me, how are you really going?' Priscilla didn't wait until they were at the coffee shop to begin their chat.

'I think I'm falling apart.' Tabbie tried to swallow away the thickness in her throat.

'We all have days like that.'

'Weeks?'

Priscilla glanced at her as they stopped at traffic lights. 'Yes, sometimes. Last time we spoke, it wasn't good with Danny. Is that still bothering you?'

'Kind of.' Tabbie told Priscilla the whole story. 'Steph reckons I should move on, but part of me just isn't ready to.'

'What does moving on look like?'

'I guess finding another boyfriend.' Tabbie glanced at Priscilla.

'Do you have to find another boyfriend straight away?'

Tabbie shrugged, looked out the window, then back to Priscilla. 'It's just that I keep thinking about him. How do I forget about him?'

'Get busy. Move your focus onto something else. Maybe another boyfriend isn't the answer. Maybe a new interest is.' Priscilla parked in front of the local coffee shop. 'So it's mostly the break-up that's bothering you?'

Tabbie nodded as she pushed the door open. 'And some other stuff.'

They ordered hot chocolates and slid into a booth. 'What else has been going on?' Priscilla folded the napkin in front of her.

Tabbie filled Priscilla in. She cringed as she relayed the way she'd treated Jaya and Steph.

'Could Jaya's words have affected you more than they would have on any other given day because you were already feeling down about Danny?' Priscilla asked as the waitress delivered their mugs.

'Maybe. But that doesn't excuse me dumping her to help Steph. And then dumping Steph and moving home.'

'Did you consciously decide to leave Jaya out last year?'

'No, but I remember making a decision not to be her keeper at parties.' Tabbie hugged the hot chocolate in her palms.

'That sounds like a healthy boundary you needed to set. She's going through a big change with her parents' divorce. I know you were there for her the year before last, and it was really taxing on you. You invited her to youth group, you prayed for her, you tried to make her see that she could have fun in a safe way. But she chose to continue going to parties and getting drunk. That was her choice. We all have freewill and we can only do the best we can with the knowledge we have at any given time. In the last year, did Jaya come to you and ask for anything other than taking her to parties?'

'No. That was pretty much the only time she wanted to hang out with me—when she didn't want to go to a party on her own.'

'So, in some ways, she wasn't being altogether fair on you.' Priscilla sipped her drink. 'Learning to forgive is a powerful tool. There are studies proving it.'

Tabbie stirred her hot chocolate.

'Not only is it written in the Bible that we are to forgive, forgiveness can actually benefit our health. Can you find it in your heart to forgive her?'

'But I'm the one who needs to be forgiven.'

'That's not your responsibility. You can apologise if you feel you need to, but you have no control over whether she will forgive you. What you do have control over is whether you forgive or not.

To forgive simply means letting go of controlling the situation and handing it over to God to deal with.'

'I'm a little lost. Shouldn't I always be there for my friend? Wouldn't Jesus have done that?'

'You are a gorgeous girl. You are so selfless. What you've done is put boundaries in place. That's not being self-centred. If you were meant to spend more time looking after Jaya, I'm sure you would've sensed it. Remember how you had that urgency to go to Stephanie's apartment when she was living with her boyfriend? You felt compelled to visit her.'

That's true. Tabbie thought back to the day she'd had a vision of Steph lying at the base of a staircase, so she went to check on her. If she hadn't turned up when she did, Steph might not be alive today.

'If you think you've made a mistake, pray about it. There's no burden too heavy for God to heal.'

'But if I can't be there for my friends when they need me, how can I be a leader at youth group?' Tabbie pushed her cup away.

'You do it with a whole lot of grace. Sure, you'll make mistakes. We all do. There's no pressure. This isn't something you have to do. But you love God, and I see the overflow of that love in everything you do.' Priscilla twirled her blonde ponytail in her fingers and flashed a bright smile.

'I don't know if I can be available for everyone,' Tabbie said. 'I don't know if I'll have the time with school as well.'

'Gosh, I can't be there for everyone either. I just do the best I can.'

'You make it sound so simple.'

'It is. Everyone tries to complicate it.'

Tabbie reached for her cup and drank the last of her hot chocolate.

Chapter Twenty-one

TABBIE

TABBIE CLUNG TO THE SEAT of an overcrowded bus. As it turned another corner, her thoughts returned to her conversation with Priscilla. She still wasn't sure about the whole 'leader' thing. Was she really capable of leading girls almost her age?

Priscilla swung the church door open just before Tabbie reached it. 'You're here early. Great! We're setting up the chairs. Would you mind giving us a hand?'

'Love to.' The band was rehearsing. She glanced at the bass player, willing him to somehow morph into Danny. She cast the thought away as she pushed another chair into place.

Shelly returned. 'We need someone at the Fizz Hut. Our regular volunteer is away. Would you be okay with selling snacks tonight?'

'I'll need some willpower to not eat too much if I'm there all night.' Tabbie laughed.

'I won't leave you there for too long. I'll try to find someone else to help you.'

While on duty at the Fizz Hut, she discovered a lot of people made a beeline from the front door straight towards her, especially those who came on their own. Some girls were quiet, making their purchase then leaving quickly. Some boys were annoyingly flirtatious, and some kids were happy to hang out for a chat while they ate their potato chips or sipped their soft drinks.

When Shelly appeared with Ina, her replacement, Tabbie's shoulders dropped. She wasn't ready to leave. She'd enjoyed helping more than she thought she would. She grabbed her lemonade and purse and began to move before looking up. Her hand hit a solid stomach, splashing the drink down her shirt and all over her arm.

'Hey,' he said. 'Sorry.'

'No, no. My fault.'

'Let me get something to wipe that up.' He reached over to the Fizz Hut and grabbed a couple of napkins. His voice was deeper, but she'd remember the face anywhere.

'Joey! Where've you been?' *And when did you get so tall and so brown and so…*

'On the family yacht.' He shrugged. 'And it's Joe. I'd rather you call me Joe.'

Tabbie nodded. She'd call him whatever he wanted. Her body tingled all over. 'Your family has a yacht?' She couldn't take her gaze off him.

'Nanna and Pop bought it to bring the family together.'

'Were you waited on hand and foot?' She imagined being on a yacht, lying on a deck chair with a mocktail. Heat rushed up her neck. 'It must have been great.'

'It wasn't a cruise ship.' He chuckled. 'It's a real yacht with real working sails. They put us all to work. Both on the deck and in the kitchen.' Joe shook his head then drank from a bottle of water. 'If you call being stuck on a yacht with a bunch of socially awkward people who haven't spent time together for at least ten years great… yeah it was out of this world.'

'Okay, I'm getting the picture,' Tabbie laughed, imagining the awkwardness. 'So it was more like a nightmare?'

He nodded.

'How long were you stranded for?'

'Six weeks!' He flashed a wide smile, white teeth glowing against his fresh tan.

'So, Joey—'

'Joe,' he corrected her.

'What's with the change? You're all grown up and need a more mature name?' She tried to make a joke, confused at why she was so flustered.

'This probably sounds weird, but every time I hear Joey, I'm taken straight back to Suzie. So it would be great if you could keep it to Joe.'

Tabbie felt another flush rise up her neck as a brick fell in her stomach. *How could I have forgotten?* 'Yeah, I miss her too. I can't imagine how you…' Her voice choked. She didn't know how to continue. Stuck in awkward silence, she glanced at his arms, senses heightened at the way his sleeves clung to his biceps. Memories of her fantasy man, Mr Biceps, came flooding back, followed immediately by memories of her reality. *Danny.* The one who had Mr Biceps' biceps but...

'You weren't here much last year.'

'You were?' she asked.

'Yeah. I reckon Danny was onto a good thing. It just took me a while to catch on.'

Now that he'd mentioned Danny, she had to ask, 'Have you heard from him? Danny, I mean.'

'Yeah. We messaged a lot before I went out on the yacht.' Joe waved to a friend, smiled at her, and walked away.

Does that mean he hasn't heard anything lately either? She pushed the thought away and came back to Suzie. It had been more than a year since she'd died. Tabbie missed her. She hadn't expected Joey to still be grieving the loss of his girlfriend.

Tabbie glanced from side to side, feeling alone in a crowded room.

$\mathcal{S}$TEPHANIE

The sun slipped over the horizon, sucking the daylight with it. Stephanie flicked the light switch on. She put her baby down in her cot. Another night in her stuffy box of an apartment. She turned the cold water on in the shower and stepped under the flow to refresh herself. Uneasiness followed her as she dressed.

She'd only gone as far as the local convenience store for bread and milk since her fortnightly payment. Her nerves took over every time she attempted to leave her apartment. She didn't want to bother Tabbie. Things could be worse. At least she had a roof over her head. *Right?*

Steph double-checked the locks were fastened on the front door and windows. She turned off all the lights, then plonked herself in front of the TV. She watched the beginning of the news then turned it off and sat in darkness.

Thud. Rattle, rattle.

She jumped from the couch. Her hands trembled. The outline in the opaque window could be only one person. She crawled on her hands and knees to her bedroom, closing the door behind her.

'Hey, Steph, open up. I've got a bottle of your favourite.'

Her mouth watered at the thought. She shook her head, swallowed, and stayed still, leaning back against the door. *Please, go away.*

'You can't be 'sleep already. S'too early. I just wanna say g'bye to you an' specially baby Lola 'fore I 'ed off.'

Her whole body froze. *Especially Lola?* He'd already been suspected of kidnapping his daughter. *What if he intends to take Lola?*

Stephanie reached for the doorknob, swung the bedroom door open and crawled into Lola's room. Again, she closed the door and leaned against it. Lola stirred. 'Shh, baby,' Steph whispered, trembling. 'It's okay.'

Silence.

She hoped Lola had drifted back to sleep. The room was too dark to see anything with the blackout blind closed.

The rod. She crawled across the room and slipped her hand under the blind to make sure the rod was in place. Of course it was. She hadn't opened the windows since the police had been. Was OCD another title she'd have to deal with? She thought back to how many times she checked everything was locked over and over every day.

'Steph!' Warren called. 'I know ya home. I saw the telly.'

She bit down hard on her lip. Blood spurted onto her tongue.

'S'okay. I'll come back 'n a bit.' His voice was so soft, she barely made out the words.

She focused on the cot, hearing Lola's gentle sleepy breaths.

Stephanie breathed in deeply, holding her breath before releasing it, a technique she'd learnt in rehab. *Breathe, count, release slowly, repeat.* Her mind cleared a little. She needed her phone. Not daring to stand in case he saw her shadow, she edged the door open and crawled to the kitchen. She felt around on the top of the bench where she always left her keys and phone.

With her mobile in hand, she crawled back into Lola's room.

     Spiralling Solo

Chapter Twenty-two

THE MUSIC BEGAN TO PLAY and the crowd surged towards the auditorium. Tabbie slid into a chair and sensed Joe's presence before she saw him standing beside her. Her heart flipped and did a strange squeezy thing. She clenched her teeth, willing her physical reactions to stop betraying her. But the fresh soapy aroma of the grown-up boy from her dance classes hit her. She lost all sense of control as his arm brushed hers when they sat down. She couldn't have been more distracted when the pastor said her name. 'Tabbie,' he began. 'I was watching you worship and James 1:27 came to mind. Do you have a heart for the orphans? Widows?'

Orphans, yes. Tabbie nodded. *Widows?* She wasn't sure.

'I believe you will be more significant than you could ever imagine. What you are going through now will stretch you and prepare you for what God has in store for you. Remember to stay humble and don't lose heart.'

Tears sprang over her lashes. *What is he talking about?* She'd heard the preacher single people out a few times, but no one had ever spoken to her in that way before. *Stretch and prepare?* What had he been talking about before he mentioned her? Maybe it would have made more sense if she'd been listening. The past few weeks had been challenging, but could all the turmoil be preparing her for something ahead?

Distracted by the hand resting on her shoulder, she glanced at Joe. His eyes were closed. Praying for her, she assumed. Did he have any idea what his touch did to her? Perhaps it was a sign there were other boys. How could she be a leader when her body continued to betray her? She needed self-control.

Steph came to mind. She'd had trouble with self-control. The word *hypocrite* hovered in Tabbie's mind. Maybe she should talk to Steph. Maybe they could learn together.

After the service ended, Tabbie raced outside without saying goodbye to anyone. She found her mother and jumped into the car. Her mind soared as she tried to work out what the preacher had meant and where the attraction to Joe had come from. As she replayed the night in her mind, something else distracted her.

Stephanie. She hadn't married Jason, but was she technically a widow? 'Mum, I'm worried about Steph.' It was as if the words came out on their own.

'Yeah?' Her mother glanced at her. 'She has to learn to stand on her own feet. But keep checking in on her. Let her know we're here if she needs us.'

Tabbie nodded, then said a silent prayer asking God to watch over Steph.

$\mathcal{S}$TEPHANIE

Thump, thump, thump.

Steph scuttled back until she hit the wall. She'd sat in paralysing silence for what felt like half an hour, hoping he was gone.

'Hey, Stephy, let me in!' Warren called.

She held her mobile and punched in triple zero. Before her call was answered, sharp clunking shuddered against Lola's bedroom window. *What's he hitting the glass with?*

A male voice boomed through the phone. 'Name and address please.'

If she spoke now, she'd wake Lola, and Warren might hear. Stephanie felt for Lola's soft play mat on the floor and lifted it over her head to muffle her voice. She whispered her name and address.

'There's a guy, Warren… umm… Oh! I can't remember his last name… the police were here.' Her words fell out in a jumble. 'They told me he's dangerous… he's outside my window. He's hitting my window. I'm scared.'

The man asked her more questions then asked her to stay on the line.

A loud crack made her jump. Glass clattered to the floor. She gasped, then held her breath as she dropped the mat. She blinked, trying to let in more light. The room was still pitch-black. Outside noises were no longer separated by the window.

A siren blared.

Stephanie felt the floor around her, checking for glass. She couldn't feel any between her and the cot. Lola stirred. Steph breathed short, sharp gasps. Her hands shook as she reached into the cot and patted Lola's back, hoping to soothe her.

Lola stopped fussing, but Steph continued to rub her back.

One, two, three sets of shoes scuffed past the window. Men yelled. A muffled thwack made her jump.

Lola cried. Stephanie pulled her out of the cot and rocked her. Another scuffle and more voices. She couldn't make out the words. She stepped backwards until her back was against the wall. Frozen with fear, all she could do was cling to Lola.

Three sharp knocks sounded on the front door. 'Stephanie, are you there? It's the police.'

The voice was nothing like Warren's. *But what if he's got someone with him?* How would she know without seeing first?

Another round of knocks sounded on her door, louder this time. 'Ms Stronge?'

The voice sounded oddly familiar. She held Lola tight and edged her way out of the bedroom and into the kitchen. She pulled the blind a fraction from the window to look outside. Tobacco-breath and his offsider stood at the door.

With Lola quiet against her shoulder, Steph opened the door, leaving the chain attached and peeked through. 'Where is he? W-Warren?'

'The other officers have arrested him.'

'Broke the window,' was all she could say. 'Smashed.'

'Can we turn some lights on?' Tobacco-breath asked.

She stepped aside and they walked past, leaving her trembling against the wall.

'Which room has the shattered window?'

She pointed to Lola's room.

Tobacco-breath flicked light switches on, then stood at the doorway while his partner took some pictures.

'Good thing the blind was down to stop the glass from shattering across the room. Either of you hurt?' Tobacco-breath's partner asked.

Steph looked down and saw nothing. She checked under her feet. Both were clear. She shook her head.

'But you were in the room when the window was broken?'

Steph nodded. 'Lola was in her cot.'

'There are shards of glass just below the window. You didn't stand on any?' said Tobacco-Breath.

Stephanie shook her head.

Tobacco-breath's partner held out a rock with a piece of paper stuck to it in his gloved hand. 'Does this mean anything to you?'

She gasped as she read the note. *Crass. Embarrassing.*

'Do you have friends or family you can stay with tonight?' Tobacco-breath asked, the stale cigarette smell of his breath infusing her apartment.

Stephanie stared through them. Tabbie was busy with school and youth group. She didn't want to bother Tom and Francine.

'We'll tape the window up, but it won't be secure until it's replaced. You'll need to call the property manager first thing in the morning so they can make arrangements.'

She nodded.

'We've got all we need from here. We'll be outside for a while. But best you grab your valuables and stay out for the night. Maybe a motel?'

Are they offering to pay? She shrugged and shook her head. She glanced at Lola, asleep on her shoulder. The police suggested she lock the door behind them, but that seemed pointless with a gaping hole in the bedroom window. Then she sat on the couch and flicked through the TV channels. Nothing appealed to her, but silence was worse than white noise.

Chapter Twenty-three

TABBIE

TABBIE CHECKED HER PHONE. No reply from Steph. Maybe she'd gone to bed early. Or maybe…

She ran up to her room, grabbed her pillow and pushed it into place like she was shoving away her thoughts. She fell into bed hoping everything was okay with Steph and she hadn't let her down. Tomorrow would be a new day. She closed her eyes. Maybe her thoughts would be clearer in the morning.

She tossed and turned with visions of Stephanie in the forefront. Was it a sign? She rolled over again. All she could see was Steph. She couldn't ignore it.

Tabbie grabbed her phone. Still nothing from Stephanie. She dropped it on the floor and pulled her doona over her head hoping to smother herself to sleep. But she lay wide awake.

In the early hours of the morning, she traipsed downstairs and used the light from inside the fridge to illuminate the room enough to pour herself a glass of milk. It had helped her sleep in the past.

Hopefully it would work again.

She tiptoed back to her room so she didn't disturb her parents. Her phone lit the room. She rushed to it.

Call when u wake up. S x

Maybe Steph needed her. Maybe that's why she couldn't sleep.

I'm awake now. Need to chat?

Yes.

Knowing Steph was probably nearly out of credit, Tabbie rang.

'Hi,' Steph whispered.

'What's up?'

'Oh, um. I've got to be quiet. I'm holding Lola.'

'Is she okay?'

'Yeah, she's sleeping. Just… something crazy has happened. That guy from next door threw a stone and shattered one of our windows.'

'What! When?'

'A few hours ago.'

'Why didn't you call straight away?' Silence. 'Are you okay? Do you need to get away from there? I'll get Dad to come and pick you up.' Tabbie left her bedroom to wake her father.

'The cops taped up the window. But I can't sleep.'

'We can come pick you up now.'

'You can wait till the morning.' Stephanie's whisper dropped even lower.

'We'll be over soon.' Tabbie hung up and nudged her father's shoulder. 'Dad, it's Steph.'

'Huh?' He sat up, his eyes half-opened. 'She needs us?'

'Yeah, I think so. Someone tried to break in, and now she's there alone with a broken window. She said she'd be right, but I think we should go.'

'Right, give me a minute to change.'

Tabbie threw on a pair of shorts and a t-shirt, then raced downstairs to wait for her father. He emerged soon after covering a yawn with his hand.

Ten minutes later, Tabbie tapped on Steph's door. Steph didn't come. What if she'd fallen asleep? Maybe she should have waited until daylight. She knocked again in a round of little taps. She couldn't hear Lola and didn't want to wake her with a thunderous bang. 'Steph, it's Tabbie.'

Steph opened the door just a crack, then slid the chain off. As soon as Tabbie was through the door, she wrapped her arms around Steph.

'What time did it happen?' Dad followed them inside.

'Not sure exactly. Maybe around eight or nine.'

'Why didn't you call us straight away?' Dad asked.

'I didn't want to bother you.'

Tabbie raised her eyebrows. 'You know you're family. Which means you can call at any time—night or day. That's how family works.'

'Should we grab some of your things and take you back to our place?' Dad held Steph's shoulder. 'Or would you rather we stay here with you?'

'I don't know.' A slight slur curved her words.

Dad walked around, investigating, as Tabbie lowered her voice to ask. 'Have you been drinking?'

Stephanie's eyes widened. She shook her head.

'It's just that your voice…'

'I feel like I've lost it. My voice… my mind…'

'What is it? Did something else happen?'

Stephanie swayed from side to side as she staggered across the room.

'Should we call an ambulance? Where's Lola?' Tabbie rushed forward to help as Steph collapsed, knocking her head on the corner of the couch.

'Dad! Call the ambulance. Something's wrong. Steph collapsed.'

'I saw.' He held his phone to his ear.

Lola whimpered.

'You check on Lola, I'll stay here with Stephanie.' Dad crouched, checking Steph's pulse.

   Spiralling Solo

Tabbie walked towards Lola's room but was stopped by tape across the door. She checked Steph's room and found the baby sleeping between two pillows. Tabbie gently picked her up, waking her in the process. Lola cuddled into her shoulder.

'What's happening, Dad?'

'They're sending someone out. They should be here soon. Did you ask her if she'd taken anything?'

'Just if she'd been drinking. I didn't think about anything else.'

'I told them it was unlikely. But can you see if there's anything in the kitchen or bathroom that she might have taken?'

Tabbie checked the benches, the cupboards, the drawers, and the bins. 'Nothing here.'

Lola pushed away from Tabbie, crying, 'Mumma.'

'Let me guess. Now I've woken you up, you'd like a bottle?' Tabbie went to the pantry where Steph kept the formula. There was only enough in the tin to make up half a bottle.

Blaring sirens pierced the air. Dad rushed outside to meet them.

Steph lay on the couch. She stirred as they ran some tests on her.

Lola pushed the empty bottle away. 'Mumma.'

Tabbie searched for her favourite elephant and saw it in her cot, on the other side of the tape. She found another squeaky toy, hoping it would be enough to distract her.

The paramedics concluded that Stephanie was suffering from shock. They continued running tests, then suggested Steph make an appointment with her local doctor and recommended monitoring her for the next twenty-four hours.

'Don't you worry,' Dad scratched his greying beard. 'She's like a daughter. I'll be keeping a close eye on her for the next couple of days.

Tabbie knew her parents felt they'd failed Stephanie when she'd ended up pregnant and in rehab. But seeing her father right now gave her a greater understanding of how deeply he cared.

'I'm fine,' Stephanie said after the ambulance officers left. 'Really. You don't need to keep an eye on me.'

Tabbie put Lola on the floor and filled a glass with water. 'Here, drink this. They said you're a bit dehydrated.'

'Thanks.'

'You look really skinny. Have you been eating?' Dad asked.

'Yeah, you know, it's busy…'

It hit Tabbie. When she'd checked the fridge and pantry, not only had there been no drugs or alcohol, the shelves were virtually bare. 'Would you like to go wash your face or something? I'll watch Lola.'

'Thanks.' Stephanie stood slowly. 'Actually, I might have a shower.' She swayed as she began to walk. Tabbie rushed to her side. 'I'm okay.' Stephanie seemed steady enough as she walked down the hallway.

'Just yell out if you feel wobbly again,' Dad said.

Tabbie waited until the water was running. 'Dad, I don't think she's been eating. There's nothing in her fridge.'

'Right.' The crease between her father's eyes deepened. 'I'm not taking no for an answer this time. She's coming home with us for a few nights.'

She hoped Stephanie would accept their kindness and not feel disempowered.

Spiralling Solo

Chapter Twenty-four

STEPHANIE

STUPID! WHAT AN IDIOT. Tabbie had warned her about Warren, but she'd ignored her. Tabbie kept asking if she was okay on her own, and she'd lied. What a failure. She turned up the water pressure, but the force of the shower didn't wash away the heaviness weighing on her heart. She held the wall to steady herself as her cloudy thoughts swirled like a storm. She wanted to be independent and cope on her own. But how could she with no money? No job? The government money only covered rent, nappies, and baby formula.

She shut off the water, dried herself, got dressed and reluctantly returned to the lounge room.

'Right, let's grab anything valuable and head back over to our house,' Tom said.

Stephanie nodded. Surreal numbness took over. Nothing she owned was valuable.

'Were the police going to let the property manager know, or do you have to?' Tom checked the windows in the kitchen and lounge room.

She shrugged. *What did they say?* She couldn't remember.

'Never mind. We'll call them when they open and work it out then. It's best if you stay with us until we know the unit is safe.'

'But…' She hated relying on them.

'Only for a couple of days. Until you're back to yourself. Then you can decide where you want to be.'

Steph took a shallow breath. Her chin trembled as tears formed. She rushed to the bathroom before Tom and Tabbie saw them. 'Just getting some things,' Steph called.

Steph woke with a clear mind for the first time in days. She'd been wandering around the Morays' in a hazy fog, trying to make out what her life was meant to look like. But today she was ready to be independent again. 'I'm heading home today.'

Tabbie stopped chewing her toast.

'Are you sure?' Francine raised her eyebrows.

'Yeah. I want to check that childcare centre close to home. Umm… I'd love to have someone else's opinion. Are you busy today?' Steph looked at Francine. 'I don't really know what to look for. But I… I need to get a job.'

Francine grabbed the pot of coffee and poured three cups. 'I've got some time after ten. I'd be happy to check it out with you.'

'I'd come too, but it's a school day.' Tabbie took another bite of toast.

'And I know how you hate to chuck sickies.' Stephanie tried to make a joke but her tone was all wrong.

'I know.' Tabbie giggled. 'I can't help it. It's just the way I am.'

Steph smiled, thankful Tabbie hadn't taken her comment the wrong way.

'I'll pop back and pick you up. Is that okay?' Francine wiped the benches.

'You sure? Um…' Steph hesitated. 'I just feel like…' *A failure. A bad mum. Completely hopeless.*

     Spiralling Solo

'You know, I've been thinking.' Tabbie sat down beside Stephanie. 'This year doesn't look that hard. Maybe I could come stay with you again.'

'No.' *Why is this family always so nice?* Steph looked Tabbie in the eye. 'Your parents wouldn't let you. Not to mention the grades you hope to pick up.'

'Let's talk about it again later.' Tabbie pushed her chair out and rushed off with a smile.

$\mathcal{T}$ABBIE

'Tabbie, love,' her father said across the dinner table. 'How did Steph settle back into her apartment?'

'I haven't spoken to her, but her texts sound like she's doing well.'

'Maybe you should give her a call and check in properly.' Dad put his fork down. Her mother paused, knife and fork mid-air.

'Why?' Tabbie's shoulders tensed.

'I'm worried about her. She's been home a week, so I rang to check on her myself. She didn't seem herself.'

Her dad was ringing Steph? He must be worried. He had an uncanny wise-woman type of perception that seemed to be showing up more often. She'd sensed something wasn't right as well. Why hadn't she acted on it?

'I'll call her after dinner.' She pushed the food around her plate. She needed to keep a closer eye on Steph.

After dinner, Tabbie grabbed her phone and checked the last few text messages from Stephanie. She was either putting on a brave face or everything really was fine. She rang but Steph didn't answer.

Stephanie replied almost immediately.

Tabbie turned her phone off for the night. Her chest tightened.

The next night, Tabbie walked into youth group, trying not to admit to herself that she wanted to see Joey. When he didn't turn up, the night seemed lacklustre. At least this week she heard every word the speaker preached and walked out refreshed.

'How's everything going with Steph?' Priscilla asked her after the service.

'She says she's okay, but I'm staying over there tonight to make sure.'

They shuffled their way through the crowd, then stopped outside near a bunch of younger girls in fits of laughter. 'Would you like me to pick you up in the morning and go to the beach?' Priscilla asked.

'Thanks, but I think I should hang out with Steph for a while.' She wavered. Beach hangs were the best. But maybe Steph needed her.

Tabbie looked up. Mum was parking the car. She said a quick goodbye and watched Priscilla join the group, laughing along with them. It felt like forever since she'd laughed like that. When did life get so serious?

'Make sure you call me if you need a ride home.' Her mother pulled into the kerb outside Steph's apartment.

'Okay, but I'll probably jog home. I need the exercise. See you tomorrow.' She jumped out and walked down the dimly lit driveway.

Warren's apartment was dark. *Thank goodness he's gone.* A few more paces and she stood in front of Steph's and tapped the door with the tips of her fingers.

'Shh.' Steph opened the door. 'Lola went to sleep ages ago, but she's stirring.'

Tabbie nodded, tiptoed inside and placed her backpack down quietly. 'Mum said the childcare centre was clean and comfortable.'

'Lola started there yesterday.' Steph nodded. 'It was horrible. She screamed when I left.'

'Oh, no. Did she settle down?'

'They said she did.' Steph bit her lip as she glanced towards Lola's room.

'Were you okay? Why didn't you get in touch?'

'You were at school.'

'Mum was home.'

'I came home and cried.' Steph's shoulders tensed into a shrug. 'I felt miserable. I couldn't do anything until I had to pick her up. I couldn't bear to take her back today.'

'Oh, Steph.'

'I still don't have a job. I didn't do anything around here. I haven't done much at all.'

'Except look after Lola.'

'Yeah, but that's not going to pay the rent.'

'What if Mum goes with you, or takes you to some interviews?'

'I've got to get the interviews to start with.'

'True.'

'Most places want you to apply online and I don't have—'

'What about the library? You could use their computers.'

Steph shook her head. 'I thought about it, but Lola gets restless in her stroller if we aren't moving.'

'You should have asked me to bring my laptop.'

'I know.' Stephanie's jaw jutted forward. 'But I'm sick of relying on you.'

'But we're family. We're here to support you.'

Tabbie searched Stephanie's puffy eyes. Why couldn't she accept their help?

'Have you heard from Danny?' Steph asked.

'No. Nothing since "time to move on". I guess he really meant it. You told me before the email to move on. I should have listened. I thought he was the one.' A shiver ran down her spine.

'Just like I thought Jason was the one. Look at the mess that got me into.' Steph frowned. 'I reckon our judgement is completely skewed when we fall in love.'

'Yeah, funny.' Tabbie nodded. Maybe she'd had been blinded by Danny's biceps and hotness. 'I remember saying something along those lines when you were falling for Jason.'

'It was great advice. Wish I'd listened to you.' Steph's frown lifted. 'You went to youth group? How's that going?'

'Joey's back.' Tabbie's heartbeat raced away from her. Why did she feel like she'd cheated on Danny just because she found Joe attractive? She took a deep breath. 'Do you remember him? He's the one Suzie—'

'The dancer?' Stephanie rolled her eyes.

'Yeah, that's him. Well, he's been away with his family, and I haven't seen him for ages. Anyway, he's lost his boyish look. He's tall and tanned and you should see his biceps!'

'Is he still dancing?' Stephanie flicked the TV on, muting the volume.

'I didn't think to ask about that.' Tabbie couldn't stop the bubble of laughter rising in her. 'I was distracted by his biceps.'

'Shh, Lola.' Steph raised her eyebrows. 'Nice switch, one set of biceps to another.'

'Ha ha. Can we change the subject?'

'Sorry.'

'I'll have to avoid looking at Joey's biceps. I'm not going for a rebound relationship.'

'So no fantasising then?' Steph laughed.

'No.' Tabbie laughed a little too loud. She'd let her mind wander, but she needed to stop.

'Shh. Lola.' Steph pointed.

Laughing felt good, but she quieted herself at Steph's request.

'What's Joey been up to since losing Suzie?'

     Spiralling Solo

'Well, he grew tall, tanned, and hot.'

'You are so fantasising.'

'Am not.'

'Are too. Tabbie, what's going on with you? I never expected you to fall for someone else so quickly.'

'I haven't fallen for him. I just noticed his biceps.' She laughed at herself.

'Are you hanging around in the morning?' Steph asked.

'I don't have plans. What have you got on?' Tabbie asked.

'I don't have much here for breakfast.'

Tabbie eyed Stephanie up and down. She was thin. 'Have you been grocery shopping since you came back?'

'Yeah, just for the necessities.'

'I've got an idea. I've got some cash on me, so how about we go out for breakfast?'

'Okay.' Stephanie turned. 'But what about Lola? It's just that she just hates sitting in the stroller unless we're moving.'

'What about a highchair? Let's see how she goes. We can grab takeaway if she's restless.'

Tabbie was determined to make sure Steph ate at least one good meal.

Chapter Twenty-five

$\mathcal{S}$TEPHANIE

STEPHANIE STARED AT THE BIG BREAKFAST on the café menu, salivating. 'What are you getting?' She chewed her lip.

'The bacon and egg muffin. You?'

'Looks good. I'll get the same.' She'd look like a pig if she went for the Big Breakfast. Though right now she could eat that—and more.

'Want a coffee?' Tabbie's gaze was fixed on the board behind the counter.

'Are you getting one?' Stephanie didn't want to abuse her friend's generosity.

Tabbie nodded.

'Sure, if you're getting one.'

'How about we get some pancakes to share as well? Or would you rather a blueberry muffin?'

'Really?' Stephanie's stomach groaned with joy at the thought. 'Are you that hungry?'

Tabbie smiled, nodded and proceeded to order enough food for four people. She grabbed a highchair and led the way towards a table on the sidewalk. Her phone buzzed with a text message.

'Who was that?' Stephanie asked.

'Priscilla.'

'What did she want?'

'She's just checking if I want to go to the beach for the day.'

'And?' Stephanie parked the stroller behind her chair and lifted Lola out.

'Well… I'm with you.'

'But you could still go.' Steph slipped Lola into the highchair and sat down. She hated being the reason Tabbie missed out.

'Would you come with me?' Tabbie smiled, eyebrows raised.

'With Lola and all?' A day at the beach would be nice, but…

'Why not?' Tabbie poked Lola and giggled with her.

'There isn't enough in the nappy bag for all day. We'd have to go home and get sorted. And then there's the car seat, and—'

'What if Priscilla grabs the seat from my house on her way here? What else do you need? We could grab something from the supermarket next door. We should leave that car seat with you, then you'd have it to put in anyone's car.'

It would be handy to have the car seat. Tabbie made everything sound easy. Just grab it from the shop. Except for the money.

'It'll be fun. What do you say?'

'Maybe. The weather is nice.' She looked out at the patches of fluffy clouds floating with hardly a breeze.

'Yay! We're going to have a great day.' Tabbie pulled her phone out again and punched in another message.

Stephanie looked at Tabbie. *What have I done?* Did she really want to hang out with a bunch of teenagers? She didn't even have sunscreen or a shade cover on the stroller.

Tabbie's phone buzzed as their breakfast was served.

'This looks amazing.' Stephanie could hardly hold back from scoffing it down.

'It sure does. Go for it.' Tabbie pushed the pancakes towards Stephanie and checked her phone. 'It's all sorted. Priscilla is stopping by my place, then she'll have time to meet us at around nine-thirty.'

Steph focused on the food in front of her. Lola sat surprisingly content in the highchair playing with her bottle and elephant. When they finished, Tabbie led them to the supermarket. 'What do you need?' She grabbed a trolley.

'Sunscreen for Lola.'

'Sure. Does she have swimmers?' Tabbie went straight to the baby product aisle. 'Hey, these squeeze packs look easy. How is she going on solids? Does she like custard? Or fruit?'

'Maybe the fruit would be better. I haven't tried them.' Stephanie watched, unable to speak as Tabbie threw several of each into the trolley. Then she grabbed a tin of formula, regular nappies, and swim nappies. 'Really, Tabbie, that's stacks.'

'I'm sure you'll make use of it.' Tabbie added a packet of biscuits, crackers and chips as they walked past the displays near the checkout. 'What about other things? You're out of coffee, hey?'

Steph nodded. 'But Tabbie, I don't have enough—'

'It's okay. I told you I had some extra cash on me.'

Steph followed Tabbie through the grocery aisles as she filled the trolley. Thank you didn't seem adequate.

'We'd better drop this back at your place so you can get the milk in the fridge.'

'It's going to take ages for me to pay you back.'

They loaded some bags over the stroller handles and carried the rest. 'This one is on me. Didn't I say that earlier?'

How was she ever going to show the Morays she could manage on her own if she couldn't even buy her own groceries?

   Spiralling Solo

When Priscilla pulled up, Shelly jumped out of the front seat. 'Hey, Stephanie, so good to see you again. Would you like to strap Lola in the car seat while I put the stroller in the boot?'

'Okay, thanks.' Steph unbuckled the stroller straps and pulled Lola into her arms.

'Now, how does this thing fold down?' Shelly asked, laughing.

'Like this.' Tabbie pushed the foot release peddle.

'Yep, I was just about to try that.'

'Sure you were!' Tabbie bumped Shelly's shoulder.

'Stephanie, your little girl is absolutely beautiful.' Priscilla smiled as she started the car.

'Thanks.' Steph tried to swallow the thickness in her throat. *Yeah, Lola is beautiful.* She'd inherited her father's features and incredible good looks.

'I take my hat off to you,' Priscilla said. 'I dreamed of being a young mum but haven't met the right guy yet. I guess she's a lot of work, though.'

'Yep. She's all that.' Work, work and more work—not to mention expensive.

'Do you see your family much?' Shelly asked. 'They're in Toowoomba, aren't they?'

'Mum and my sister are. But Dad is further north. I rarely speak to my parents but I talk to my sister a lot…' She paused, not wanting to dump April's dramas on them.

'How's she going?' Shelly asked.

'She'll be fine.' Steph wanted the conversation to stop.

'And Lola's other grandparents?'

'I don't talk to them. They're business people and travel heaps.' Stephanie pulled at her fingernails.

'You're amazing. It must be such a blessing to have Tabbie and her family around.'

Stephanie smiled and clenched her teeth. They didn't think she could cope on her own either. She had to prove them wrong.

'Yeah.' Tabbie turned to Steph. 'You might be living by yourself, but we're here for you, hey?'

Stephanie forced another smile. She should be thankful for everything Tabbie had just bought, but instead she felt hopeless. Tabbie raised her eyebrows. *Is she reading my mind again?*

When Priscilla parked the car at the beach, Steph's feet tingled at the thought of sand between her toes. Lola had been good so far this morning, but how long would that last? She glanced up and down the street, searching for the nearest bus stop.

'Do you want me to get the stroller out of the boot? Or would it be easier to just take the picnic blanket?' Priscilla asked.

She released a long breath. 'My stroller wheels are too small to handle sand.'

'Can I carry Lola?' Shelly was already pulling her out of her seat.

Steph watched as Lola turned and leaned back towards her.

'Can I carry the bag?' Priscilla asked.

Stephanie noticed Priscilla's perfectly manicured fingers grab the nappy bag. She glanced at her own hands, the chips in her nails held telltale signs of a mum without money. 'Your nails are gorgeous. Wish I had the money—'

'I've got a friend who could do them for you at a fraction of the price.'

'Maybe when I get a job.' Steph forced another smile. It was a nice thought to park for the future.

Lola squirmed. 'Mumma, mumma.'

'Thanks, but I'll take her now.' Steph bounced Lola on her hip.

They reached a large group on the beach. Steph didn't recognise anyone and hung back. She grabbed a wisp of hair caught in the sea breeze and attempted to tuck it behind her ear, but her jagged fingernail snagged more hair and caused a messier tangle.

Chapter Twenty-six

TABBIE

TABBIE NOTICED STEPH PLAYING with her fingernails and hanging back from the group as it erupted with hellos and hugs. She scanned the faces but couldn't see the one person she hoped to see. She groaned on the inside for letting her mind wander. Again.

Tabbie returned to Steph's side and gently grabbed her arm to pull her into the group. Steph resisted. Tabbie followed Steph's gaze toward the water. And there he was. With a body like that, he'd draw everyone's attention.

'Oh, he's here,' Tabbie said, hoping to break Steph's trance.

The group had relaxed onto their towels, but Tabbie and Steph still stood, staring at Joe as he headed up the beach towards them.

'Hey, will she come to me?' Priscilla jumped up, and Lola reached out to her.

'Enjoy having your arms free for a bit.' Tabbie spread out a towel and sat on one side of it.

Steph plonked down beside her while Priscilla entertained Lola on the picnic blanket.

His tall physique cast a shadow in their direction before he bent to grab his towel. He straightened and seemed even taller from where Tabbie sat.

'Joey?' Steph whispered.

'Yep.'

'You're right about the change,' Steph whispered. 'That and seeing your jaw drop. Otherwise, I wouldn't have recognised him. And he's single?' She glanced at Joe again.

'Not sure. I didn't ask. But—'

'Can you introduce me?' Stephanie pushed her shoulders back.

'But, Steph, you know him.'

'I doubt he'd remember who I am.'

Joe shook his hair, the spray of water hanging in the rays of sunshine.

'Urgh.' Tabbie bumped her arm. 'Seriously, if you drool any more, I'll have to pull this towel up and wipe your face.

'What?' Stephanie blinked then smiled. 'Was not.'

'Was so.' Tabbie flicked her hair off her face as she stood, picked up Lola and walked towards him.

He stood with the towel around his waist, still facing the ocean. Tabbie reached up and touched his arm to get his attention. His muscles twitched.

'Hey, Joe. How are you?'

'Yeah, good.' He turned, then beamed a smile. 'Hi. I didn't know you were here.'

'Just got here.' Tabbie saw Steph in her peripheral vision. 'Do you remember Stephanie?'

Steph blinked and her mouth moved, but nothing came out.

What's up with her? Tabbie turned back to Joe, his eyes virtually popping out of his head.

'Hi,' Steph almost squeaked.

Joe smiled then reached down and let Lola grab his finger. 'Babysitting for the day, are you?' He poked the baby's tummy.

Lola giggled.

'Ah—' She glanced down and Steph shook her head slightly. Tabbie realised she wanted to be just Steph for a moment, not Lola's mum.

'Was the water nice?' Steph's cheeks were blushing.

'Yeah, bit of a rip, but the temperature's great.'

'Nice. So how was your week, Joe?' Tabbie wanted to make idle conversation.

'I've been checking out some dance studios.' His gaze fell back on Steph.

'You still dance?' Steph asked.

'Yes! That's where I remember you from.' His smile was wide and heart-melting. 'You left just after I came to the studio at Hill Top.'

'Mumma,' Lola reached out for Steph but stayed in Tabbie's arms.

Joe seemed to miss the exchange and ruffled his fingers through his damp hair, his gaze glued to Steph.

'Yeah, Steph was the star dancer before she left and some crazy clumsy girl took over.' Tabbie laughed, but her joke fell flat.

$\mathcal{S}$TEPHANIE

'You still dance?' Joe asked.

'No.' Steph pulled at her fingernails.

Joe nodded, as if deep in thought. 'Yeah, now I remember. You were really good. Maybe you should start again.'

Memories flashed in her mind. She watched the waves, wishing they'd crush her past. She glanced at Tabbie, willing her to change the subject and saw care and concern in her eyes. How Steph envied her. If only she was as nice as Tabbie, she'd never have danced in a club or for that creep.

Lola lunged out of Tabbie's arms and into Steph's.

'Do you miss dancing?' Joe said.

'My dancing days are over.' Stephanie wiped dribble from Lola's chin.

'Have you thought about teaching?'

A rumble exploded from Lola's bottom. Steph felt the dampness on her arm as Lola squirmed and whinged.

Joe looked from Steph to Tabbie. He clearly had no idea Lola was hers. He really thought Tabbie was babysitting.

'Want me to change her?' Tabbie asked.

'It's okay. I'll change her.' She needed to get her arm cleaned up as well as her baby. 'Might be easier up on the grass.'

'Wow, so you're both babysitting? Do you look after her often?'

Steph smiled as she grabbed the nappy bag and walked over the sand dunes, towards the grassy area.

'You could say that.' Tabbie's voice carried in the wind.

Damn. He was hot. And he seemed totally interested in her. If only she could continue the charade forever. She wondered where the conversation went as she laid Lola down on the change mat. Would Tabbie be telling him the truth?

Chapter Twenty-seven

TABBIE

Joe watched Steph until she'd reached the grass. Of course he'd be attracted to her. Steph's natural beauty turned heads everywhere. Tabbie shook her head, wishing her hair fell in that naturally beautiful way. 'Wow, it's hot today. I'm going for a swim. Want to join me?'

'Thanks, but I think I'll catch a few rays.' Joe lay back and closed his eyes.

He'd just come out of the water, so why would he want to go back in? But she was sure he'd have jumped at the chance if Steph had asked him. She wandered down to the water on her own. Why was she so attracted to him? Was it just the rebound thing people talked about? 'Maybe I just need to find myself again,' she said to the ocean, but it sounded weird. She knew where she was. She knew who she was. She didn't have a problem with being single—she'd been single her whole life, until Danny. She just missed having a boyfriend to talk to and think about. No, not just a boyfriend. She missed Danny.

She splashed over and under the waves, focusing only on the water and letting everything else wash away.

$\mathscr{S}$TEPHANIE

Lola rolled off the mat, crying while Steph tried to wipe her arm clean with a baby wipe. She pulled Lola back and began to change her, holding her in place under her leg while she cleaned her bottom. Lola's cries escalated. She grabbed a fresh nappy from the bag and fastened it into place. Lola rolled away as soon as Steph moved her leg. Wrestling her back onto the mat, Steph dressed her in a clean romper suit. Finally, when they were both cleaned up, Steph walked back and forth under the trees, rocking Lola until she fell asleep.

'Hey, Steph,' Priscilla joined her. 'Can I take her for a while?'

'Thanks, but she'll probably wake up if I try to pass her to you.' Steph continued rocking back and forth.

'I love cuddling babies. Anytime you want a break, I'm here.'

'Actually, she might be happy to sleep in the stroller.' Steph glanced towards the car. 'Would you be able to grab it for me?'

'Yeah, of course. Back in a minute.'

Stephanie carefully lay Lola in the stroller then pushed it back and forth to keep her asleep.

'You're an awesome mum,' Priscilla said.

Steph smiled. She was nothing but a struggling teen mother. She turned to reply, realising Joe was behind Priscilla. He'd heard.

'You're a mum?' His eyebrows pushed creases into his forehead.

She nodded. And there it was—that look in his eyes that shouted the opposite of what she'd sensed less than an hour earlier.

'Wow, sorry. I thought you were babysitting. I guess you're busy up here.' He combed his fingers through his hair. 'I'm going in for a swim. Might catch you later.' He raced away from them.

Exactly what she'd thought. Most guys wouldn't be interested.

'I could mind her if you'd like to go for a swim.' Priscilla put her hand on Steph's shoulder. 'I can walk up and down the esplanade to keep her asleep.'

'Thanks. A swim sounds perfect.' Steph left the stroller in Priscilla's hands and set off.

Joe was halfway to the water by the time Steph peeled off her clothes. She wished she owned a rashie to cover her stretch marks. Too late now. She ran to the water so she could hide in the whitewash. Joe and Tabbie bodysurfed past her. She bobbed up and down, hoping they'd come back in past the break.

They stood in the shallows, deep in conversation. Steph tried to make out what they were saying by lipreading and their body language. A sheet of water crashed over her and she tumbled over and over until she found her footing. She flicked her hair out of her face then spat out a mouthful of sand. Spinning around, she searched for Tabbie and Joe.

Well, that was dumb, following him like that. The smartest thing she could do now was head back to Priscilla before anyone noticed her.

$\mathcal{T}$ABBIE

Joe ruffled his hair. 'So the baby is Steph's? I had no idea.'

'Yeah.' Tabbie wiped water from her face and nose, making sure no snot had escaped. The last thing she wanted to do was talk about Steph behind her back. Joe glanced towards the esplanade. Steph was out of view.

That'd be right. He couldn't keep his eyes off her even after he'd discovered she had a baby. Why did it bug her?

'Stephanie didn't seem interested, but have you ever thought about teaching dance?'

Tabbie shook her head. 'No. Dancing was never really my thing.'

Joe raised his eyebrows. 'Reckon we could sway Steph to think about it?' He glanced back towards the esplanade.

'You'd have to ask her yourself.' Of course, it was really only Steph he was asking about. He'd just included her to be polite. Why was he affecting her so much?

'I will. Did she ever think about going professional?'

'You'd have to ask that as well.' She looked at her feet. 'Do you run the studio you're at?'

'No. But I hope to.'

'That sounds exciting.' Her thoughts jumbled. If only she could keep that green monster from surfacing. She needed to get away from Joe before she said anything she'd regret. Something familiar caught her attention in her peripheral vision. Steph? Joe had noticed her too. His gaze transfixed. His expression said it all.

Someone called out, 'Hey, Joe. You playing this game?'

'Sure am.' He flicked a smile backwards and ran up the beach towards the group about to play volleyball.

Tabbie caught up with Steph on the dry sand.

'I don't know why I came today,' she said.

'You came because I asked you to.' Tabbie went to put her arm around Steph but tripped over a footprint and her fingers got tangled in Steph's hair as she tried to stay upright.

'Ow!'

'Sorry.' *Yep. Definitely a klutz.*

'You're acting weird.' Steph fingered her hair back into place. 'I shouldn't be here. Your friends are awkward around me and I'm awkward around them.'

'No way. I'm the same, aren't I? I'm a klutz sometimes—sorry. Priscilla loves having you here. Plus, I think Joe has a thing for you.' Tabbie's heart tugged as she voiced the words and gave Steph a side hug.

'I thought he might, until he realised I had baby baggage.' Stephanie shuddered then shook Tabbie's arm off her shoulders.

'I have a feeling that didn't put him off.' Tabbie rubbed her arms as they prickled with goosebumps. 'He wants to talk you into teaching with him. Dancing. I reckon he has a crush on you.'

Stephanie shook her head. Tabbie shrugged. If Steph wasn't interested, maybe Joe was fair game. *Oh! Stop it.* She had to stop thinking that way.

'Do you think the others will be ready to leave soon?' Steph pulled her shorts and T-shirt over her wet swimmers.

'You've had enough?' Tabbie watched Joe spike the ball as she shook out her towel and wrapped it around her shoulders.

'It's just hard with Lola. But I could catch a bus if you all want to stay longer.'

'No. No. I'll check with Shelly after this game.'

But a shadow had fallen over Steph's expression. 'I'll go take Lola off Priscilla's hands and check the bus timetable.' She headed off the beach.

What was bothering Steph? Was she still getting over the Warren debacle or was it something else? Maybe bringing her today hadn't been the smartest decision.

Chapter Twenty-eight

$\mathcal{S}$TEPHANIE

STEPH DUSTED THE SAND off her feet and found Priscilla sitting on a park bench, rocking the stroller back and forth. 'Was she okay for you?'

'She sure was. Just call me the baby whisperer.' Priscilla pulled her shoulders back and glanced at Lola.

'When were you thinking of heading home?'

'Soon. Why?' Priscilla stood.

'I'm ready to go.' Steph took over rocking the stroller. 'But if you're not ready now, I'll check when the next bus—'

'No, it's okay. I'm ready too. I'll round up the others.'

Priscilla made her way back to the beach. Babysitting was easy, being a mum was different. Steph pushed the stroller towards the car, hoping they wouldn't take too long. If she could transfer Lola into the car seat and keep her asleep, the drive home would be more pleasant. If she woke up, she'd be expecting a bottle. But that wasn't going to happen; Lola hated cold milk and Steph had no way of heating it.

'Seriously, hurry up,' she said to the breeze.

*T*ABBIE

Priscilla and Shelly sang softly to the music on the radio as Tabbie glanced at Steph, slumped low in the back seat. She was brooding. It would have been nice to hang around at the beach for a bit longer. The mood in the car suppressed any conversation.

Priscilla pulled up at the kerb outside Steph's home. Tabbie shoved open the door and rushed to pull the stroller out of the boot. 'Did you want me to hang around?'

'No, I'll be right.' Stephanie grabbed the stroller, waved and headed towards her apartment with Lola on her hip.

'I'll get my things then.' Tabbie didn't feel like dealing with Steph's mood. It was disappointing, especially after the great start to the day.

'Is everything really okay with Steph?' Priscilla asked.

'Other than how selfish and ungrateful she is?'

'She does have a baby to look after,' Shelly said.

'Yeah, I know. She just frustrates me at times.' Tabbie pulled the elastic out of her hair.

'Do you think it's only selfishness, or is something else going on?' Shelly asked.

'There's always more going on with Steph.' Tabbie looked out the window. 'Sorry. I shouldn't have said that.'

'Is there anything we can do to help her?' Shelly asked.

'She doesn't want help. She's determined to make it on her own. I keep wondering if I should move in with her again or help her out with the rent.'

'But you aren't working,' Shelly said.

'Neither is Steph.' Tabbie wondered if she should tell them how empty Steph's fridge and pantry were.

'I guess some people in the world survive on less.' Priscilla glanced at Tabbie in the rear vision mirror. 'How's school going? You moved home to get focused.'

'Well, I'm not focused right now.' Tabbie forced a laugh. 'I spend most of my time checking on Stephanie.'

'She has to run her own race.' Shelly turned to face her. 'I know you mean well, but you need to keep your boundaries.'

'Yeah, I know. But she's my best friend and has no family around to help her.'

'She has to want help. All you can do is offer.' Priscilla focused on the road. 'Let us know if there's anything we can do.'

'I'll have another talk to Mum and Dad. They might have some ideas.'

'Sounds like a plan,' Priscilla said as she turned into Tabbie's street.

Tabbie spent the afternoon alone in her room, working on an essay due Monday. That night she tossed and turned like the night was never going to end.

'Mum.' Tabbie wandered downstairs the next day to the laundry. 'I know it sounds crazy, but I think Steph needs me there. I think I should move back in with her.'

'Hmm.' Mum stopped sorting the washing. 'Yes, she needs support, but you can't neglect everything else because of her. She's responsible and independent.'

'Yeah, I know, but I'd be saving myself so much time. Steph's place is closer to the aquatic centre, school, and church.'

'Love, who are you trying to fool? If Steph isn't coping, she knows she's welcome here, but she appears to want to make it on her own.'

'But she refuses to move in here.' Tabbie shrugged. 'Can you talk to Dad about me maybe moving back in with her?'

'I already know what he'll say.'

Tabbie closed her eyes and had a flashback of Steph bleeding at the bottom of the stairs. It was something she never wanted to go through again. 'I'm going for a run, then I'll be at Steph's.'

'Please don't go scheming with her about this,' Mum called as she left.

'I won't,' Tabbie snapped back.

She knew she shouldn't take it out on her mother, but she didn't know how to help Steph right now. If she moved back in, maybe she could stop her from making mistakes. Mistakes like falling for Joe… as if she had any control over that situation.

She reasoned with herself that she and Joe had a bond—Suzie. Tabbie had been the one who'd set them up. Thinking about it made her miss sweet Suzie all over again. She blinked away the tears swelling and pushed her legs to run faster.

Tabbie arrived at Steph's gasping for breath as she knocked her knuckles hard on the front door. She pulled her hand back. *Hope Lola isn't sleeping.* Steph opened the door as far as the chain would allow.

'Heya,' Tabbie forced a smile. Now she was there, she wondered why she'd felt the urge to visit. 'You're still in your PJs. I thought you would've been up for hours.'

'I've been up for a while.' That familiar shadow hung over Steph.

'You're not okay, are you?' Tabbie asked.

'Why are you here so early?' Stephanie shrugged and lifted the chain. 'Why aren't you at church?'

'Because I felt like going for a run.' Tabbie pushed the door open. 'And I've been worried about you since we dropped you off yesterday.'

'Don't be silly. I'm fine.' Steph filled the jug and flicked it on to boil.

'Really?' Tabbie grabbed two mugs from the sink and washed them.

'Shh. Lola's asleep. It's a wonder your knocking didn't wake her.'

'Sorry.' Tabbie glanced over her shoulder. Lola's toys covered the floor in front of the TV. 'It's unlike her to sleep at this time.'

'Yesterday must have worn her out. The quiet is nice, so if you stop banging things around, it might last a bit longer.' Steph's ponytail whipped the air as she opened the cupboard to grab the coffee.

The musty oiliness hit Tabbie. 'How long is it since you washed your hair?'

'Give me a break. I ran out of shampoo and conditioner last week. You know, that and the salt water yesterday.'

'We could have bought some yesterday.' Tabbie sighed.

If she still lived there, she'd have been able to share hers. Would smelly hair put off a possible employer?

'Why don't you come back with me and wash your hair at our place?'

'I'll be right.' Steph bit her lip and inspected her fingernails.

'Pretty sure Mum's cooking a roast. There's always loads for everyone.'

'Then you'd have to bring me back. It's such a hassle.'

'You know it's not a hassle. Why are you always stopping us from helping you? Come and enjoy a night with the Morays. Why not stay the night?'

Chapter Twenty-nine

How could she give up homecooked roast and clean hair?

Francine arrived later in the afternoon and Lola protested as Steph tried to strap her into the car seat. Francine sang *Twinkle Twinkle Little Star* to calm Lola down. Steph would have to remember to sing more often, because Lola seemed to like it.

'Peter might pop in tonight,' Francine said as she drove into their garage.

A tingle ran down Steph's spine. *Peter.* He was in love with Phoebe. Why did she have a physical reaction at the thought of him? That was the only way she'd have any hope of actually being a Moray. As much as they tried to make her feel part of the family, when it came down to it, blood was thicker than water and they'd always choose their own ahead of her and Lola.

'How have you been sleeping?' Francine asked.

'Yeah, good,' Steph lied as she unbuckled Lola. She hadn't slept well since the shattered window ordeal.

'I hope you're hungry, I've made enough to feed the whole street.' Francine laughed.

Stephanie walked up the porch stairs, holding Lola in one hand and hitching up her shorts with the other. The baby fat and some had fallen off. At least the lack of money was good for something. 'Yeah, I am pretty hungry.'

Stephanie's mobile phone rang during dinner.

'Do you need to get that?' Tom asked.

'No, it can wait.' The Morays didn't take their phones to the table, and she didn't want to be the odd one out. Knives and forks clinked as they all waited for the phone to quiet. It did. But, started again straight away. 'Or maybe I should.'

She left the table and grabbed her phone. *April.* A sniffle came through the phone as she answered.

The front door opened. She glanced up. Yes, Francine said Peter might pop in. She turned her back hoping he didn't see her.

'Hey, Steph.' He saw her. 'Are you here for dinner?'

She nodded, pointing to the phone at her ear.

'Sorry, didn't realise you were on a call.' He waved and went through to the dining room.

'Steph!' April yelled on the other end of the phone. 'Would you listen for a minute?'

'Can I call you back?'

'You keep saying that, but you don't.'

'I don't have much credit.'

'Neither do I, and I want to talk to you.'

Laughter flowed from the dining room, distracting her. She pressed the phone against her ear and tried to focus on April.

'I'll catch up another time, Steph,' Pete said as he passed her. 'Phebs is waiting in the car. See you soon.'

'Who's that?' April asked.

'Peter.'

'Tabbie's brother?'

'Yep.' His only interest was Phoebe. There it was. They were still a couple.

'Where are you?'

'I'm at the Morays', in the middle of dinner.'

'Why didn't you say?' April mumbled something under her breath.

'I'll call you later.'

'Really?'

'As soon as I have enough credit.'

April groaned and hung up.

'My, we've got a coming and going table tonight,' Francine said with a chuckle. 'Who was on the phone, Steph?'

'April. She… I think she's lonely.' Steph returned to her seat.

'Did you cut the conversation short because of us?' Tom asked.

'It's okay.' Steph shrugged.

'Will you call her back later? I do worry about her,' Francine said.

'I would but—'

'You can use our landline,' Tom said.

Francine nodded.

'Thanks, I'll call her after dinner. No rush.'

Thirty minutes later, Stephanie dialled April's number on the Morays' ancient corded wall phone.

'You seriously have the best friends. No one here cares. No one ever invites me to dinner.' April's voice wavered.

'Is Mum home?' Steph played with the spiral cord.

'Yeah. In front of the telly.'

'Why don't you ask her to take you to a movie or something? Sounds like you could do with a night out.' Steph looked up. Francine stepped out of view, probably still listening to every word. 'I've gotta go. Talk soon.'

'Sorry, love.' Francine came towards her. 'Didn't mean to eavesdrop.'

'That's okay. She's just down at the moment. She should be talking to Mum more.'

'Hmm.' Francine busied herself with putting away leftovers.

Steph grabbed a tea towel and dried while Tabbie washed the pans.

'How's April going?' Tom returned to the kitchen and filled the jug.

'She's pretty miserable. Don't blame her. Mum and Dad don't care about either of us. But she still has to live with Mum.'

Everyone stopped and looked at her as if she'd dropped a bombshell or sworn at them. Lola's squeals accented the moment. 'I was hoping she'd stay asleep.'

'I'll get her.' Tabbie dried her hands and ran out of the room.

Francine spoke first. 'I'm sure they do care, Steph. Maybe they're busy sorting their own stuff out.'

The Morays were too caring to even consider some parents were so horrible.

'Would you like to take some leftovers home?' Francine asked while putting plastic containers in a pile.

'Are you sure?' Her mouth watered so much she could eat the rest now.

'Of course.'

'Were you staying here tonight?' Tom made a pot of tea.

'I wasn't going to—'

'You know you're always welcome. This can stay in the fridge till the morning.'

'We can put up the new port-a-cot mum and dad bought.'

They bought a cot as well?

'I bought some cute onesies, just in case. Would you like to see them?' Francine rushed out of the kitchen, tickling Lola on the way past. Lola giggled and watched her until she was out of sight.

'So are you staying?' Tabbie raised her eyebrows.

'Um, okay. Alright. Is it still okay for me to wash my hair?'

'Of course. Why didn't you jump in the shower as soon as we got here?'

Stephanie shrugged. Nothing like that was easy when she had Lola to think about.

'I'll get you a towel.'

'You're staying then?' Francine returned and took Lola from

Tabbie. 'See, wouldn't it be easy to come and live here? There're more hands here to take care of this little one while you shower.'

'Thanks, but I'm only staying tonight. I need my own space.'

After showering, Stephanie settled Lola in the portable cot Tom and Francine had purchased. An ache hit her insides as she realised how much money they'd spent on her. She looked around the room that'd been hers when she'd first returned to Sydney. Now it was an elegantly decorated guest room.

She lay diagonally across the queen-size bed, enjoying the extra room after sleeping in a single bed. The bed she'd let Warren in to. Her skin prickled at the thought of the creep. She pushed the thought away and rolled over.

The next thing she knew, light streamed through the window. The peaceful sleep had nourished and warmed her spirit. *Wow.* Imagine sleeping like that every night. She closed her eyes again.

'Mumma.'

Lola? She stretched.

'Mumma!' Lola fell backwards in the cot kicking her legs.

Steph yawned, still trying to wake herself up.

'Would you like to sleep a little longer, love?' Francine appeared in the doorway. 'I can take Lola for you. You must have been in a deep sleep. She's been making little noises for a little while.' Francine picked her up. 'Oh, you need changing.'

Steph went to take her back but Francine wouldn't hear of it. She whisked Lola away.

'Hey.' Tabbie peeked through the doorway. 'See you later.'

'You leaving already?' Steph rubbed away sleepy dust.

'Yeah, I have to check something for one of my assignments.'

'On my way out the door, Tabbie,' Tom called up the stairs.

'Chat soon.' Tabbie threw her school backpack over her shoulder. 'Coming!'

It would be so easy to give into their offer and move in. But she couldn't do it to them. Not again. Everything would be better if she could just find a job.

Chapter Thirty

'I wish Steph would move in with us,' Dad said as they drove away. 'Things don't sound very good with her sister, either. If you hear any more about April, would you let us know?'

'What can you do, though? Invite her to come live here?' Tabbie glanced at him.

'You know me too well.' He scratched his greying stubble. 'I'd hate to see April go through what Steph's been through.'

'Okay. I'll suss it out.' She waved goodbye and headed into school.

When the bell rang at the end of the day, Tabbie dragged her feet towards the aquatic centre. Another day, more laps, more reminders of Danny. The more she tried to stop thinking about him, the more her mind returned to questioning what went wrong.

She needed to focus on here and now. April and Steph. Joe. What was it with that crazy attraction? She changed into her swimmers and climbed into the pool, hoping the water would help her escape her thoughts for a while.

 Spiralling Solo

Two laps in, she knew some of the triggers she had to remove. The photos of Danny beside her bed and in her purse. Four laps in, she stopped swimming. Who was she trying to kid? She was still in love with Danny. Her attraction to Joe was just so confusing.

The water wasn't offering any therapy today. She did one more lap, letting the water wash away her tears, and then she was ready to head home.

She'd heard over and over that time healed everything, but would it heal crushed dreams? Maybe one day she'd move on from Danny and fall in love with the right person. Joe wasn't the right person. She knew that. But he was just so hot!

She dried off and checked her phone. A text from Stephanie.

> Hey, it's kind of lonely here but no, I don't want to move 😊
> Was just wondering if you want to come over this arv?

> Sure. See you in around 15 😃

Maybe a visit with Steph was the distraction she needed.

Lola greeted her with giggles and squeals.

'Hiya. Lola's happy.'

Steph pushed herself up off the floor to open the screen door. 'Yeah, it's nice when she's like this.'

While they focused on Lola without conversation, an idea toyed in Tabbie's mind. If Steph was beside her…

'Want to come to youth group this Friday?'

'No way. You saw the way everyone looked at me at the beach.' Steph's shoulders shook like a chill had rushed through her.

'Everyone loved having a baby around. And Priscilla put her to sleep without any problems.'

'Did you see Joe's face when he discovered I had baggage?'

'Baggage?' Tabbie shook her head. 'What baggage?'

'Solo-mum-with-baby kind of baggage.' Steph dipped her chin.

'I must have missed that. You think it bothered him? I thought he was kind of into you.' The more she built that story, the quicker her attraction to him would dissipate.

'Anyway, to answer your question, no. I don't feel like hanging out with a bunch of high school kids.' Steph moved to the couch and flicked the TV on.

'Okay.' Tabbie shrugged. She was left to face Joe alone.

'Hey, Tabbie!' Joe came towards the Fizz Hut on Friday night.

Tabbie gripped the serving table. *Why does the guy have to be so ridiculously good-looking?* She reminded herself she was on duty.

'Can I grab a packet of chips?'

'Sure. Which flavour?'

'Plain.'

She grabbed the packet and knocked over the display. Heat rushed up her neck. Joe didn't laugh or make a joke of her. Just smiled as she handed him a packet.

'I'm dancing at the shopping centre tomorrow. It's a display performance with the kids. You know, a bit of entertainment while advertising our studio. Why don't you come down?' He offered her a chip. 'Bring Steph if you like.'

She took a chip. Could she forget to mention it to Steph and go on her own?

Joe walked away.

No, she'd do the best friend thing and invite Steph. In the corner of her vision, Joe played basketball with a bunch of guys. She put her blinkers on and reset the display of chip packets. When the band started playing in the auditorium, Tabbie closed the Fizz Hut and headed inside in search of answers. Moments after she'd found a seat, her hair stood on end as she sensed Joe moving to sit beside her. She sang the songs and looked up, but not at Joe. Why was she so attracted to this guy when she wasn't over Danny? None of it

     Spiralling Solo

made sense. Could God heal her broken heart?

She plonked down onto the chair as soon as the music stopped. Her mind wandered as the preacher spoke. *What if God has brought Joe back into my world for a reason?* He was different now. He'd never spent so much time with her in the past. Maybe it was only because he wanted to see Steph again.

'So do you think you'll come tomorrow?' Joe's voice snapped her back to reality.

Everyone was dispersing. She'd spent the entire service lost in her thoughts instead of listening. 'Yeah, sure. What did you say it was? A demo of some sort?' She walked with him, aware of his closeness as they moved through the crowded room.

'Yeah. The school I'm looking at buying into is doing a display to recruit students. Everyone will be dancing—from toddlers through to our performance team.' He waved to a group of guys. 'Anyway, would be great to see you and Steph there.'

'I'll ask her.' Something churned inside her stomach.

'Did you need a lift home?' He'd started to walk away but turned back.

'Thanks for the offer, but I'm going to hang out and help clean up.' Her heart went off on a wobbly beat. She needed to get away from him.

'Oh, yeah, I hadn't thought about that. Guess it's a big job. Are they looking for more volunteers?'

'Probably.' *Yeah, great, just what I don't need.* Joe volunteering alongside her. 'Maybe check with Shelly.'

'Cool. I'll chat with her Sunday.' He leaned towards her. Was he about to hug her? But then he turned and was swallowed by the crowd. Was that a sign, her own desire imagining things or a random moment? She tidied up and left more confused than when she'd arrived.

Lola woke Steph at her usual early hour on Saturday morning. After changing her nappy and giving her a bottle, Steph turned on her phone.

A text message buzzed.

Joe is doing some performance thingy with a bunch of his students. I was thinking about going. Wanna come with? T x

What time?

Not sure, I'll have to check.

Twenty minutes later Tabbie replied,

11 am. Wanna go?

Yeah, of course I want to see that hot bod dance!

Her phone buzzed with an immediate reply from Tabbie.

No more concerns about baggage?

A shiver ran down her spine. Tabbie was right. She had way too much baggage to be thinking about Joe. He was eye candy. Nothing more.

A couple of hours later, Steph consciously held her jaw in place as Joe stole the show with his tricks and acrobatics. The whole crowd cheered and clapped. In one dance he spun a partner around the floor. Right now, Steph would do anything to be spun and lifted the way Joe danced with that girl. She grabbed Lola's favourite squeaky elephant and shook it in her face to stop her whining.

'Is that how he danced a couple of years ago?' Steph glanced at Tabbie then back to the stage.

'Almost.' Tabbie didn't take her gaze off the dancers. 'Nah, not really. He was a lot smaller back then. Short. No muscles. He was a great partner. I just sucked as a dancer.'

'Stop being so hard on yourself. You were great before you stuffed your ankle.'

'I was only noticed when you moved away and Jaya lost interest.'

Joe pulled off his jacket. His arms gleamed with sweat. Steph's heart thumped at the sight of his t-shirt clinging to his chest. 'Get out of here. Now that is worth admiring. What a body. He must spend a lot of time in the gym.'

Tabbie nodded.

'Who's drooling now?' Steph nudged Tabbie's shoulder and laughed.

'Am not! I wouldn't have noticed if you hadn't said anything.' Tabbie reached for Lola.

'Did you ever have a crush on him back then?' Steph asked.

'No, definitely not, he was…' Tabbie bit her lip. 'He had Suzie back then.'

'So now you've given up on Danny, you're crushing on Joe?' Steph raised her eyebrows.

'So not!' Tabbie focused on Lola.

Steph let it go and enjoyed the last dance of the show. Tabbie was lying, but she couldn't blame her. If she'd let true feelings emerge in the moment, she'd knock over the barrier and dance on the stage with him right there and then.

He emanated all she'd dreamed about until…

Oh, how she'd love to reverse her life back to before she moved to Toowoomba, and begin afresh.

Chapter Thirty-one

Steph's face glowed.

'Watching them dance lights you up.' Tabbie raised her eyebrows. 'How are things going with the job search?'

'I thought a job at the corner shop would be easy. But they didn't call back. Maybe I'm being too fussy.'

'Being fussy is good, especially after what you've been through.'

'It's just hard.' Steph grabbed a flyaway piece of hair and tucked it behind her ear. 'Most jobs need qualifications or availability to work a rotating roster. That's virtually impossible with Lola. I wish I didn't need the money. Then I could just be a mummy and not have to worry.'

'You know that's what my parents offered?' Tabbie said.

'And you know I can't accept it.'

Lola fussed and whinged in Tabbie's arms. 'I know, but I don't understand why you won't let Mum and Dad help you more.' She picked up Lola's toy and tried to hand it to her, but she pushed it away. 'I reckon you'd make a great dance teacher.'

'What? Are you serious?' Steph shook her head and found a rusk for Lola. 'I think I should stay away from dancing forever.'

'But look at you, you're glowing.' Tabbie smiled at her. 'You could teach girls not just about dance, but about how hard it can be if they chase money and sell themselves short.'

'Yeah, that'd be fun.'

'I'm serious. Joe said—'

'But then they'd know where I'd been—and I don't want anyone else to know.'

'What if you could stop other girls from going through what you went through?' Tabbie bit her lip. 'You'd be like a mentor as well as a teacher.'

'I'm not mentor material. Look at me.' The music stopped and the crowd cheered. 'I don't think many parents would want me mentoring their girls.'

'You're looking at it all wrong.' Tabbie thought about Jaya and Suzie and how the four of them used to talk about what their future would look like. They'd all gone off track. Suzie was gone, Jaya was an emotional rollercoaster, and Steph had taken paths none of them thought she would. 'You made some crazy decisions—stuff happens. You've turned things around. People who judge you on your past need to get a life.'

'Tabbie…' Steph leaned towards her. 'You might find this hard to believe, but not everyone sees the world the way you do.'

Another song began to play and a group of younger girls ran out to dance.

'Yeah, well, everyone needs to stop judging other people.' Tabbie handed Lola over. 'Just think about it. Teaching little girls how to dance might be the answer to finding an income.'

'Pft!' Steph said, but her face continued to glow. A fresh sparkle returned to her eyes.

Tabbie had missed that sparkle. She'd rarely seen it since Stephanie moved to Toowoomba with her family.

The dancers jumped off the stage after their finale and passed out flyers. Joe was swamped, but he pushed his way toward them. 'What did you think?'

Both girls crooked their necks to look up.

'Great.' Steph fluttered her eyelashes.

'Yeah, great.' Tabbie had to stop looking at him. She turned her attention to Lola.

'Did it make you want to dance again?' Joe asked Steph. 'How about you, Tabbie?'

'And risk another major injury?' She laughed. 'I don't think so.'

'We need another teacher,' he said to Steph.

'Um, I'm a little occupied right now.' Steph glanced at the stroller.

'Does she go into care or something?'

Steph shook her head.

Joe rested his foot on the front wheel of the stroller, raising his eyebrows as he leaned towards Steph. She shook her head and stepped backwards, pulling the stroller with her.

Joe stumbled. His mouth flew open then he laughed and turned to a girl tapping his arm. He gave the girl a flyer then smiled back at Steph. 'Why don't you come down on Monday? Just check it out.' He turned away. 'I'll see you later.'

'Admit it, he's hot. You've moved on from Danny and you're crushing on him, hey?'

'No.' Tabbie shook her head. 'I've been praying for a sign that it's over with Danny. I haven't seen a sign yet.'

'Well, let me know when that sign shows up.'

Tabbie handed a flyer to Steph. 'You should keep that and check it out, like Joe said.'

'What would I do with Lola?' The little girl kicked her feet and squealed at the sound of her name. 'I've tried daycare and it didn't work. I can't leave her crying like that every day.'

'Mum's happy to help. Remember?'

   Spiralling Solo

'How much do you reckon she'd charge? I don't have anything left over at the moment.'

'Maybe she'd just do it. Worth asking her.'

'Yeah.' Steph kept her focus forward.

But will Steph ask? Or am I jumping in and trying to fix things again? Tabbie watched the path in front of the wheels as she walked. When it came down to it, it was easier to help Steph than deal with her own issues.

Chapter Thirty-two

STEPHANIE TABBIE

STEPH TINGLED ALL OVER as she thought about visiting Joe's dance studio. It might be fun to dance again, especially with him. Maybe she could teach. Would she have to get a qualification? A course would cost money. She swayed between wanting to give it a go and pushing it out of her mind.

Money. That's what it came down to. Her breath shortened as she walked up the small hill with Tabbie. She was so unfit. She couldn't even contemplate Joe's offer until she was fit and had more money.

Maybe she should take Francine up on her offer to mind Lola. But what if Francine got a job? It was all too hard. Besides, would she even be able to dance after having Lola? Her mind flicked back to when she'd thought she finally made it in the dance industry. Auditioning for music videos. But her childhood dream had been squashed when she'd ended up in a twisted spin-off from the porn industry. A shiver ran down her spine.

Could she really guide girls away from that sleazy destructive path? It'd looked so glamorous but, in reality, for her it had been the opposite. If only she'd found a reputable dance company. How many sharks lingered out there, ready to lure in innocent girls? Girls needed to know what to look for. But who was she to tell them?

'Seriously, tell me, have you got a thing for Joe?' Steph asked as they neared her front door.

Tabbie didn't reply, but the deep shade of pink in her cheeks told the truth.

'Knew it! You get embarrassed so easily.'

'No, I'm not interested. It's just, well, he's just changed so much.' Tabbie covered her cheeks with her hands. 'And he's into you, not me.'

'Me, the mumma of the bubba? Nah. Maybe he was for a moment, until he knew about Lola.'

'Which means if he'd noticed me at all, I'd be second choice.'

'I didn't mean it like that.' Steph unlocked the front door.

'Anyway, he couldn't take his eyes off you.' Tabbie pushed the stroller inside.

'Yeah, right!'

Tabbie shook her head, filled the jug and turned it on. 'Coffee?'

Lola squealed and kicked her legs.

'Yeah, thanks. I'll put her in the cot.' Steph changed Lola's nappy and gave her the squeaky elephant before closing the door.

'The year you were gone…' Tabbie added a dash of milk to each cup. '…and then when you were here but off doing your own thing, I realised I'd rather have you 'round and play second fiddle than not have you 'round at all.'

'Aw, thanks. You're going to make me cry.' Steph forced a sniffle and wiped at alligator tears.

'Need a tissue?' Tabbie smirked.

'Thanks for not dumping me.' Steph smiled and filled the sink to do the dishes.

'It was easy.' Tabbie hugged the cup in her palms. 'Especially when I started thinking of you as a sister instead of a friend.'

'The family thing again.'

'Yeah.' Tabbie sipped her coffee on the couch. 'Hey, want to come to church with me tomorrow? You can have another chat with Joe about dancing.'

'No thanks. It's… too awkward.' She left the dishes and sat beside Tabbie.

'Who knows, you might find some hope or something there.'

'But what if the church is what turns people away from God?' She grabbed the remote.

'What do you mean? Working out who you put your faith in is a good thing.'

Stephanie looked to the ceiling. Why was Tabbie so adamant church and God were the only way? 'For some of us, the constant fear of the church roof caving in on us keeps us away. It's different for good girls like you.'

'No way. The church is there for everyone.' Tabbie's shoulders tensed. 'Are you sure it's not your own guilt making you feel uneasy?'

'My own guilt?' *Is she serious?* Did she really not notice the way people watched her? Judged her?

'If I remember correctly, you weren't completely comfortable with the way you jumped into bed with Jason so quickly.' Tabbie put her cup down and sat forward.

'I wasn't, but what are we meant to do when… you know, someone is so hot?' *Self-control.* Something she obviously lacked. And what did that have to do with going to church?

'God's forgiveness is a pretty amazing thing.' Tabbie shrugged.

'Who says I need God's forgiveness?' She needed to take control of this conversation.

'If you're forgiven, then you don't have to walk around carrying all that guilt. It's awesome.' Tabbie moved closer.

'What? Like a Monopoly *Get Out Of Jail Free* card?' It sounded too easy. It would never work for her.

'It's not easy. It's a choice. Ask for forgiveness and repent. It's amazing. The first time I focused on doing that, it was like a weight lifted off me.'

'What sin did you commit? Dropping rubbish in the street?' Steph tried not to eye-roll. 'And what does repent even mean?'

'It just means turning from your old ways. And there're loads of things I've done and said that I'm not proud of. Instead of being down on myself all the time I hand it over to God.'

'So you're saying I should hand over the stuff that happened with Jason?' *Maybe she's onto something.*

'Yeah. Then take some action to change your old ways.'

'Hand it over and change?' That was the catch. *Change.*

'Yeah.' Tabbie smiled, nodding.

'Just like that, hey?' *If only.* 'So, wise one, how do you actually do all that?'

'Prayer.'

'What? Like, "Here God, have my junk." And then I need to change and become an angel like you.'

'Yes… no. It takes practice to leave your junk with God and not keep taking it back. I have to keep handing over my worry about Danny.'

'But you haven't done anything wrong with Danny?'

'Worry is a sin.'

'Are you serious?'

Tabbie nodded.

'But everyone worries.'

'That's right. We're all sinners.'

'Where do you get all this from?'

'Youth group, church and the big book I like to read.' Tabbie flicked a piece of fluff off the couch.

'If we're all sinners, why do so many Christians look down on people like me? Why are Christians so judgemental?'

The clock on the wall ticked and a loud car screeched outside, reminding her of Jason's reckless driving. A shiver rippled down her spine as she waited for Tabbie to answer. Maybe she'd stumped her. Maybe there wasn't an answer.

'You're right. People need to stop judging. But I guess we're all on a journey and the people who look at you without acceptance are probably dealing with issues themselves.'

'You think so?' Stephanie felt the beginnings of tears prickle.

Tabbie nodded. 'Can I pray for you?'

'Sure.' Stephanie swallowed, pushing away the tears. 'Whatever makes you feel good. Maybe you should pray for all those judgemental people dealing with issues too.'

'Mmm. I will.' Tabbie pushed herself off the couch and left, leaving her cup on the floor. 'See you during the week sometime.'

Steph followed Tabbie to the door. Did she need to work out her faith? Had she been too harsh? Maybe Tabbie needed to relax a little. She meant well, with all her forgiveness talk but how could anyone truly live life confined by church guidelines?

With Lola still sleeping, Steph played some music. She began with a short warm-up and stretched then moved in time with the beat. She couldn't believe she'd run out of breath before the first song finished. It was dumb to even think about Joe's offer. *Ridiculous.*

She fell onto the couch and flicked the TV on. Drawing in a shaky breath, she blinked away the pools welling in her eyes. A knock on the door made her jump.

'Hey, just me, I left my phone...'

Steph swiped away her tears before letting Tabbie in.

'What happened? What's up?'

'I couldn't put dancing again out of my mind. And I tried a few steps and… I'm so pathetically unfit. It would be stupid for me to even go and see on Monday.'

'No way. You couldn't be that bad.'

'I'm so bad even you'd laugh.' Stephanie reached for a tissue.

'What if you went for lessons until you increased your fitness level?'

'Yeah right, and who's going to pay for that? Everything costs money.'

'I'm sure there's a way around it. How about you get your fitness up first? You could start by coming for a run with me?'

'Lola.' Did she have to remind Tabbie every time?

'I know, but those jogging strollers—'

'Yeah, right. Do you know how much they cost?' Steph raked her fingers through her hair.

'Maybe you could leave her with me and go for a jog or something.'

'If I liked running.' She punched her fist into the couch.

'True.' Tabbie looked around the room. 'What about taking Lola for more walks, and find a few hills to climb. And maybe build your fitness up here in your apartment.'

'Why do I feel like you'll have an answer to everything?'

Tabbie shrugged and retrieved her phone from the bench. 'Maybe I could ask Joe to give you complimentary private lessons, personal-trainer-dance style.'

'No way. That would be way too embarrassing.' Steph had had enough. 'I thought you said you forgot something.'

'Yeah.' Tabbie was focused on something on her phone. It buzzed several times. 'It's all set.' Tabbie shoved her phone into her pocket. 'I'll talk to Mum, but I'm sure that will be fine too.'

'What's all set?' *What did I miss?* 'Who were you texting?'

'Joe. He's happy to give you free private lessons to get you back into shape.'

'What?'

'I've gotta go. My phone. Just came back for this.' She held it up. 'Mum's outside. I'll ask her about looking after Lola on the way home. See you later.'

'But… Tabbie!' Stephanie yelled as she left. 'I can't do it. I just won't turn up.'

Chapter Thirty-three

TABBIE

TABBIE KEPT WALKING even though she'd heard Steph call out to her. Maybe, just maybe, it could work. Encouraging Joe and Steph to hang out would be best for everyone. Something might spark between them. If that happened, her attraction towards him could die a natural death.

'I was about to come in and get you,' Mum said as she opened the car door.

'Sorry. Steph seemed upset when I walked in, but I think it's fixed now.'

'You fixed it?' Her mother pulled away from the kerb.

'Yeah. Joe's going to help Steph get back into dancing.' Tabbie smiled as the muscles between her shoulder blades pulled in a spasm.

'Are you sure that's a good idea?' Mum's voice deepened.

'Yeah, of course it is.' *I hope.* 'Steph wants a job. If she could teach dancing, it'd be perfect.'

'You aren't stepping in too much, are you? By organising Steph's life for her?'

She was doing it again. But someone had to push Steph in the right direction. 'She kind of needs *you* too.'

'And what's that for, love?'

'Would you be able to mind Lola?' Tabbie bit a fingernail.

'Of course. But I wish you'd let Steph work through this herself. It's easy for you to ask me, but she's not good at asking for help herself, and she needs to learn how to. She knows I'll say yes. I've offered so many times.'

'I guess so.' Tabbie needed to change the subject. 'Want to come to church with me tomorrow morning?'

'Are you planning to give Steph a break and start organising *my* life?' Her mum laughed.

'Mu-*um*!' That wasn't what she was trying to do at all.

'Thanks for the invite, love, but I prefer my traditional church. I'm glad you started going, though. You reminded me of what I was missing.'

Tabbie stared out the window, recalling how she'd fallen asleep last time she visited her mother's church.

'We worship the same God and read the same Bible. It's just a different expression. All that noise is a bit much for me.'

'Okay.' She'd have to keep going on her own. She grabbed her phone and texted Steph.

> All sorted for Monday. Mum is available to mind Lola ☺

> I can't believe you asked Joe ☹ I didn't want you to.
> I'M NOT GOING!!!!

Tabbie dropped the phone in her lap and focused on the trees passing by.

'Everything all right?' her mother asked as they pulled into their driveway.

'Fine.' Tabbie climbed out of the car. 'I wish I could get Steph to come to church.'

'You have to let her make her own decisions. Maybe she'd prefer my style of church now she has Lola.'

'Doubt it.' Tabbie ambled upstairs, praying for Steph. She opened her bedroom door and saw her laptop sitting on her desk. Out of habit she opened it to check her emails. *What am I doing?* As if there would be anything new to see. All she was doing was replaying the old hopeful story in her mind.

She went downstairs to watch TV. Everything reminded her of Danny. An ad for *World Vision*. A holiday show promoting an African adventure. News headlines about how many Australians lived in poverty. The poverty around Danny right now would put most Australians on the affluenza list. *Not Steph, though.* She was doing it tough.

Tabbie's phone rang. *Shelly.* 'Hey,' Tabbie answered.

'What's up? You sound like you're about to cry.'

'Just... Never mind.' Tabbie flicked the TV off.

'We're off to the beach tomorrow after church. Thought you and Steph might like to come with us.'

'I'll be there, but Steph won't.'

'Oh, have you already asked? Why not?'

'She said it's not her scene.' *Should I tell her Steph felt judged by everyone?*

'That's a shame. We loved having her join in.'

'Yeah, I know. Thanks for the call. See you in the morning.' Tabbie threw her phone on the couch and ran back upstairs. She mightn't be able to change the way Steph felt judged or the extreme levels of wealth in Australia, but she could take away the reminders of Danny. She grabbed the photos of Danny and threw them in the bin. Then she pushed her bed so it was up against the wall. She shoved her desk so it faced the window and slid her bookshelf across the room, knocking half the books onto the floor.

'Everything okay in there?' Her mother poked her head around the doorway.

'Yeah, just need to move things around.'

'And what are they doing in there?' Her mother reached into the bin.

'What's the point in keeping them?'

'Memories? How about I put them in a box in my wardrobe? You might want them again one day.'

'Mum, I need to move on. I need to forget about him.'

'You two were pretty close last year. Be patient and allow time. You might want to keep them as memories, or you might still want to throw them out. Just wait a little while before making that decision.'

Tabbie awoke the next day to rattling windows. She drew her curtains back to find the gusty wind had shed the trees of their leaves while the sun hid behind layers of clouds. The temperature dropped in response. She reached for her dressing gown. She checked the time and messaged Shelly and Priscilla.

Hey, could one of you pick me up? Please. I slept in. Nice day for the beach – HA!

Shelly replied almost immediately.

I'll come get you. B there in 15.

Tabbie dashed in and out of the shower. She threw on a pair of jeans, a long-sleeved t-shirt and a jacket. She grabbed her mascara and lip gloss, then ran downstairs.

'No breakfast this morning?' her mother asked.

'No time. Late for church. Shelly will be outside in a minute.'

'What about a slice of toast? An apple?'

'Apple sounds great. Thanks.' She grabbed one and ran outside.

'Are you planning to play volleyball in that?' Shelly asked.

'You aren't still planning to go, are you?'

'Yeah. The guys want to win after we beat them last week. Go grab a change of clothes. We need you on the team if we're going to win.'

'I've already made you late. You sure —'

'We have time. Go.' Shelly pointed towards the house.

As Tabbie raced back into her room she kicked her toe on the shelves she'd moved last night. Her tights were near her side table. Her now bare side table. Her heart tightened. He was gone. Off her side table and out of her life. She went to shove her clothes into her backpack but kept missing.

'Everything alright up there?' Mum called as Tabbie tripped through her bedroom doorway.

'Just rushing. That's all. See ya.' She kissed her mum on the cheek as she raced past.

That morning the preacher talked about temptation, nailing her attraction to Joe. It was temptation. Not a sign from God.

The weather continued its dark mood, chopping the waves up and sending sand into their legs with stinging force. Tabbie bashed the ball with everything she had, and it had paid off with a win. After the game, they dashed to the car in search of a café for hot chocolates.

'Danny.'

Had she heard right? Sitting in a booth with the girls, she turned to the guys in the ordering line. *Dare she ask?* Her heart ached.

If Joe was there, she'd ask him. But he hadn't turned up. That was a good thing. Hopefully the image of his face and physique would fade if she didn't see him as often. Because she obviously wasn't over Danny. How had she come to a place where her mind wandered from one boy to another? Neither of them were interested in her.

'Okay.' Shelly sat beside her. 'You won the game for us, but where is all that aggression coming from?'

Tabbie shrugged and hoped someone else would say something to take their focus off her.

'If it was something to do with Jaya or Stephanie, you would have said something by now. Has it got anything to do with Danny?' Shelly asked quietly.

'No. Oh, maybe.' Tabbie released a long slow breath.

'What's up?'

'I can't seem to get him out of my mind. I took the photos of him out of my room, and now I'm hearing his name above the crowd. And then there's—' She stopped. Others slid in beside them, halting the conversation.

$\mathscr{S}$TEPHANIE

Steph checked the time. She'd made the right decision. She hated hanging out with Tabbie's friends. Today was a step in the right direction. She needed to get fit again.

She took two steps outside only to return for a second blanket to wrap around Lola. Thankfully, Lola drifted off to sleep within minutes of leaving home.

At the first hilly incline, Steph's chest heaved and she gasped for air. The next hill tore shreds off the first. Her legs trembled and her heart pounded in her head. She stopped to catch her breath.

Ahead the path split. A sign pointing left indicated a steep incline. She turned right.

A few minutes later, she found herself at the bottom of a thousand concrete stairs. Steph took one look at her flimsy stroller and returned to the steep path. Lola wriggled and whinged. Within a few more strides, Lola screamed. Steph reached into her bag for something to distract Lola.

'Oh! Stupid.' In her determination to get fit, she'd forgotten to pack any toys or food. There were no shortcuts home. She'd have to retrace her steps. Lola's cries sent prickles down her spine. 'It's okay, shh, shh.' She tried to soothe Lola.

She didn't dare pull Lola out of the stroller for fear of it rolling away. Her heart hurt as Lola's face grew redder. *Selfish.* That all she was. Selfish for wanting to get fit. 'Sorry, baby girl.'

As soon as they reached a flat spot, Steph pulled Lola out and hugged her tight. She pushed the empty stroller home with Lola on her hip. Stephanie poured her attention over Lola, content with stretching to finish her workout. When Lola was ready for a nap, Steph pushed her body back into another workout until her muscles turned to jelly and collapsed on the floor. How did having a baby leave her so out of shape?

She imagined herself in front of a class of girls, teaching them how to dance. A smile formed on her lips as she remembered how much she'd loved her first dance teacher. Could she become that person for someone?

She grabbed her phone to text Tabbie.

'I've changed my mind. Is your mum still available tomorrow?'

Chapter Thirty-four

TABBIE

HAD THE GUYS HEARD from Danny? Or was she hearing things? And what was stopping her from asking if she'd heard correctly? *Pride. Embarrassment.* The first thing she did when she arrived home was fling open her laptop, hoping for an email.

Nothing.

She shoved her chair away from her desk and stood. The carpet locked up the wheels, tipping the chair over. Telling Shelly had made the wound raw again. 'I'm going for a run,' she said to her father as she left the house. 'See you later.'

How stupid to even hope Danny might have emailed. A light drizzle spattered her cheeks and sent her nose dripping. She sniffled, pushing herself to run faster to warm up.

If she did email again, would he reply and confirm it was over? The wind picked up, turning her tears into icicles. She had to stop thinking about Danny. She needed to focus on something else.

Steph.

Tabbie stopped at a bus shelter to text and found a message waiting for her. Steph did want Mum to babysit. Tabbie replied.

Steph replied immediately.

Maybe she should have helped Steph instead of going to the beach. She put her phone away and continued her run. With each step she tried to let go, hoping the light rain would hide her misery. Saturated and shivering, she turned and headed home. Homework needed her attention.

With or without Danny, she wanted to pass Year Twelve and get into university. She pleaded with God to give her something—anything. *Help me get over him and close that door for good or…*

She was already thinking of herself again! She clenched her teeth and returned her thoughts to Stephanie, praying for God to bless her.

$\mathscr{S}$TEPHANIE

Stephanie punched in Francine's number and hit *Call.*

'Hi, Steph. Tabbie mentioned you might be after a babysitter tomorrow.'

'Yes…'

'What time would you like me to come over?'

'Is eight-thirty okay?'

'Sure is. See you then.'

Steph smiled so wide her cheeks hurt. Outside, a sweetly singing bird caught her attention. She opened the window, shivered with the chilly breeze, and breathed in the delicious scent of fresh garden after misty rain. She had to accept it would take a while to build up her fitness, but she needed to at least be able to show them she could dance to get the job. Hopefully her body would hold up for that.

She kicked her leg up, surprised it went higher than the last time she'd tried. She slid down to the floor, almost in perfect splits. She jumped back onto her feet and spun on the ball of her foot. Although everything ached, her core felt solid and held her upright. She flopped onto the floor and laughed.

'I'm going to give it a go.' Steph got up and peeked in on Lola. 'I might be crazy, Lola,' she whispered. 'But I'm going to have a second go at the career I dreamed of years ago. I don't know how we'll afford it, but there has to be a way.'

As she lay in bed that night, memories came flooding back. She tossed and turned, waking from nightmares of BJ, her drug-dealing ex-boss. Giving up on sleep, she got up at four and made herself a cup of tea. Ugly memories continued to play in her mind. Who was she kidding? As if she'd make a good dance teacher.

She picked up the Movement Academy flyer from the table.

MA ~ Movement Academy ~ Come join us!
Classes for all levels and styles.
Now offering Certificate IV in Dance.

She hadn't noticed that last line before. She assumed she'd have to get some qualification, but a Cert Four? *Urgh!*

It was pointless. Everything hurt—her stomach, her legs, her shins, her calves, not to mention her pounding head. What numb-brained idea made her think she could pull it off while she was so out of shape? What if the nightmares she'd had last night became a recurring thing? *No.* She needed to put a stop to this today. Francine could have the day to herself.

Lola stirred. Stephanie went to lift her out of the cot and her arms trembled with pain. She turned the TV onto kids' shows to distract Lola and lay on the couch.

The next thing she knew, someone was knocking on the door. *Francine!*

Why hadn't she texted earlier, when she'd decided she wasn't going?

'Sorry,' Steph said as she opened the door. 'I must have fallen asleep on the couch.'

'That's okay. I'm early. Where's that gorgeous Lola?'

'Gosh, she was here. I'm not used to her moving quickly.'

Francine and Stephanie dashed different directions.

'Found her,' Francine called. 'Like all kids, she found the toilet brush.'

'Gross!'

'She'll probably do worse.' Francine picked Lola up then wiped her clean.

'I should have called.'

'Why? What's up?' Francine blew raspberries on Lola's tummy. Lola squealed with delight.

'I'm not going.' Steph looked away. 'Sorry I've wasted—'

'Really? What have you got to lose?' Francine paused in the hallway with Lola on her hip. 'How about we go in so you can see what the studio is like.'

'But everything hurts.' Steph flexed her toes and groaned as pain shot up her calves. 'I did some exercises yesterday, and now I can barely move.'

'Remember how you used to dance through the pain at school? Stephanie Stronge never gave in to a few sore muscles. Nothing would stop you back then.'

'But—' Steph crossed her arms.

'I'll change Lola, and we can leave in fifteen.'

'But—'

'Off you go. Jump in the shower. Hot water will help your muscles.'

She obediently went to the bathroom and stepped into the shower. Surely she could talk Francine out of taking her. She needed to take control. She had the choice—get into Francine's car, or let this opportunity slip away like water through a plughole. Steph dried off, pulled her clothes on to Francine's sweet voice singing *Twinkle Twinkle Little Star.*

'Hey, thanks for the encouragement,' she said. 'But I can't go.'

'Nonsense. Lola and I are both ready. I'll wait in the car.' Francine tilted her head. 'Steph, I'm usually in favour of you making your own decisions and working out life yourself. But this might be exactly what you need to prove to yourself you're an overcomer. What happened to you isn't what happens to every girl who dances. Be brave. Go for your dreams.'

'My dreams died when I worked in the club and for that monster.'

'That's all in the past. Your future is going to be great.' Francine pulled Lola's fingers away from her hoop earrings. 'Look, if you really don't want to stay after you talk to Joe, I'll bring you straight home. But at least turn up. Now, let's go.'

Stephanie took a deep breath, grabbed her bag and followed Francine out the door. Her resolve to stay home dissolved, even though the hot shower had barely relieved her muscles and she was likely to injure herself if she tried to dance in the condition she was in.

Her thoughts raced as they drove through the local traffic. What if Joe asked her to dance? Why hadn't she thought of that earlier and prepared something? Her hands shook as she pulled at her fingernails, racking her brain for a routine.

'Feeling a little nervous?' Francine glanced at her as she drove.

'That's an understatement.'

'Take a few slow deep breaths.' Francine took a deep breath herself as she pulled into the car park at the dance studio.

Steph sighed. Dancing a solo in the school performance was the happiest moment of her life. Just before everything slipped into a downward spiral with the move north. She loved that dance. But right now, she couldn't remember the music or moves. 'I think I'll fall apart if nothing comes from this,' she dared to whisper as the desire to succeed pushed her out of the car.

'Mumma!' Lola screamed.

'You know what they say? What doesn't kill you makes you stronger.' Francine climbed out, pulled Lola from the car seat and settled her on her hip.

'What if I die on the way to trying?'

'Try smiling. It might trick you into forgetting your nerves.' Francine rubbed her shoulder.

'Mmm.' A bottle of bubbly about now would calm her.

'Take another deep breath. You'll be fine.'

Yes, breathe. No, I don't need alcohol. She didn't do that anymore. Just the thought of it brought the scent. The taste.

'What's bothering you the most, Steph? That you're not in shape, or what happened in the past?'

'Both, I guess.' Tears prickled then rolled down her cheeks.

'Come over here.' Francine led Steph away from the building. 'No one needs to know. All Joe knows is how good you were in high school.'

'But what if he asks about after school?'

'Leave it out. He doesn't need to know the whole story.'

Lola reached out and landed in Steph's arms.

'But isn't that lying? I'm sick of lying.'

'Unless Joe asks you a specific question, you don't have to bring it up. Now put your big girl pants on, walk in there, and see what he has to offer.'

'You make it sound simple.'

'I'll hang around out here until you're finished.' Francine put her arm around Steph's shoulder and gave her a squeeze, then took Lola back from her.

'Thanks.'

'Mum, mum, mum!' Lola cried.

'She'll be right. I take her for a walk in the garden. Off you go.'

Lola's cries echoed in her ears as she walked through the door. She glanced back, took another deep breath, and walked towards Joe.

Chapter Thirty-five

TABBIE

TABBIE WATCHED THE CLOCK, knowing Steph was at Joe's studio while she was in maths class. She couldn't concentrate, so she closed her eyes and prayed.

'Tabbie?' Her teacher's voice interrupted her.

'Sorry, Miss. I'm a little distracted today.'

'I thought you were napping on us.' The teacher smiled and turned back to the board.

Tabbie didn't know how she'd cope in Stephanie's shoes. How do you put the past behind you and move on? How could she put Danny and everything about him behind her and move on? *God, please help me. I've asked for a sign.*

No signs.

And silence from God.

Tabbie picked up her pen and glanced out the window. Something awful might have happened. Maybe she should contact the ministry where Danny's family were missionaries.

She pushed herself to focus. It was hopeless. She was falling behind. She doodled in her notebook and waited for the bell. She used to love school. She was lonely without her friends around. She hadn't invested time into developing deeper friendships with anyone outside her group.

At lunch break she rang Steph, but the call went through to voicemail. 'Hey, it's me. Just wanted to see how you went today.'

$\mathcal{S}$TEPHANIE

Stephanie was heaving deep breaths. Joe had led her through a few combos before putting a full routine together and asking her to perform it in front of the studio manager. She'd managed to push through the pain, and both Gabriella and Joe's faces lit up when she'd finished.

'Hey, would you like to hang around and see what our full-time students do?'

'I'm not sure. Francine is outside with Lola.' She'd already been there too long.

'The students will be here any minute. Why don't you go ask if she's okay to stay a bit longer?'

Steph found Francine rocking the stroller back and forth under the trees. 'Joe asked if I could stay a bit longer. Would that be okay?'

'No problem at all. She only fell asleep a few minutes ago.'

Steph turned and followed a group of girls her age into the studio. Her cheeks heated up as she watched them dance. She thought she'd done alright, but these girls were amazing. It was torture to watch.

Joe dismissed the class and came to her side. 'What did you think?'

'They're pretty good.' *What is he expecting me to say?*

'Would you like to join in? They've only been going for a month. It's the first class of full-timers this studio has had.'

'They've only been going a month? They're amazing.'

'Most of them have danced their whole life.' Joe smiled and nodded.

'I don't know.' How could she even compete? She'd only danced through high school.

'If you're still thinking about becoming a teacher, you'll gain some invaluable skills.'

Stephanie bit the edge of a sharp fingernail.

'You don't have to give me an answer today. Sleep on it. I'll chat with Gabriella and give you a call in the morning.'

His smile sent her heart racing again. It'd be easy to turn up and see Joe daily.

'Sorry, Francine.' Stephanie rushed towards the shaded area near the car park. 'I didn't think the lesson would go so long.'

'It was no problem at all. Lola and I have had so much fun.'

Stephanie pulled her daughter out of the stroller and squeezed her into a hug.

'She slept for nearly an hour. It's lovely and peaceful here under the trees.' Francine folded the stroller and opened the boot. 'Would you like to go out and grab a bite for lunch?'

'No thanks.'

'My shout.'

'Are you sure?' Steph kissed Lola's cheeks.

'I wouldn't have asked if I wasn't sure.' Francine jingled the keys as she climbed into the front seat.

'Thanks.' One less meal to find money for. They stopped at a sidewalk café, and Stephanie ordered a chicken wrap.

'How did you go? What did you do?'

'I danced a little. Not great compared to the girls doing the course. I'm so out of shape.'

'But you didn't come straight back out, so something must have gone okay.'

'It felt great, actually. Joe asked if I'd like to join the full-timer course. But the cost… there's no way I could afford it.' Steph's voice trembled. 'Right now, I need income.'

'What about paying it off? You might be able to study now and pay later.'

'But it's a full-time course. It might be five days a week.' She just wanted Francine to stop talking about it.

Chapter Thirty-six

*T*ABBIE

TABBIE NEEDED FRESH INSPIRATION. *Direction.* The missionary group. She was going to call them. She went to her laptop to find their number.

'Hello, how can I help you?' a soft, shaky voice answered.

'I was just wondering if you could help me with some information regarding mission trips? I'm in Year Twelve and looking at my options.'

'Of course, dear. Now where were you looking at serving?'

Dared she say it? *Rwanda, near the Burkleys?* 'Maybe somewhere in Africa.'

'If you go onto our website, you'll find an application form and there's also a schedule of short-term mission trips you can apply to go on. Our next trip to Africa won't be until the middle of next year. But if you're looking for something during your summer break, we have a team going to Indonesia. I think there's a few spots left in that one.'

'Thanks, I'll have a look. While I'm on the phone...' She knew she shouldn't ask but... 'I have a friend in Rwanda at the moment with your organisation. Danny Burkley.'

'Yes, I know the family.'

'Do you have any news on them?' she said, almost breathless.

'I'd love to share something with you, but you know about privacy and how everyone is nowadays. I'm not able to give out any personal information. I'm sure you understand.'

'I was hoping to call them. Do you have a phone number?' Tabbie rushed her words.

'Sorry, dear, we don't. I'll send an email to let him know you enquired.'

'No, it's okay. I have his email address. Thanks for offering.' Tabbie took a deep breath.

'Is there anything more I can help you with today?'

'That's all, thanks.'

The crunch of pebbles on the driveway and the hum of the family car sounded as Tabbie hung up. She pushed the phone call out of her mind.

'So?' she asked as her mother walked through the doorway. 'Details?'

'Haven't you spoken to Steph? I'll let her tell you about it. Why don't you ring her now?'

Tabbie grabbed her phone.

'Hi,' Stephanie almost sang. 'What's been happening?'

'That's what I want to know.' Tabbie pushed her foot hard on the tiles. 'You didn't reply.'

'Yeah, sorry. Busy day.'

'How did it go?'

'It was good to dance again. But I can barely move. I might need a wheelchair tomorrow.' Stephanie laughed.

'It is good to hear you sound happy.' Tabbie relaxed a little. 'What happens now?'

'Not completely sure. It was different from what I expected.'

'Are you going to keep going?'

'Nah. I need income, not an extra expense right now.'

'It's great you went.' Tabbie took a deep breath. 'I'm so proud of you.'

'Ha, thanks. Gotta go and deal with a smelly nappy.'

'Okay, talk soon.' Tabbie found her mother outside at the clothes line. 'Steph sounds happy. Shame things didn't work out, though.'

'What did she tell you?' Her mother threw some pegs into the basket and looked at her.

Tabbie replayed the short conversation.

'So she didn't tell you about Joe asking her to hang around and watch the class he took? She didn't mention the fact he's calling her tomorrow about doing the course so she can teach?'

'No. What? Wow, that would be a dream come true for her.'

Her mother went on to fill in the missing details of the day.

'That's impressive. Finally, everything might be falling into place for Steph.'

'Seems that way.' Her mother beamed a huge smile. 'And I'll be Lola's nanny.'

'I thought you were looking for a job.'

'I was looking because I need to keep busy. We don't really need the money, so this is perfect.'

Yeah, perfect. Tabbie left her mother with the washing and retreated to her room. Steph was getting to hang out with a hot guy while doing what she'd always dreamed of. All Tabbie had was school. Boring Year Twelve. What was it all for? To get into uni, to do what? *Work with Danny.* No, work with children somewhere in the world. *Blah!* Why weren't things turning out for her? She pulled out her phone to text Stephanie.

She threw the phone onto her bed as it buzzed with a reply.

Tabbie poked her tongue at the phone and pushed it away. It buzzed again.

Tabbie didn't reply. She wanted Stephanie to see what the silent treatment felt like. A few minutes later her conscience got the better of her. She grabbed her phone and punched in a reply.

She lay on her bed, staring at the ceiling. Jealous of Steph seeing Joe? *Am I?* Or was she trying to keep her mind busy but looking in the wrong place?

Danny. What if he truly couldn't get to a computer or phone?

Now the wind had blown away the clouds and rain, the scents of summer lingered in the air again. It would've been a great afternoon to head to the beach, but public transport would take too long. If only Priscilla and Shelly wanted to go to the beach midweek, she'd be set. But no, they had commitments.

Her textbooks stared at her. She should be studying. But instead, she picked up her phone.

Chapter Thirty-seven

STEPHANIE

STEPHANIE AWOKE TO A FULLY LIT ROOM. Sitting up, she stretched away the sleepiness. Pain darted up and down her legs.

'Mum, mum, mum, mumma,' Lola called.

Steph forced her aching muscles to move. She pulled Lola from the cot, changed her nappy, and warmed up a bottle before checking her phone. Two text messages. One from Tabbie. The second was from an unknown number.

> Hi, this is Gabriella from M.A. I'm not sure if the message I just left worked. Please call me as soon as you can.

Stephanie looked at her settings. There were no messages or missed calls. She shivered. She wasn't ready to talk to Gabriella. The super-confident lady intimidated her. Joe said he'd call, so she'd wait to hear from him.

She opened her fridge. Bare. Income from a basic job would at least put food on the shelves. A pipe dream wouldn't. Francine's voice echoed in her mind. *You might be able to study now and pay later.*

She turned the TV on to entertain Lola, took a deep breath, and called Gabriella. 'Hi, Gabriella. I'm, um, Stephanie Stronge. You sent me a text?'

'Yes, thanks for ringing back. Joe and I have talked.' Gabriella paused.

Steph bit her lip. Why couldn't they have just texted that there was no room for her?

'As you're probably already aware,' Gabriella continued, 'Joe's taking over, but I'm still the manager at this point in time.'

'Oh, I hadn't heard.' Stephanie released a breath. Great. Joe probably didn't even have a say in who Gabriella chose. It was pointless. She knew it was. Why did she even bother returning the call?

'It doesn't matter. I thought I'd mention it in case you were expecting Joe to call. That's the reason it's me and not him. Anyway, what we'd like to offer you is a partial scholarship to join the class that's just started.'

'Partial scholarship?' She hadn't read anything about a scholarship in the prospectus.

'It's a new initiative. If you choose to do the Cert IV, you'll be able to apply for government study support. By offering you the partial scholarship, we'd like you to help us with a few classes each week. Like an assistant teacher. So basically, the course won't cost you anything, just a few extra hours assisting. You could call it a traineeship, I guess. If you accept our offer, we'd like you to sign an agreement to work with us for at least one year after graduation.'

Stephanie swallowed. Her tongue was lost in her dry mouth. It sounded too good to be true.

'I know it's a lot to take in,' Gabriella continued.

'I… um… I don't know. Maybe not at this point in time.'

'Really?' Gabriella's voice squeaked through the phone. 'But it's a great opportunity. We'd like you to give it a go.'

The phone almost slipped from Steph's sweaty palm. Opportunities that sounded too good to be true usually were. She blinked, unable to focus as she glanced from the ceiling to floor. She needed to stay away from dancing. She needed to stay away from the past that haunted her.

'How about you think it over?' Gabriella interrupted her thoughts. 'We don't need to know straight away. Maybe pop in and we can go over some of the finer details.'

'Thanks.' Stephanie shook her head. 'Bye.'

Leaving her phone on her bed, she went to sit with Lola in front of the TV. Joe wouldn't be involved with anything dodgy, would he? What did she really know about him? She would have jumped at the opportunity a couple of years ago. But a couple of years ago, she was naïve and willing to say yes to anything.

Her attempt to send Lola to childcare was a disaster. What if Francine's situation changed and she couldn't look after her? *No.* It was too hard. She'd leave it for today and send a text tomorrow to decline their too-good-to-be-true offer.

She remembered Tabbie's text.

Tabbie replied an hour later.

Steph wasn't in the mood for Tabbie's reasoning and questioning. She had it all planned out in her head. As soon as Tabbie arrived, she'd ask her to mind Lola while she went for a walk. She needed to get some fresh air to clear her mind.

Chapter Thirty-eight

Tabbie

'Seriously, Steph?' were the first words out of Tabbie's mouth as she entered. 'I thought everything was falling into place for you. Why didn't they offer you something?'

'Um…' Stephanie shrugged. 'Look, can you watch Lola? I need to go for a walk.'

Steph was at the door before Tabbie could answer. She breezed out as Lola began to cry. Tabbie went straight to the baby but nothing she did consoled her. She changed her nappy. Changed her clothes. Made her a bottle. Turned some music on, played with her, and tried kids' shows on TV.

Nothing would settle her down.

Tabbie rang Steph but it rang out. She sent a text.

Hey, Lola's really unsettled. Can you come back?

Steph didn't reply. After another fifteen minutes of whinging and crying passed, Tabbie rang her mother.

'Try taking her for a walk.'

Tabbie found the stroller in Steph's bedroom. As she turned, she saw Steph's phone sitting on her bed. Tabbie strapped Lola in and pushed her outside.

Just down the road, people crowded around a bus stop. Tabbie had to excuse herself so she could get the stroller through without going onto the road.

'Get a good welfare payment?' asked a man with a grey beard and walking stick.

Tabbie avoided eye contact, wanting to tell him how rude he was.

'Yes,' someone spoke loudly. 'Seems these days young girls are popping out babies just to get the payments.'

Tabbie didn't look up to see who was talking, instead she pushed her legs to walk quicker.

A lady around her mother's age leaned over the stroller, stopping her. 'She looks flushed. You should check her temperature. She might be coming down with something.'

'She's fine.' Tabbie steered the stroller around the woman, clenched her teeth, and started to jog. She kept her pace steady until she was well away from the crowd, then slowed down.

She took a deep breath and swallowed, trying to add moisture to her dry mouth. With nothing to drink in the nappy bag, she stopped at the first café she came to and grabbed a chocolate milkshake and muffin. 'Nice to have you quiet again, Lola. Hopefully you'll stay that way for a few minutes.' She pulled the stroller in close and sat down at a table.

Lola screamed and kicked the table. The milkshake tipped. Tabbie caught it just before it spilled everywhere. 'Maybe I spoke too soon.' She undid the stroller clasps and sat Lola on her knee.

'She's a bit young for that, don't you think, lovey?' A woman glared over her spectacles as a map of creases appeared on her face.

'What? What's life without a treat?' Tabbie said to Lola.

'You know, the obesity problem is growing in this country.' The woman flicked through a magazine.

'I hardly think a tiny amount of milkshake would send a baby into obesity.'

Did the lady really think she was about to give Lola the whole milkshake? Maybe she should. It might cheer Lola up.

'Don't be too sure.' The lady shook her head, letting her turkey neck flap, then concluded her argument by pulling the magazine up in front of her face.

'Whatever.' Tabbie turned Lola to face her. 'You are perfect, even when you won't stop crying. Don't let anyone ever tell you otherwise.'

Tabbie sucked up the last of her milkshake with a slurp, strapped Lola back in the stroller, and left the café.

A minute later, Lola started to cry again. Had Steph encountered these nasty people on her walks? If she had, why hadn't she told her? *Maybe she'd tried. I've been preoccupied. Maybe I didn't listen.* That didn't stop her from being annoyed with Steph for taking off on her. She stopped to plug Lola's screams with a pink smiley face dummy then continued down the path. Thankfully the dummy worked and Lola drifted off to sleep. But maybe she'd needed some time out. But to leave her phone as well?

Parenting could wait a while, that was one thing Tabbie knew. It was much easier to watch Lola a couple of months ago. She slept more back then. Tabbie turned the corner and headed back up Steph's driveway. She shuffled through the bag for the keys then looked up.

Her palms prickled with sweat.

Her breath caught in her chest.

His tall frame cast a shadow as he knocked on the door. His shirt pulled tight across his back. Her heart raced.

'Hey,' she said as he was about to knock again.

'Oh, hi.' Joe turned to face her. 'I was just about to—'

'See Steph? I don't think she's there.' Tabbie held the key up, hoping he'd move back a little. She needed space between them.

'Will she be back soon?' Joe looked from her to Lola.

Tabbie followed his gaze. *Does it bother him that Steph had a baby?* She'd told Steph he wouldn't care, but… She stopped that train of thought. 'I hope so. Lola's a bit unsettled this afternoon.'

'She seems peaceful now.' Joe smiled as he made room for Tabbie to open the door. 'Maybe I should come back.'

Lola stirred.

'Hopefully Steph won't be too much longer. I might need a little help entertaining this little possum if she wakes up.'

Joe followed her through the door and stood in the corner of the room.

'You want a drink of something? Take a seat,' Tabbie said as she poured herself a glass of water.

'Oh, okay. I'm right for a drink. Thanks, though.'

'Mummummuumm!' Lola called.

'Hey, hey, shhh.' Joe walked over to the stroller. 'Is it okay if I pick her up?'

'If she goes to you, yes, please do.' Until Tabbie could stop her body reacting to Joe, distance and distraction were her friends.

Lola reached up to Joe and giggled as he tickled her.

That was a good sign… for Steph.

Tabbie drank the water and refilled the glass, willing Stephanie to come home.

'Just let me know if I should go. I can give Steph a call later on.'

'It's fine. You're entertaining Lola better than I was.'

'Did Steph talk to you about her decision?' Joe glanced up, eyebrows raised.

'Not really. She took off as soon as I got here. Mum said everything went well yesterday, then Steph sent me a text to say otherwise.'

'She was amazing. Like, I mean, really amazing.' His face lit up. 'She would dance rings around most of our students. It's hard to believe she hasn't danced in over a year.'

'Maybe that's why she's gone for a walk. Her muscles have probably taken a battering. She might be trying to walk it out.' *Or maybe she wanted to run away from her daughter and reality for a while.*

'Did she say why she said no to the scholarship? I know she's short of money—I thought the scholarship would help her out.'

'Scholarship?'

'Yeah. She didn't tell you?' Joe grabbed a toy off the floor for Lola.

Tabbie shook her head and glanced outside just as the screen door rattled.

'Didn't know you planned to entertain while I was gone.' Stephanie pulled the door open, glancing from Tabbie to Joe.

'Yeah, Joe is doing a great job entertaining Lola.' Tabbie swallowed back a giggle when she noticed Steph's tight lips.

Stephanie rushed to take Lola out of Joe's arms.

'I just came by to ask why you said no,' he said. 'And see if I can change your mind.'

Steph's face glowed with a hint of pink.

'You're a gifted dancer.' Joe kept his gaze glued to Stephanie. 'I'd hate to see that wasted.'

STEPHANIE

'You're treating me like I've done something wrong.' Steph stormed into the baby's room, away from Tabbie and Joe, and busied herself changing Lola's nappy.

'What's stopping you?' Tabbie followed her.

'I can't.' Steph's stomach twisted into a knot. 'It sounds too good to be true. It won't work.'

'But this is Joe.' Tabbie said in a hushed tone.

'I can't trust anything when it comes to dance.' She fastened the fresh nappy and pulled Lola into a tight hug. She had to stop making mistakes for Lola's sake.

'Oh.' Tabbie rested her hand on her shoulder. 'I think I see where you're coming from.'

'Good. Now help me get Joe out of here.' Steph glanced towards the door.

'Sure. Let me see what I can do.' Tabbie left the room. 'Hey, Joe, she's having trouble understanding why you've offered her this scholarship.'

'Ah.' Joe groaned.

What's Tabbie doing? She wanted her to get rid of him, not engage him in conversation.

'We want her in our program. I'd love her to teach at the studio.' His voice was loud, like he wanted her to hear him.

'Because?' Tabbie's voice was raised too.

Steph went to the doorway and peeked around the corner.

'It's…' Joe shrugged. 'Steph, are you coming back out here?'

Steph brushed Lola's hair into place with her fingers, taking her time to join them.

'Look, Steph, will you at least consider it? Why not come in, give it a trial for a week and see how it goes. No pressure to stay. You're just so gifted.' He scratched the stubble on his chin.

'I don't know. I don't get why you're…' She stopped before mentioning the scholarship. 'I still need to work out how I'm going to pay the rent here. I have Lola to think of. It wouldn't work.'

'What about the study allowance? Mum's already said she's happy to be Lola's nanny.' Tabbie paused, then looked at Joe. 'Maybe you should come back later. Give Steph a bit more time.'

'Sure. I should have rung before coming over.' He went to leave but turned back to face Steph. 'Talk soon, hey?'

Steph shrugged and stared at the door until the crunch of his footsteps diminished on the driveway.

'It sounds like an opportunity you would've jumped at a few years ago.'

'But it's all different now. What's he really after? He was playing with Lola when I turned up. Why did you let him hold her?' She clung to Lola.

'It's Joe.' Tabbie threw her arms out wide. 'I've known him for years. I didn't think there was any harm in it. I'm sorry.'

'And a scholarship? Like, why would he offer that? I don't trust him.'

'Steph, this is Joe. He's okay.'

'How do you know? Really?' Tears blurred her vision. She'd trusted too many times and got it wrong.

'Steph.' Tabbie put her arm around her and led her to the couch. 'You can't treat everyone like the bad guy.'

'But I only attract bad guys.' Steph wiped the tears running down her cheeks with a tissue.

'Why don't you do what Joe suggested? Go in next week and see what it's like. What have you got to lose?'

'But Lola—'

'Leave her with Mum. She'll be safe with her.'

'Why is everything so hard to work out?' Stephanie kicked a toy in front of her feet.

'Because you're thinking about everything instead of just taking one step at a time. You don't have to plan for the next five years. Just go in and see what it's like. If you don't want to take the scholarship you don't have to.'

TABBIE

Tabbie went to boil the jug. It was easier to think about Steph than what was going on in her own life. 'Tea or coffee?'

'Tea, thanks.' Steph yawned.

Tabbie wanted to shake Steph and tell her she was crazy not to grab the opportunity. She poured the hot water and jiggled the tea bags. As if Joe would be involved in some underground illegal scheme. Maybe she should go and meet Gabriella and check the studio out for herself. If something wasn't right, hopefully she'd get a gut feeling straight away. She'd been getting those gut feelings more and more lately—and they were usually right.

Tabbie took the cup to Steph. 'Here you are.' *Silence.* 'Steph?' Tabbie touched Steph's shoulder but she was motionless. She took the cup back to the kitchen. Staying at Steph's all afternoon wasn't what she had planned. She had a history assignment due tomorrow. Tabbie went back to Stephanie and shook her gently.

'B'there 'n a minute.' Steph slid down until she lay on the couch. Within moments a gentle snore vibrated through her body.

'Sometimes you're impossible!' Tabbie grabbed her phone to ring her mother. 'Any chance you can come pick me and Lola up?'

'Why? What's happened?'

'Steph's fallen asleep.' Tabbie glanced at her friend. 'I need to get an assignment done.'

'You can't wake her?'

'I tried. Please? I really need to come home. Now.' Her voice still didn't stir Steph.

'Of course, love. Be there as soon as I can.'

Tabbie grabbed Lola's nappy bag and checked there was enough packed for a couple of hours. She took a deep breath and headed outside with Lola on her hip, the nappy bag in hand, and more weight on her shoulders than she'd planned to leave with.

Chapter Thirty-nine

STEPHANIE ROLLED OVER. The room was dull and eerily quiet. What time is it? Had she put Lola to bed? *Tabbie?*

Rubbing her eyes, she stood and saw a cup of tea on the bench. She touched the side of the cup. Stone-cold. Her shoulders shook as a chill rushed through her body. How long had she been sleeping? Biting her lip, she looked towards the locked door.

She dashed into Lola's room, then to the bathroom. *Where's Lola? Where's Tabbie?* Maybe she'd taken her for another walk. She grabbed her phone.

You fell asleep. I couldn't wake you. I got Mum to pick us up. Text when you wake and Mum will drop Lola back.

She sighed with relief. How did that happen? Why did she fall asleep? She punched in Francine's number. 'I'm so sorry. I can't believe I fell asleep. I don't know what would have happened if Tabbie wasn't here. I'm…' *Hopeless* was the only word coming to mind. Tears bubbled up over her lashes.

'Don't be too hard on yourself. You've had a physically and emotionally draining couple of days. I'm sure Lola would have woken you. I'll bring her back over now. See you soon.'

She didn't deserve Francine's kindness. It was the second time within a week she'd fallen asleep without making sure Lola was safe. *Completely irresponsible.*

That night she lay in bed, wide awake until well after midnight. Lola slept in the room beside hers and the apartment was locked, but her mind raced. She thought back to how she'd felt when she used to dance. Her muscles tingled while her insides buzzed. She shut the thought down, but the music continued to play in her ears. New choreography flashed in her mind. Spins, tricks, and leaps turning emotion into story.

Was she turning down a genuine opportunity? *What if Tabbie's right?* Maybe Joe isn't the bad guy. Now that she thought about it, he'd been nothing but kind to her. He hadn't tried to touch her or ask her out. Could they actually be offering her a real career and not some B-grade drug-infested underground nightmare? Eventually her mind must have shut off and fallen asleep.

The next day she thought about ringing Gabriella. The first time she reached for her phone, a dirty nappy grabbed her attention. Then every time she went to make the call, Lola screamed for her attention. Finally, with Lola napping, she tried again.

'Hello, you've reached Movement Academy. Please leave your name and number and I'll call you back as soon as I can.' A recording of Gabriella.

Steph sighed and hung up without leaving a message. Maybe it was easier not getting in touch after all. A text from Tabbie came through as she hung up.

> I've made an appointment with Gabriella and Joe straight after school. They have 15 mins before classes start. I want to see if what they're offering is legit. Want to come with me? Mum can pick you up and mind Lola. T x

Steph picked at her fingernails. Her mind darted from thought to thought. She couldn't decide if she wanted to go with Tabbie or stay home. Why was her brain fogging over again?

'Knock, knock,' Francine called through the door in her bright and breezy way.

'Hi, thanks for not banging. Lola's sleeping.'

'I thought she might be. I hope I wasn't too loud. Tabbie told you I was coming, didn't she?'

'Um… she said you'd come if I was going. But I didn't reply. I'm not sure I want to go. Sorry to put you out.'

'No, no. I'm happy to take you to the studio or just visit.'

She loved the way Francine spoke to her rather than turning everything into an argument like her mother used to do.

'I do think it would be good to find out all the information you can. Can you transfer Lola to the car without her waking?'

'Not likely. I won't go. I'm sorry. My brain hasn't been working well today. It's like it's taking a holiday.'

Francine pulled Steph into a hug. 'You're really worried, aren't you?'

Steph nodded.

'Tabbie told me a bit of what happened yesterday afternoon. It's possibly anxiety. It can leave your brain feeling foggy which may cause difficulties in decision-making. That could also be why you fell asleep so quickly.'

'So I should stay home, hey?' She wasn't up to talking psychology.

'I don't think that's the best thing to do.'

'Why not?' Stephanie slumped onto the couch.

'If you don't go, you might look back and wonder.'

'But what if it's all too good to be true?' Steph pulled her ponytail out and ruffled her hair.

'Then you tell them it's not for you. Some people call it having good boundaries.'

'Yeah, they talked about that a lot in rehab. Not going is having good boundaries.'

  Spiralling Solo

'Saying no straight away without looking into it is putting a wall up. Similar but different.' Francine looked in on the sleeping baby. 'Now, can I pack a few things for Lola?'

'Um… I'll do it.' Stephanie hesitated. What was she so scared of? If Tabbie was by her side and Francine not far away, surely she'd be safe. Wouldn't she?

'I'm so glad you've come in, Stephanie.' Gabriella slid two more chairs into the narrow office. 'Now let's answer some of your questions.'

Tabbie fired questions at both Joe and Gabriella, asking what was expected of Stephanie. She asked them to explain what would happen if Steph pulled out and why they were offering a scholarship and if it would be affected if the studio changed hands.

'Look, I'll be honest.' Joe rested his elbow on his knee as he leaned forward. 'I'm taking over, and I want Steph on my team. I reckon she'll make a great teacher, and that's pretty much the bottom line as to why we're offering the scholarship. If I was to sell, then we'd have to have another conversation with the new owner. But right now, I plan to own and run this studio for at least five years.'

'But I'm a mum. What if Lola's sick?' Steph clenched her teeth.

'Take the day off.' Joe shrugged. 'We don't expect anyone to come in if they come down with a virus.'

'That's right.' Gabriella smiled. 'I'd rather not catch what's going around. I wish everyone would stay home when they're sick.'

'I was talking about Lola though, not me.'

'Same thing. It won't be an issue.' Joe sat back in his chair.

'But you're right to be concerned.' Gabriella glanced from Joe to Tabbie then stopped to focus on Steph. 'You see, the reason I'm stepping back is because my husband and I are ready to have a family. We've started IVF and I'm finding it hard to cope with everything.'

'Oh.' Steph suddenly felt guilty for having a baby she didn't plan.

'Once you've finished the Cert...' Gabriella shuffled some papers on her desk. '...your hours will be mostly mornings, with our toddler classes. I'm hoping to continue teaching in the afternoons.'

'We can work it all out when the time comes.' Joe cleared his throat. 'I reckon your gifting will be to teach the older girls. And once you have confidence, I'd like you teaching our full-time classes.'

'But why?' *It still sounds too good to be true.*

'Call it a gut feeling.' Joe shrugged. 'We'll work out which classes and the hours you'll be needed down the track.

Steph pulled at her fingernails. It seemed so up in the air with all the 'we'll work it out when the time comes' talk. Laughter and shouts from outside distracted her.

'Thanks for that info,' Tabbie said. 'We'd better go. Your students seem keen to come in.'

'If you have more questions, give us a buzz or pop back in at any time.' Gabriella smiled warmly as she walked them out.

Joe tapped Gabriella's shoulder. 'Hey, Gabbie, could you please get the girls started? I'd like a word with Steph outside.' He looked at Tabbie. 'Is that okay?'

Tabbie shrugged and looked at Steph. Steph nodded, and Joe led her outside to the path, then headed towards some trees.

'How can I convince you?' Joe stopped in the shade and ran his fingers through his hair.

She glanced sideways to make sure Tabbie was close enough if she needed her.

'How about you come, join in for a few days and then decide? What have you got to lose?' He scratched his stubble. 'Trial it for a week.'

A knot pulled Steph's stomach when Joe didn't move. He obviously wanted an answer from her. Without thinking she wrapped her arms around her middle to hold the pain. She couldn't give him what he wanted. She walked towards Tabbie in the carpark, leaving him hanging.

 Spiralling Solo

Chapter Forty

TABBIE

'I DON'T KNOW. What do you reckon?' Stephanie asked Tabbie.

'Just have a go,' Tabbie said.

'Don't throw away your talent.' Joe had followed them. 'If you decide not to come here, don't stop dancing. You're too talented to waste it.'

'But I'd be starting so late. They've been going for weeks.'

'You'll catch up no problem. Look, I'd better get inside. Please come in tomorrow morning and give it a chance.'

Tabbie watched Joe saunter back inside. 'I've got a good feeling about Gabriella, and Joe is one of the nice guys.'

'That's what my friends in Toowoomba said about Jason. And they were wrong.'

'I know it's hard to trust again.' Tabbie's mind flashed back to the guy she'd narrowly escaped. 'How about you give it a go? Trust in yourself with baby steps.'

Stephanie kicked a stone towards the car tyre. Tabbie waved at her mum, still pushing Lola around, signalling they were ready to leave. She'd been granted a one-day extension to get her history assignment in. She needed to get home and work on it.

'Hey, are you doing anything this afternoon?' Steph leaned against the car. 'Maybe going for a walk will help me collect my thoughts. I can't seem to think clearly at the moment.'

'I've got to work on an assignment. Why don't you take Lola for a walk?'

'Yeah, I was planning to, but just hoped you might come with us.'

'Sorry.' Since she'd experienced how cruel some people could be, she understood why Stephanie preferred company. The hairs on the back of Tabbie's neck tingled as Steph put Lola in the car seat. She had to let Steph fend for herself this time. She needed to focus on her history assignment, not Stephanie's future.

Soon after, they pulled up outside Steph's. With the nappy bag on one shoulder and holding Lola with her other arm, Steph hip-bumped the car door closed.

Tabbie put her window down. 'I'll come over tomorrow.'

'It's fine. Don't worry about it.' Steph's lips were tight as she turned and rushed towards her front door.

Tabbie jumped out of the car. 'Mum, I'll be back in a minute.'

'Steph…' Tabbie jogged to catch up to her. 'Do you know you're amazing to cope the way you do?'

'I'm not coping well.' Steph flung open her front door and let it slam behind her.

'You are.' Tabbie followed her inside. 'I copped all sorts of comments, judgment, and parenting advice when I took Lola out the other day. It's crazy the way people spoke to me. If that's what happens when you're out on your own, I get why you question yourself.'

'I keep asking you and your mother to help me out. I can't seem to do this without you. I'm a long way off amazing.'

'Asking for help is natural. It doesn't take anything away from your amazingness.'

'It's a sign of weakness.' Tears flowed down Steph's cheeks. 'I'm weak because I can't do it all on my own.'

'I don't think we were ever meant to do it all on our own. God's plan was for a man and woman to create a baby and bring that baby up around family and community. It was never a job to be done alone.'

'Yeah, I know I stuffed up.' Steph spat the words out. 'Why do you make everything about God's plan?'

'Sorry. Does it really bother you that much?' Tabbie clenched her teeth to stop herself from saying anything else.

'Only because I don't get it, I guess.' Steph wiped her tears with the back of her hand.

'I only started getting it after I'd been going to church for a while, hanging out with Christians, and reading the Bible.' She chewed her lip and continued in a lower voice. 'There's so much good stuff in it.'

'It doesn't make sense to me. It's such an ancient book. I don't get how something written in the Dark Ages can have any impact in today's world. I mean, everything has changed so much since when Jesus was supposedly on earth. What relevance does it have to a single mum? The Bible won't pay my rent.'

'Mumma.' Lola pulled at Steph's leg.

'You're right, but its principles are guidelines to live by. And when we do, life becomes wonderful and fulfilling.' She couldn't stop. She had to get Steph to understand. 'And when we accept Jesus as our Lord and Saviour, we're given eternal life.'

'I know that. You've told me a million times.' Stephanie sat on the floor with Lola. 'But it just doesn't make sense to me. So many people find other religions just as good as you find Christianity. Why choose one religion when there are so many that make people happy?'

'It's more than just happiness. It's about joy and fulfilment. Have you found a religion to satisfy that searching inside?'

'I'm not searching. I was meaning other people.'

'Why don't you check it out? Find someone who is completely filled with joy. Someone who doesn't have to keep doing certain things to make everything all right. Someone who knows they're forgiven even if they do the wrong thing. Someone who—'

'Enough! You don't have to get all high and mighty on me.'

She'd gone off on a tangent again, exactly what Steph hated her doing. 'Sorry. I didn't mean to preach at you.' Tabbie combed her fingers through her hair. 'Christianity is different from other religions.'

'You've already told me that. You're the one into the spiritual stuff—not me.'

Lola pulled Steph's hair. 'Ouch!' She untangled Lola's hand from her hair and shook a rattle in front of her face.

'I know. But…' Tabbie tried to gather her thoughts. She wanted Steph to understand how God loved her, no matter what. She thought for a moment before trying again. 'What I meant—'

'I thought you had an assignment to do. Isn't your mum waiting?'

Steph had just told her she wasn't interested. She needed to stop.

'I didn't mean to snap at you. But you said you couldn't hang out. Look, if ever I find I'm searching for that spiritual something, you'll be the first person I come to.' Steph took Lola into the bedroom.

'You're right.' Tabbie followed Steph to where she was changing Lola's nappy. 'I shouldn't have gone on about it. I'll see you soon.' She put her arm around Steph in a shoulder squeeze, waved goodbye to Lola, and left.

Tabbie sighed as she walked back to the car. Thoughts flashed to the times she'd tried to talk to Suzie and Jaya. Everything she'd said had fallen on deaf ears. They just weren't interested in her beliefs. She needed to shut up about it and get on with living out her faith.

'That took a while.' Her mother lowered her chin as Tabbie climbed in beside her.

'Yeah.' Tabbie pulled the car door closed with a thud.

'She'll be okay. The offer is a lot for her to process.'

'True.' Tabbie looked at her mum. 'When we get home, I need to get my history assignment done. Can you help me? I can't get my head into it.'

'You know History isn't my strong point.'

'Pleeease?' Tabbie clasped her hands together and smiled.

'Alright.' Mum laughed. 'Oh, sorry. I should have told you straight away. Jaya rang. She said you weren't answering.'

Tabbie sent a text to Jaya while her mother was driving. Jaya replied immediately.

> I need you to come meet me. I wouldn't ask if it wasn't really important. You know that.

'Jaya?' her mother asked.

'Yeah, she wants me to meet her. But I can't.'

'Are you sure you shouldn't ring and check in with her?' Mum parked the car in their garage. 'I can make a cuppa while you talk, then we'll get on to that assignment.'

'Okay.' Tabbie walked into the house, and waited for Jaya to answer.

'Where have you been? I've been calling you all afternoon.' Jaya's voice boomed into her ear.

'What's so urgent?'

'Can you come over?'

'Can't it wait till tomorrow? I've got an overdue assignment to finish.'

'It's to do with Danny—'

'What?' Tabbie's heart raced.

Jaya was silent.

'Can't you just tell me over the phone?'

'I'd rather not.'

Tabbie's heart sank. It could only be bad news if she had to tell her in person.

'I'm flying up to see Dad tonight. I won't see you till the end of next week. He's not dead or anything like that.'

'Thank goodness.' Tabbie released a breath. 'Why can't you just tell me over the phone?'

'You wouldn't believe me. I want to show you something.' Something in Jaya's tone rang warning bells in Tabbie's gut.

'I'm sure it can wait until you get back. I've really got to do this assignment.' Tabbie couldn't hang up fast enough. Jaya had been ultra-gossipy lately. She tried to push the conversation out of her mind. Surely if it was anything of substance, Jaya would have given in and told her over the phone.

'Everything okay?' her mother asked as she passed her a cup of tea.

'Just Jaya talking in riddles.'

'So we don't need to pick her up or anything?'

'No. I'll grab my books.'

Once she'd finished, Tabbie hated to admit most of her assignment was her mother's suggestions, word for word. Her mind continued to bounce back to the conversation with Jaya, leaving her with a billion what-ifs and maybes about Danny.

Chapter Forty-one

TABBIE

ON THE WAY TO YOUTH GROUP a week later, Tabbie's stomach churned. She'd finished all her assessments for the term, so she should have felt lighter. But she didn't. She felt weighed down, wishing she'd connected with Jaya again.

Joe leaned on the fence outside the church. His silhouette took her breath away and sent her heart thumping. Why did he have that effect on her?

'Hey, hi. I was waiting for you.'

'You were?' She almost choked on the words.

'I was hoping Steph would turn up at the studio after our chat.'

Of course it was about Steph. As if he'd be waiting for any other reason. She wanted to slap herself on the forehead.

'Do you reckon I should talk to her again?'

'Maybe.' That familiar guilty feeling settled in Tabbie's chest. Had she neglected Steph again? 'Give her a call and check.'

He nodded and crossed one foot over the other, still leaning against the fence.

'You've got a thing for her, haven't you?' Tabbie struggled to quiet the jealous tone.

'Ahh...' He ran his fingers through his hair. 'She's an amazing dancer.'

'You sure it isn't more than that?'

'Nah.' The flush in his cheeks told her otherwise. 'I think she's got some kind of block. I'd love to help her through it.'

She looked deep into his eyes. A strange desire to kiss the boy in front of her overwhelmed her. His focus locked on her for an awkward eternity. *What's going on? This isn't a movie set.* She turned to walk inside to the service, wishing she had an icepack to cool her cheeks as she sensed Joe following her.

He grabbed her attention during the soft shuffling after the preacher stopped speaking. 'Is anything happening tomorrow?'

'I'm sure something is, but all I'm planning to do is sleep.' Loud music played. The service was finished.

Their arms rubbed as the crowd bottlenecked through the doorway. Warmth rushed through her. *What is it about this guy that keeps igniting something I don't want ignited?* She shook it off and took a deep breath. 'Hey, have you heard from Danny?'

'Yeah, I have.'

'How is he?' Tabbie's chest tightened.

'Pretty good. Not an easy life over there.'

'No. His family is amazing to do what they've been doing. I...' She paused. 'Does he have a new email or something?' She blinked, hoping her eyes wouldn't start leaking.

'No, same one.' Joe glanced at her. 'You haven't heard from him?'

Tabbie shook her head.

'I'd better head off. I'm teaching first thing tomorrow morning. See ya.' He jogged off leaving Tabbie alone in the crowd.

She was about to head out to meet her mother when she heard someone mention Danny.

'Yeah, must have sent me the same email,' one of the guys said.

'Reckon he's found an African girl,' another guy said.

Enough. She didn't want to hear any more. She left through the side entrance. Tears prickled and a golf-ball sized lump floated in her throat. *What's going on?* One minute she wanted to kiss Joe, and the next she was upset Danny had found someone else.

She arrived home and checked her emails.

Nothing.

Releasing a silent breath, she groaned, then climbed into bed and lay under her doona letting let her tears flow. Next she knew, her room was bright, yet no early morning sunlight cast shadows across her bed. She wiped her sticky, salty teary eyes and reached for her phone.

9:40 am.

How on earth had she slept through her alarm and the usual morning sounds of the house? And she'd missed a text from Shelly.

Hey, I'll be there at around 10. It's a gorgeous day. The beach will be perfect. S x

Tabbie yawned. Too late to cancel—Shelly would be on her way by now. She dashed out of bed and down to the kitchen. It was empty, except for a note on the bench.

> *'Good morning sleepyhead. Dad and I are heading out to the markets. See you around lunch time. Love Mum.'*

Tabbie shoved a piece of bread into the toaster. She grabbed her towel and changed into her swimmers. Scrunching her hair on the top of her head, she pulled an elastic around it, poured coffee into a keep-cup, then shoved toast into her mouth. She opened the front door just as Shelly pulled into her driveway.

As she watched the streets pass by, Danny invaded her thoughts. She wanted to be firm in her resolve to move on and get over him. If only…

'Something's bothering you.' Shelly slowed the car to a complete stop behind a sea of brake lights on the motorway.

'Sorry, Shelly. Yeah.'

'Tell me all your woes. Looks like we'll be here for a while.'

'Danny.' Tabbie balled her fist, pushing it into the car seat.

'The infamous Danny.'

'I overheard some guys talking last night.' Tabbie looked out the window. 'He's been in touch with them, plus Joe's heard from him.'

'And not you?'

She shook her head.

'Tabbie, Tabbie, Tabbie, why do you always expect the worst? Just wait and see what happens. Sit back and focus on school, youth group, and your friends. If it's meant to be, I'm sure it'll be in God's perfect timing.' Shelly glanced at her and grinned.

'But I asked God for a sign.'

'And has He given you one?'

'Maybe that was the sign.'

'Maybe, maybe not. We live in a fast-food world. We expect God to give us the fast answers, but He doesn't always work like that. His timing is perfect and something we can't fathom. That's part of the mystery.'

The traffic cleared and, as they travelled the rest of the way in silence, Tabbie mulled over Shelly's words.

She'd barely set two feet on the sand before Joe caught her attention again. She blinked and redirected her gaze. Being attracted to him while thinking about Danny was doing her head in. She needed to take Shelly's advice.

'Hey,' Joe called as they got closer.

'Thought you said you had classes this morning.'

'I did—only a few early classes then I came straight here.'

'Oh.' She wondered why his eyes sparkled more than usual.

'Plus I wanted to tell you about something.' He dipped his chin and opened his eyes wide.

Tabbie swallowed hard.

'Danny emailed.' Joe ran his fingers through his hair.

'What did he say?' Her heart contorted in her chest. She braced herself for the news she didn't want to hear.

'He'd heard some of the guys were spreading rumours, and he wanted me to squash them. Any idea what those rumours might be?'

Tabbie shrugged. She didn't want to admit what she'd heard to Joe.

'He asked if you've been keeping safe, suggested I keep an eye on you, make sure you don't twist an ankle or—'

'What? I don't understand.' Tabbie swallowed hard as tears welled. 'Why haven't I heard from him?'

'You haven't received any snail mail?'

She shook her head.

'Game on.' Joe took off towards the volleyball court, then called back, 'Are you playing?'

Tabbie shook her head and walked towards the water. Had something gone missing? Why was he emailing the guys but not her? Joe's words gave her goosebumps on goosebumps. He wanted to squash any rumours and was worried about her twisting her ankle again. A smile crept across her face, warming her whole body as the cool ocean water lapped her feet.

The inkling of hope soon washed back out to sea as doubt rose. Could it really be so? There must be a reason why Danny hadn't emailed her. She turned around to head back up the beach when she was swamped by a group of boys who'd barely hit puberty. 'Hey, beautiful. Wanna come for a walk with us?'

A chill shuddered down her spine. *Where had they come from?* She opened her mouth, but before she could get any words out, Joe was right there beside her.

'I guess not,' a boy spoke before they all ran off.

'Thanks. I think.'

'You're welcome. Just keeping you safe. Danny…' Joe winked but didn't say any more.

'I don't understand—'

Joe ran back to the game as her words drifted in the salty breeze.

Chapter Forty-two

$\mathcal{S}$ TEPHANIE

STEPHANIE ENJOYED A SILENT MOMENT as she lay in bed. They wouldn't leave the scholarship open forever. She needed to make a decision. She thought about the text Joe sent this morning.

The offer is still open if you'd like the scholarship.

There hadn't been any creeps lurking around the building. Francine said she'd be available to mind Lola all year, so the concern of putting her into full-time care wasn't really an issue. It was only a year.

If she took the scholarship, it could lead to teaching full-time, an opportunity she'd thought was out of reach. She threw her legs over the side of the bed and wandered towards Lola's bedroom. Eyes still closed, her little chest rose peacefully with each breath.

Steph poured herself a black tea. No milk again. Grabbing her phone, she punched in Francine's number and hit call.

'Hello, Steph,' Francine answered. 'What's up?'

'Hi.' She sipped her tea, finding the courage to continue. 'I'm wondering if I could take you up on your offer of looking after Lola so I could accept the scholarship.'

'Of course you can, but you still sound a little unsure.'

'Um…' Steph took another sip. 'It's okay if you've changed your mind, but you said you were happy to mind Lola.'

'Oh no, absolutely it's still okay.'

'Are you sure? Like for the whole year? I don't want to put you out.'

'I understand why you want to double-check. You're becoming very responsible, Steph. I'm proud of you. I've had a look at my calendar, and there are a few days that might be a little tricky, but it would only be three or four days you might have to take off. I'd love to look after her. She's like family, both of you are.'

'Do you think I should accept the scholarship?'

'If it's what you want, yes. It's a great opportunity.'

Stephanie hung up with the words *like family* echoing in her mind. It was a nice thought, but blood was always thicker than water. Deep down, she knew she'd never really be a Moray, but she'd always be family to her sister.

'I've been offered a scholarship at a dance school!' she told April. 'Can you believe it?'

'No.' April sighed. 'How on earth did you find that? I didn't think you'd be able to dance after you'd had a baby.'

'Gee, April, thanks for the vote of confidence.' Stephanie wished the bouncy, happy, optimistic April from a few years ago would return.

'Well, I just thought you wouldn't want to dance again.'

'Anyway…' Stephanie went to the sink and filled it with water. She'd get to the dishes when she hung up. 'I'll be qualified to teach dance in a year.'

'I guess that would be kind of cool.' Clicking on a keyboard followed April's words.

'How are you?'

'I found a support group online. Heaps of other girls have similar stuff going on. Some deal with things differently to me.'

'Differently as in?'

'Some hurt themselves.'

'In what way?' Steph cringed at the thought of her sister joining them.

'Like cutting and stuff.'

'You don't, do you?' She held her breath.

'Nah.' More tapping on a keyboard.

'Did you ever ask about being a gym coach?' How could she trust April wasn't hurting herself?

'Huh?' April sounded vague. 'Gymnasium or gymnastics?'

'Gymnastics, of course.' Although any gym would keep her sister off the internet. 'Teaching might run in the family.'

'Coach? Nah. I don't want to go back to that. What's the deal with the scholarship?'

'I've missed a few weeks, but they said I'll be able to catch up. Francine's offered to mind Lola. I'm kind of nervous, but I'll give it a go.' Steph tensed, an uneasy feeling rising in her. 'Are you listening to me?'

'Yeah, I'm listening.'

'Be careful. There are loads of trolls online. You can't fully trust them if you don't know them in real life.'

'Mmm, gotta go. See ya.' April hung up.

Steph threw her phone on the couch and went to finish the dishes. She hoped April was safe. It was hard enough going to a face-to-face support group and trusting new people there. Internet support groups were a whole different level.

Thoughts of April still plagued her mind when Tabbie arrived that afternoon. 'April's in some online support group. Some are self-harming. I'm worried she might copy them. She said she wasn't, but how do I protect her?' Stephanie picked at her frayed fingernail. 'Do you have a file? I'm sick of catching my nails on everything.'

'It's hard when you're so far away.' Tabbie pulled a nail file out of her purse. 'Mum might know what to do. Is it okay if I tell her?'

'If you want, but what could she do?' Steph dragged the file across the top of a fingernail. Francine hadn't been able to help her when she was April's age. She doubted her sister would be any different.

Chapter Forty-three

TABBIE PULLED THE ELASTIC out of her hair as Steph sniffed at the air.

'You smell like the pool. Didn't you shower after doing laps?'

'Not this time.' She needed to talk about Danny, process what was going through her mind. But Steph went into a longwinded speech about how she was going to give the scholarship a go and then about April and teaching gymnastics. 'Joe—'

'I know, I should call him and tell him I've decided to take up the offer. It'll be a bit of a perk having him to feast my eyes on every day.' Steph inspected her nails and handed the file back.

'Maybe you should focus on the course.' Tabbie hadn't meant to sound snarky.

'I will, I will. You sound jealous.' Steph smiled. 'He's just nice to look at. That's all.' She reached out to Lola and pulled her in for a cuddle.

Tabbie nodded. She wasn't interested either, so why was she getting all hot and bothered?

'So if you're interested, go for it.' Steph raised her eyebrows.

'No—'

Lola started to whinge.

'I can put in a good word for you if you like. You know, like, hint that you're keen.' She winked.

'Thanks, but no thanks.' Tabbie reached for her phone.

'Can you help me with the bath while you're here?'

'Sure.' It was pointless trying to sort her thoughts with Steph's mind elsewhere. Tabbie sent her mum a text asking her for a lift home, then ran the water for Lola.

Twenty minutes later, Tabbie climbed into the car beside her mother. 'You know how you were worried about April?'

'Hmm…' her mother said, keeping her focus on the road.

'Well, Steph says she's spending a lot of time with an online support group with randoms. Steph's worried about her hurting herself.'

'With everything she's gone through, April would be in a high-risk category.' Mum rubbed her chin, deep in thought. 'Leave it with me. I'll have a think and chat to your father.'

On Sunday morning Tabbie heard voices above the hum of her hairdryer. She shut it off for a few seconds. *Joe? What's he doing there?*

She finished drying her hair and headed downstairs.

'Hey, good morning. Thought I'd save you the bus fare.' Joe's smile sent her heart racing.

'Thanks, but I was planning to walk today.' The thud of her heart pulsed in her ears.

'You never know, there might be cracks in the path and you could twist that ankle again.' He jingled his keys.

'I hear you have a bodyguard.' Her mother smiled.

Tabbie's face heated up. A seriously weird-awkward-wishing-the-floor-would-open-and-swallow her kind of moment she just wanted over.

'Let me save any accidents and give you a lift.' Joe turned to walk towards the door. 'Besides, there's always the possibility of a mugging. And there's safety in numbers. See you later, Mrs Moray.'

'Yeah, right! Our neighbourhood is safe.' Tabbie waved to her mother and followed Joe down the path. *Is he going to walk me to church and back?* His car was sitting outside her home. She had no words. She hadn't felt this awkward in a long time.

During the service, the pastor announced an upcoming family barbecue to bless single-parent families in the community.

Afterwards Joe asked, 'Should I escort you home, or did you want to hang out with the others?'

'Actually, I'd like to go and tell Steph about the lunch next week.'

'Great idea. I'll take you over there.'

'We'll have to catch the bus or walk.'

'Yeah, my car is...' Joe laughed. 'Nice day for a walk, isn't it?'

Tabbie fell into step with him. Yes, it was a nice day for a walk, but she'd rather walk on her own.

'Shh,' Steph said as she opened the door. 'Lola's sleeping.'

Joe stood just inside the door and smiled at Steph.

'I know you didn't want to come back to youth group because you felt out of place with Lola—' Tabbie spoke in a quiet voice.

'Why don't you tell it as it is?' Stephanie glanced at Tabbie, then Joe.

Tabbie shrugged. It wasn't anything Steph hadn't said herself. 'Anyway, would you come to a family barbeque?'

'Where, when, and how much?' Steph stared at the floor.

'Maybe I should come back later.' Tabbie wished she hadn't come with Joe. Maybe Steph would be less weird if he wasn't there.

'What are the details?'

'It's at church, next Sunday and it's free.'

'Free food?'

'Yep.'

'Sure, why not?' Steph sat on the couch. 'Free food is always good.'

'Great, I might head off. Study and all that, you know.'

'Good to see you, Steph. I'd better stay on duty and see Tabbie gets home safely.' Joe held the door open.

'Duty?' Stephanie asked.

Tabbie shrugged and followed Joe.

'Oh, I've decided to take up your offer, Joe.' Steph followed them to the door. 'I'll see you in the morning.'

'That's great. See you tomorrow.' Suddenly Joe seemed to have a spring to his step.

'You sure you aren't taking this…' Tabbie waved her hands. '…a little too seriously?'

'Just doing as I was asked.' Joe flashed his heart-melting smile.

'I'll call Mum.' She fumbled with her phone, aware of the heat rising up her neck. 'It'll be quicker than catching the bus.'

'Cool.'

'What I don't get is why Danny hasn't contacted me. It doesn't make sense.'

'I'm sure he has his reasons. I'm just doing a mate a favour.' Joe stared out towards the road.

If Danny wanted someone to watch out for her, why hadn't he asked Shelly or Priscilla? It didn't make sense. She relaxed on the drive home when Joe told them he needed to head off as soon as they got back to her place.

He climbed out as soon as they parked in the driveway. 'Thanks for the lift, Francine. Keep safe, Tabbie. I'll see you soon.'

'Too soon, I'm sure,' Tabbie mumbled as he walked towards his car.

Her mother opened the door. 'About April…'

Tabbie raised her eyebrows.

'Your father and I have talked, and we've decided to invite her down here for a while. We'll let her have the spare room. Just means you'll have to share the bathroom with her.'

'That's fine by me.' Tabbie headed towards the stairs. 'But Diane might say no.'

'Guess I'll find out when I call her.' Her mother rubbed her chin with her thumb.

Once settled on her bed, Tabbie pulled out her notes to study. An hour later, her mind began to wander. She needed a break and grabbed her phone to call Stephanie.

'Your parents are gluttons for punishment,' Steph said with a chuckle.

'That news travelled fast. Last I heard, it was just a thought.' Tabbie closed her book.

'It's seriously a crazy offer.' Steph sounded brighter.

'No crazier than letting you move in a few years ago.' Tabbie thumbed her notebook.

'But why would they want to do it again, after what I put them through?'

'You're like family, and I guess they're worried about April.'

'Exactly, *like* family but *not* family,' Stephanie's voice lowered a few decibels.

'You know what I mean. Mum and Dad treat you like they treat me.' She'd have to remember to drop the *like* and just say *family*.

'Whatever.' Steph sighed. 'It's stupid, I know, but I kind of hated that you dropped in with Joe. Is there anything happening between you two I should know about?'

'What? You said you weren't interested.' Tabbie paused. 'He's made some promise to Danny that he'd watch out for me.'

'Interesting pick-up line. Like I said, go for it. I don't know why it bothered me. Maybe lack of sleep. Wouldn't surprise me if you two were an item by the end of the week.'

'As if.' She couldn't deny that Joe had an effect on her but… 'No. Not after spending so much time with the guy. Sure, he's good looking, but no.'

'What about Danny? Let's be open about this. Maybe we both have a bit of a crush on Joe.'

'Steph!' What had changed since their last conversation? Tabbie pulled her knees to her chest, airing her sweaty armpits. 'I told you

I wasn't interested. I thought you said it was just a perk. No one can deny how good-looking he is, but do you think it would be smart to crush on your dance teacher? Who's also your boss?'

'Exactly. I knew you'd agree.' Steph's words were drawn out. 'It's pointless. Nice guys run as soon as they see Lola. Guess I always imagined I'd have a father around for my kids. I hate that she's fatherless.'

Steph's tone seemed strange. There had been a few guys who'd run straight towards Steph, not away. 'How about we chat more tomorrow? After your first day.' Tabbie hung up and threw her phone onto the bed.

Why had she even noticed Joe? She pushed her fist into her pillow. If only Danny had kept in touch with her, this would never have been an issue.

Chapter Forty-four

$\mathscr{S}$TEPHANIE

STEPHANIE'S PHONE BUZZED. April's name appeared on the screen. 'Hey.'

'Guess what?' The smile in April's voice made its way through the phone.

'Francine's invited you down here?' Steph replied in a matter-of-fact tone.

'You already know?'

'Yeah, she mentioned it to me. Will you take up their offer?' It would be good to see April, but having her around would change everything. She'd be expected to do the big sister thing and look after her, take her places, and probably help with her homework.

'Of course. Why would I hang around here?'

'The Morays have some pretty strict rules.' Steph thought back to the first time Jason had come over and how they banned him from her bedroom.

'If I don't like it, I'll do what you did and move out.'

'Yeah, and look at me now.' Moving out of their home was one of the dumbest decisions she'd made.

'You're doing okay.'

'Only okay. If I'd listened to them and stayed there, chances are I'd be doing great by now. They're nice people. Don't stuff them around.'

'I won't. Anything's better than living here.'

April was probably right, but agreeing with her wasn't going to make matters better. 'Hey, I'm starting that scholarship tomorrow.'

'What scholarship? You didn't even finish school.'

'Dancing.' Steph scratched her head. 'I told you about it. I'm going to become accredited and teach.'

'See, things are working out just fine for you.' April huffed. 'Hang on, I've got a message from someone online. See ya.'

'Don't give them your personal de—'

April hung up.

Steph stared outside contemplating what her sister was going through. Would the Morays police April's online habits?

After she put Lola to bed, she stretched her legs. How was she going to dance every day? A smile crept onto her face. Starting at Movement Academy was something that made her want tomorrow to come sooner. Her phone buzzed again.

A text from Gabriella.

Steph's phone rang straight away.

'Hey, thanks for taking my call this late. You have nothing to worry about. I'm sure your fitness will return quickly. There's a lot of dancers out there who've had a baby and get back into it. You're really talented. You'll be a great fit.'

'You sure?' Steph pointed her toes and stretched again, feeling her muscles pull.

'I am. Now, just to give you the heads-up, Mondays you'll be assisting Joe straight after your class. In the afternoon, we'll get you to move between classes if either of us needs assistance. So just be ready to go with the flow. We often get caught talking to parents at the beginning of each class, so we might ask you to start the warmups.'

'Okay, sounds good.'

'As we mentioned, there is a theory component with the course and the others have already handed in one assignment. I'll get you all set up with that tomorrow so you can catch up. Then it'll be one main assignment per month, a few short ones, and the rest is practical. Don't worry. The theory isn't hard, just necessary. See you at nine in the morning.'

'Okay, see you there.'

Stephanie's thoughts jumbled around in her head as she tossed and turned that night. She thought back to her high school dance classes and tried to remember the warmup drills she'd done over and over. Would she use those or have to learn something new? Would she fit into the cert class? Would the younger students listen to a new teacher coming in? And Lola. What if she didn't like being with Francine every day?

Eventually Steph's eyelids drooped and she drifted off to sleep.

TABBIE

'I'll wait in the car, love. Just need to ring Dad back.'

Tabbie realised she'd have to get used to her mum's new routine. Driving via Steph's and sitting in the morning traffic. She could go back to catching the bus. 'Knock, knock,' she called through the screen.

'It's open. Come in.'

'First day. Are you ready?' Tabbie waited in the doorway.

'I think so. Pinch me! I still can't believe I'm doing this.'

'It's time for good things to come your way. Enjoy the moment.' Tabbie attempted to dance and kick a leg. 'Ouch.' She burst out laughing. 'What can I carry?'

'Bit out of shape, hey?' Steph smiled and handed her the nappy bag.

'Ha ha! You don't need me to pinch you—you'll be in enough pain by the end of the week anyway.' Tabbie laughed and held the door open. 'Come on, I've got to get to school. Mum's in the car.'

Stephanie bit her lip as she pulled Lola in close. 'I think I've got everything.'

'She'll be fine, and so will you. Let's go.'

'Hey, why aren't you answering my calls?' Jaya stopped Tabbie at the gate.

'What?' Tabbie grabbed her phone to see three missed calls. 'Sorry. It was on silent. Hang on. You said you were leaving.'

'I'm leaving Friday.'

'Huh? Why?'

'Things changed again. I'm going to live with Granny. She needs company.'

'What? Weren't you meant to be at your father's this week?' Tabbie tried to piece together the last few conversations she'd had with Jaya.

'I went. He sent me back last night. He's too busy to deal with me.' Jaya rolled her eyes.

'So you're going, as in leaving Sydney?'

'That's what I said.'

'What about school?'

'There's a local public school. It will be so much better than here. It's co-ed.' Jaya nodded with a sly smile.

'Sounds distracting.'

'It'll have to be more fun than I've been having here anyway.'

The bell sounded.

'Tabbie, do you have a minute?' Her history teacher stood in the staffroom doorway.

'I guess so.' *Great.* She braced herself for bad news.

'See you at lunch,' Jaya said as she slipped away.

'You realise you've lost marks because you handed in the assignment late, don't you?'

'Yes, miss.' She held her breath.

'Stay focused, Tabbie.' Her teacher peered over the top of her glasses. 'You're capable of doing really well. Don't throw this year away.'

'I'd better get to class then.' Tabbie glanced at her watch. She felt like she should care more, but she didn't. She just wanted to pass and get through.

'I'll write you a late slip. I think we need to talk.' The teacher went into a spiel about girls who didn't work hard right until the end and didn't score high enough to get into their chosen university.

'Okay, I'll work harder.' Heat was rising up her neck. She was putting all the time she could into study. If it wasn't enough, would she score high enough in the end?

University. Did she truly want to go? What was the point in working so hard if she didn't? They kept telling her good grades would give her more choices in the future. She just didn't know.

Her teacher smiled and handed her the late slip.

Chapter Forty-five

STEPHANIE

STEPHANIE HEADED TOWARDS THE STUDIO door with an extra spring in her step. Her stomach churned with butterflies. A new beginning.

'Wasn't expecting you this early,' Joe said as the door bumped behind her.

'Am I too early?'

'No, no. I'm glad you're here. We finally have a moment alone.'

Steph clenched her teeth, her shoulders tense. Surely he didn't mean anything by that.

'You know how I'm watching out for Tabbie?'

'Yeah.' Steph glanced around the room, avoiding eye contact. *Where is this conversation going?*

'Well, I… was hoping to get to know you a little better before you started, but—'

'You know the basics. I went to school with Tabbie. I have Lola.' Steph shrugged, hoping to release the built-up tension in her shoulders.

'True, and what a cute baby she is.'

Steph nodded. *Seriously, where's he going with this?*

'It must be hard work on your own.'

'Tabbie's been really helpful and Francine will be looking after Lola while I'm here.' She didn't want to admit how hard it really was.

'So you used to dance at the Hill Top dance school before they let boys in?'

'I think boys came just around the time I left.'

'Yes, the infamous lead dancer everyone aspired to be as good as.' Joe winked at her.

'Yeah, whatever.' A chill ran down her spine.

'Tabbie twisted her ankle trying to be as good as you. Jaya stopped dancing because even after you left, she wasn't as good as you. Suzie…' He paused and looked heavenward. 'Suzie thought she had a chance with you gone. And she did… until…'

'I'm sorry about that.' Steph watched him blink glassy eyes. 'You two got pretty close, hey?'

'She was great. Her parents were ridiculously strict. I think she just got sick of them and needed an out.'

'So she took the easy out and overdosed.'

Joe's look changed and pierced her with fire.

'Sorry.' Steph looked away again. 'I didn't mean that the way it came out.'

'I don't know if it was an easy choice for her. She couldn't see a way out. Couldn't see how much God had in store for her. I don't know if she meant to overdose or if she made a mistake. The doctors couldn't confirm either way. Her parents thought they were doing the right thing, but she felt smothered. One thing was clear… her parents wanted to blame someone, so they blamed her.'

Stephanie leaned against the wall and let the silence drift between them. In the soft mood of the moment, she'd shared enough. Anything else shareable was hidden under murky memories. She wanted Movement Academy to be about her future, not her past.

　　　Spiralling Solo

'Anyway, I feel like we're connected through friends and it'll be a great baseline for us to work together. How about we get organised? Everyone will be here in around fifteen minutes. Let's use that time to catch you up on some choreography.'

Joe made every move look easy. He spoke as he danced and, when she followed, her body seemed to glide effortlessly in the right direction. The girls started to arrive, and warm-up for their routines.

At the end of the day, Steph repacked her bag, exhausted and a little flat. The girls were all nice enough, but they'd already formed a clique and she was late to the party. Gabriella and Joe stood talking quietly in the corner. She didn't want to interrupt so she followed everyone out, took deep steadying breaths and tried to find the confidence to go back inside before the younger students arrived.

Inside, Joe and Gabriella laughed. As she contemplated going for a walk, Joe appeared in the doorway. 'We've got just under half an hour before the next class. Let's go grab a cold drink and bring it back.'

'Are you sure we'll be back in time?' After sweating all morning, she was wary of getting into his car.

'Yeah, the café is two minutes down the road. My shout.'

Steph made a mental note to pack a sweat towel and deodorant as she followed him to his car.

'Tell me about Lola's dad.' Joe held his milkshake in one hand as he steered the car back to the studio with the other.

Stephanie took a long sip. 'Ouch! Brain freeze.'

Joe laughed, then glanced at her with raised eyebrows. 'Lola's dad?'

'He's not around.'

'Does he ever come to see her?'

'He got into some trouble. Now he's dead.' Hairs prickled at the back of her neck as her vision blurred with pooling tears.

'I'm sorry. What happened?'

'He was shot. There was a fire. Can we drop it?'

Silence lingered in the car. 'Sorry. Didn't mean to upset you. I hope God heals you the way he's healed me.'

'Are you into all that God stuff like Tabbie?'

'Yeah, I am.'

Great. Another one. She closed her mouth and looked away.

Steph almost fell on the floor in front of Lola after her third load of washing and cleaning her small apartment. Though she was exhausted, her week had run surprisingly well.

Her phone buzzed with a text message.

Joe and I will be there in 10 to pick you up.

'Pick me up?' she asked aloud. 'Oh, Lola, the barbeque. I forgot all about it. You'd rather not go, hey?' Her chest tightened.

They were already on their way. Maybe if she went this time, Tabbie might stop inviting her. She pulled on a clean pair of jeans and dressed Lola in her favourite floral party dress, then restocked the nappy bag.

Tabbie's perfume preceded her. 'Are you ready?'

Steph fanned the air in front of her and looked Tabbie up and down. 'Are you trying to pick up someone or something?'

'No, why?' She giggled and smelt her wrist.

'You've drenched yourself in perfume.'

'It's a new sample. Just thought I'd try it out. A little too much?'

'Did you shower in the whole sample?'

'Hi, girls.' Joe appeared in the doorway. 'Is there anything I can take out to the car?'

'Did you bring the car seat?' Steph raised her eyebrows.

'Bummer. Why didn't I think of that?' Tabbie shook her head. 'Sorry.'

'You guys go without me.' Steph shrugged. 'I'm pretty tired anyway.'

'Sorry, Steph,' Joe said. 'I didn't think…'

As if he even needed to. She should've sent a reminder to Tabbie.

'It's not too far.' Tabbie linked her arm through Steph's. 'I'll walk with you.'

'Walking is fine by me too,' Joe said. 'I'll push the pram.'

'It's okay. I've got it.' Stephanie's words came out as a whisper. Something in her wanted to keep her baby close. *Can I trust Joe around Lola?*

'I promised to help with the welcome table.' Joe increased his pace as they neared the church. 'See you there.' He took off in a slow jog.

'Why didn't he just drive?'

Tabbie shrugged.

'You sure he doesn't have a crush on you?' Steph shoulder-bumped Tabbie.

'Apparently, he's doing a friend a favour.'

'You don't really believe that, do you?'

Tabbie shrugged again.

'Hello!' Joe stood at a table as they arrived and handed them name stickers. 'Welcome.'

Stephanie tried to think of something witty but her brain got stuck on 'he's so hot'. In that moment, she wished he was playing bodyguard for her.

'You'll find the jumping castle over there, but Miss Lola…' Joe bent down and spoke to her daughter. '…I think that's for your mum because you're a bit small for that yet.' He straightened to his full height and smiled down at Steph. 'If you'd like some pampering, we have a mini spa set up in the tent for mums. They tell me there's extra arms to hold babies so you can relax. We also have Ashley, our resident barista, waiting to take your coffee order. Enjoy your afternoon.'

'It's a wonder he can take time out from being your full-time carer.' Tension sat in Steph's chest as she pushed the stroller away from the table.

'Yeah, it is a wonder.' Tabbie fake-laughed. 'Now, you deserve to be pampered. I'll take Lola so you can relax.'

A little pampering might be just what she needed. Walking into the tent felt like another world. She stepped onto red carpet decorated on each side with tall vases of long-stemmed roses and baby's breath. Silver hearts hanging from the ceiling caught her eye as lavender and rosemary filled her senses. 'Hi, I'm Eileen,' an older lady said. 'Would you like a shoulder massage?'

Lola whinged in Tabbie's arms, reaching for her. *This is pointless.* She'd be getting more tense instead of relaxing.

'You enjoy,' Tabbie said.

'But—'

'She'll be fine. We'll be outside.'

Steph bit her lip as Eileen ushered her to a cushioned seat and began to massage her neck and shoulders, releasing knots and easing the tension. *Why am I worried?* Eileen finished the massage and then applied a French manicure to her fingernails.

'Wow, my nails haven't looked this good for ages.' Steph held her hands up and admired the nail art. 'Thank you. I better go and see where Tabbie's gone.'

'Would you like some refreshments before you go?' Eileen offered her a tiered platter holding a variety of small sweet treats.

Her mouth watered. 'I guess she knows where I am if she needs me.'

'Of course she does. Take a moment to relax in the lounge.'

Eileen returned a minute later with a glass of iced tea. Steph took a sip, then bit into a cupcake as her mouth watered for more. Licking the crumbs off her fingers, she went to grab another as Eileen fussed over another girl. A smile crept onto Steph's face and then fell. If only this wasn't a one-off. She finished her drink and headed outside to where Tabbie rocked Lola on her hip.

'I can't believe they've gone to so much trouble,' Steph whispered to Tabbie. 'And for free. Why?'

'You're worth it. That's why.'

Lola lunged from Tabbie's arms to her mother. 'Wow, there's a lot of strollers here.' Steph took in the surroundings.

'Yeah, the church wanted to bless solo parents.'

'Do they all come to your church?'

'Some do.' Tabbie shook her head. 'But there are a bunch of people here I've never seen before. Some are probably from the church playgroup.'

'Single mums go to the playgroup?'

'Yeah, I should have told you about it. Sorry. Would you like to meet the coordinator?'

'Maybe another time.' Now that she was at Movement Academy, she wouldn't have time.

'Looks like you'll meet her anyway.' Tabbie angled her head toward the girls walking towards them. 'She's on her way over.'

'Hi, how's your afternoon going?' a young woman asked.

'Nice so far.' Steph suddenly felt awkward.

Tabbie filled the silence with introductions. 'Lucia, this is my friend, Stephanie.'

'Great to meet you. And is this your little girl?'

Steph nodded and wiped dribble off Lola's chin.

'Yes, this is Lola,' Tabbie said. 'I was telling Steph about the playgroup.'

'Great. Would you like to come along?' Lucia tucked her sleek shoulder-length hair behind her ear.

Steph shook her head. 'I've just started a course.'

'Fantastic. What kind of course?'

Stephanie gave her a brief outline.

'Wow. Let me know if you're performing somewhere.' Lucia beamed a huge smile. 'I'd love to come and watch.'

'So you have children?' Steph changed the subject.

'Oh, no. Not yet. I'm at uni doing an early childhood degree. I have Fridays off and like to put into practice what I'm learning.'

No wonder she looked so neat and tidy. Steph thought back to when she had time to actually do her hair, instead of tying it up out of Lola's way.

Lucia had a hundred and one stories about toddlers and what they did at playgroup. It sounded great. But Steph had classes Friday mornings. Maybe Francine could take Lola.

Chapter Forty-six

TABBIE

TABBIE JUMPED WHEN HER SHOULDER was tapped.

'Hi.' Joe laughed. 'Sorry. Didn't mean to scare you. Have you been pampered yet?'

'Well, Steph enjoyed the massage. I hung out with Lola.' Tabbie couldn't help notice the way Joe's gaze lingered on Stephanie. Probably the way hers lingered on him. *What am I doing?* She moved her gaze to the growing crowd around the food tables.

'How about you girls line up for lunch before the queue reaches the road?' Joe smiled and guided them to the line. 'I'll be on the drinks table.'

Tabbie watched him walk ahead of them. His shirt tightened around his bicep as he grabbed a jug of juice and filled cups for the kids waiting.

Steph seemed to click with the two girls in front of her in the line. An animated girl with a baby strapped to her in a pouch, joked about her koala. The other girl with a toddler on her hip nodded.

They pulled out their phones and swapped numbers. Goosebumps ran down Tabbie's back. This was perfect for Stephanie. Finally, she might be making some new friends.

$\mathcal{S}$TEPHANIE

Steph stole glances at Joe when Tabbie wasn't watching. While at the studio, everything she'd done over the past week had been alongside Joe. But whenever Tabbie was around, he was almost her shadow. Just doing what he'd been asked, apparently. She looked forward to getting back into the studio, away from Tabbie.

If only she didn't have baggage, Joe might see her differently. How she dreamed of being carefree. But she had a past. She'd have to live in hope that someone might come along and accept her as she was, child and all. Maybe. One day.

'Whatchya thinking about?' Tabbie interrupted her thoughts as they sat down at a table.

'Those girls were really nice.' She shrugged, bringing herself back to the present. 'It's different to how I thought it would be.'

'Good. I'm glad you're here.'

'So why did I feel so uncomfortable last time I came?'

'Maybe you're in a different mindset. Maybe you're at a different stage of life now.'

'Yeah, maybe.' Steph bit her lip. 'Strange to be in the next stage of life when we're the same age.'

'All things can be turned around for good. Look how well things are turning out for you.' Tabbie picked up her burger.

Lola kicked and screamed, trying to wriggle out of the stroller straps. *Great, just when things were going well.* Frustrated, Steph wanted to throw her plate at Tabbie and leave.

'Would you like me to help with your little one so your food doesn't go cold?' An older lady made a face at Lola.

Lola giggled.

'Um, are you sure?' Steph looked at Tabbie. *Who is this lady? Can I trust her?*

'Thanks, Noela, that's so kind of you,' Tabbie said to the woman, nodding at Steph.

Lola smiled at Noela.

'It's no trouble,' said Noela.

'Okay.' Steph watched Noela wheel Lola away. 'Thank you.'

'You're very welcome. I won't go too far.'

Steph actually finished her meal while it was still hot. 'It doesn't really feel natural, all this niceness. It's kind of overwhelming.'

'What? Overwhelmingly nice?' Tabbie chuckled.

Steph had expected at some stage during the afternoon, someone would approach her with the big sell on going to church. But no one did. She waited for someone to stand up and start preaching. But no one did.

On the way out, she was handed a small box tied up with a pink satin ribbon. Inside were three heart chocolates with a note.

> *You are intrinsically unique and beautiful in every way.*
> *You are God's perfect design.*

She glanced back as a tingle ran through her body. It was a nice card but… *Beautiful? Perfect design?* That felt a long way from the truth.

TABBIE

'Let's go while Joe's entertaining the kids.' Tabbie glanced at Joe playing handball.

'Hey, girls.' Joe jogged towards them as they left.

'Let me guess.' Steph glanced at him. 'You're escorting Tabbie so she doesn't fall and break something?'

'Anything is possible.' He chuckled.

'Seriously!' Tabbie shook her head, partly embarrassed and partly amused.

'I need to grab my car anyway.' Joe fell into step with them.

It had been such a lovely afternoon, and Tabbie had hoped to debrief with Steph on the walk home. But Joe was there.

'Can I push the stroller?' His upper arm flexed like it had a mind of its own.

'Thanks for the offer, but I'm used to pushing her.' Steph laughed.

Tabbie slowed a little and watched Steph and Joe, side by side in front of her, chatting about the studio. It was good to see Steph happy. As they turned the final corner, Joe glanced back at her.

'Hey, sorry, but do you girls mind if I take off? I promised a mate—'

'Of course not.' Tabbie flung her arms forward, shooing him away then struggled to take her gaze off him as he ran ahead.

'Still no feelings for the guy?' Steph asked when he was out of earshot.

'He's a friend. And Danny's best friend.'

'How about you? You seem really at ease with him.'

'I guess it's because we've been working together for the past week.'

'I kind of think he might be interested—'

'You've already tried that on me. My baggage will keep him away. Our relationship is purely professional. He can stay in the eye candy realm. Wasn't that your favourite saying?'

'Maybe a few years back. Not now, though. I try not to look just for the sake of looking.'

Stephanie rolled her eyes and turned off the path.

Heat prickled behind Tabbie's ears. *Is someone watching?* Her senses were on high alert but she couldn't see anyone. The uneasy feeling persisted. Glancing backwards, she thought she saw someone duck behind a tree trunk.

'What's up?' Steph glanced back too.

'I've got a weird feeling, like someone's watching us.'

'What? Who?' Steph's face dropped.

Realising she'd sent Steph's mind on a fear leap, she shook her head. 'Nah, nothing there. Silly how the mind plays tricks sometimes.'

Chapter Forty-seven

STEPHANIE

THAT NIGHT, STEPH DREAMED of Joe holding Lola and doting on her like the perfect father. When the sun forced her eyes open in the morning, she wiped tears away. It would only ever be a dream. Lola's morning gurgles escalated to a loud cry, demanding attention. 'What should we do today, Lola?'

'Mumma.' Lola stopped crying, squealed and reached up with a big smile.

Joe and Tabbie would be at church. So would that lovely girl she'd met who ran the playgroup. She hadn't asked the other girls she'd talked to if they went to church or if they'd been invited to the lunch like she was. What would they be up to? Maybe she could contact them. *No.* She'd only just met them, so she should leave it a few days. She'd really clicked with them. She'd have to remember to send them a text in the next day or so.

'I guess it's a good day to get some groceries,' Steph said to Lola.

On the walk home, the hair on the back of her neck tingled.

Was she being paranoid after Tabbie's comment yesterday? Or was someone watching her? Her stomach knotted. She stopped, checking every direction. There were people everywhere, but no one seemed to be taking any interest in her. She rushed home, and locked and chained her front door.

*T*ABBIE

Tabbie left home early, glad to have a moment out in the fresh air on her own to gather her thoughts before church. She'd barely gathered her thoughts when a familiar car horn tooted three times. 'Seriously.' She sighed as she opened the front door of the car. 'I thought the novelty would have worn off by now.'

'What novelty? Danny asked me to keep you safe, and that's what I'm doing.'

'What were you in such a rush for last night?' Tabbie climbed in to get out of the heat. 'Did you have a hot date or something?'

'A date?' Joe flicked a glance at her as he pulled out onto the road again.

Tabbie wished she hadn't brought it up. Now she felt like she was interrogating him.

'I promised to go back and help pack up.'

'Why didn't you say? We could have walked the whole way home without you.'

'Just wanted to make sure. You never know who is out on the streets.'

Tabbie shivered. She didn't want to mention the feeling she'd had after he'd left them yesterday. She shook her head and thought of Steph. Was Joe attracted to her, or was it just an eye candy thing for him too?

'Life will be so much easier when I get my license,' Tabbie said as Joe swung into the church car park.

'And a car to drive.' He grinned.

'Yeah, that too.' Tabbie's insides went to mush. *He's just so good-looking!*

Joe left her to chat to a group of guys. Maybe it would be easier to ignore his looks if he'd stop wearing such an exotic aftershave. As she meandered inside, she attempted to recall last night's dream. Joe was in it. But nothing was clear. They'd been at the beach. Her arm was around him, and his arm rested on her shoulders. She couldn't remember seeing anyone else there.

No. That wasn't what she wanted. She needed to stop spending so much time with him. She looked up and there he was walking towards her. 'I think we need to talk.'

'Sure.'

'You're making me feel uncomfortable.' Her tone was sharp, and she tried to soften it. 'Seriously, Joe, we're at church. I know people here. I don't need you by my side.'

'Right, point taken.' His face glowed a deep shade of red as he stalked off.

She was by herself again. If only Danny would get in touch. It had been too long since they communicated. This physical attraction to Joe confused her. She knew he wasn't the person she wanted a relationship with. Her shoulders slumped. Her mood plummeted. Maybe a chat with Shelly or Priscilla would help. They seemed to help her see things from a different perspective.

*S*TEPHANIE

Hey, Steph, want to come over for an early dinner? We'll drop you back before it's too late.

Mum can pick you up too if you like.

Two texts in a row from Tabbie.

'Just what we needed, Lola.' A shiver travelled down her spine as she wondered if someone had actually been watching her earlier.

Lola giggled then mimicked her mother's facial expression. Her little eyebrows dipped together, squeezing a crease in between.

'It's only a couple of hours away. Just enough time to tidy your toys and clean up a bit.' But anxiety took over, crippling her before she could start. Steph took a deep breath. Recognising the fear and panic, she released the breath she was holding. Mindfulness. She heard the counsellor's voice in her mind. One breath at a time. Be aware of the moment you are in. The past was in the past, and she couldn't control the future. All she could do was control her breath in and out.

Closing her eyes she focused on her muscles, starting at the tip of her head, tensing then releasing. She focused on her next breath in and out, then began to move around her apartment. One breath at a time, one step at a time, picking up and putting away one toy at a time. She'd get through this season in life, like she had the last season. By putting one foot in front of the other.

Steph bathed then dressed Lola and restocked the nappy bag. Then she splashed water on her face and applied a little makeup before brushing her hair.

Tomorrow, she'd be back in the studio, near Joe. The anticipation of excitement helped push the anxiety away. She smiled at her reflection in the mirror. It was good having something to look forward to.

She sat Lola on the seat between her and the window and pulled out her phone as the bus pulled away from the bus stop.

She read it a few times and sent the message to both the girls she'd met yesterday.

Her phone buzzed before she'd put it back in her bag. She flipped it over, hopeful one of the girls was as keen to meet up as she was.

'What?' Steph said out loud.

Chapter Forty-eight

STEPHANIE TABBIE

As soon as the bus stopped, Steph bundled Lola into her arms, and darted off the bus. She rushed towards the Morays, dragging the stroller behind her. *What if I'm being followed?* She spun around and slammed the door behind her.

Is someone playing some kind of sick joke? She swallowed hard. *Jason?* Her head throbbed.

'Steph, is that you?' Francine called.

She stood there, frozen.

'Hey, Steph,' Tabbie came out of the kitchen. 'What's wrong? You're as pale as…'

'Jason,' Steph said.

'Jason?'

'He's alive.' Steph shivered. 'That or someone —'

'Is he here?' Tabbie looked towards the door.

Steph fumbled for her phone and handed it to Tabbie.

'Will you reply?'

'I don't know. I need a drink. Bubbly, or—'

'You can do this without one.' Tabbie put her arm around Steph. 'We'll get you through this.'

'What's happened?' Francine entered the room.

Steph held out her phone and showed Francine the text.

'Could it be someone else? Like a sick joke or something?' Francine wrapped her arm around Stephanie. 'Maybe we need to call the police.'

Steph nodded. Her heart raced. Her armpits were clammy. Lola fussed. Tabbie scooped her out of Steph's.

'He was in the police protection scheme. Maybe he's still alive. The cops said he was dead. But what if they lied to protect him?' Steph shuddered.

'Or you,' Francine said. 'What if the police were protecting you?'

'Hadn't thought of that.'

'Would you like me to call the police?' Francine asked. 'Or would you like me to call the number the text was sent from?'

'Maybe I should reply and see if he—or whoever it was—replies. What do you think he wants?'

Tabbie and Francine both looked at her without answering.

'What if he wants to take Lola from me? I've never been able to say no to him. I'm petrified. I need a drink.'

'Breathe.' Francine took a deep breath in and held it. Steph followed her lead then released the breath as Francine released hers.

'You can get through this without alcohol.' Tabbie's hand rested on her shoulder as she rocked Lola on her hip. 'Can I pray for you?'

'I need all the help I can get right now.'

'Dear Lord, I pray that You fill Stephanie with strength, courage and peace.'

If only Tabbie's God could change things. Tabbie was fixated on God sorting everything out. Steph tried to focus on what she was saying.

'Only You know what lies around the corner. Please help Steph make the right decisions to keep her life moving forward. Thank You, Lord, for covering her with Your grace and goodness.'

'You didn't pray for me to say no to Jason or—'

'Right now, you need to focus on making the right choices. That's more important than getting hung up on making sure you say no to Jason. You aren't even sure if it was him.'

Steph's heartbeat thudded in her ears. *What if he's alive? What if he's as irresistible as he had been a few years ago? If he's alive, he'd have a right to see Lola. What if he'd cleaned up and put his life in order?* 'What if he's changed?' Steph asked.

But what if it was just some idiot messing with her?

*T*ABBIE

Tabbie had seen a lot of people turn their lives from destruction to the complete opposite. She'd seen miracles, but could Jason change?

She'd continue to pray and trust God would sort it out.

'I think I should call rather than text.' Stephanie took a deep breath in, her face still pale. 'If it is him, I'll know his voice straight away.'

'Are you sure?' Tabbie hoped God would intervene.

As Steph nodded, Tabbie wanted to tell her to trust in God. She wished God could make this right in an instant.

'Okay.' Stephanie closed her eyes and clenched her fists. 'Stay with me while I make the call?'

'Of course.' Tabbie's heart thumped at double speed in her chest. She couldn't imagine what it would be like to be in Steph's shoes. She wanted to find a private spot to pray. But instead, she stayed there, because her friend needed her by her side.

Chapter Forty-nine

STEPHANIE

STEPH'S FINGERS SHOOK as she hit the call back button. It rang six times before clicking through to a recorded message. 'Please leave a short message, and it will be sent as a text message.'

Steph cut the call off. *Just the phone company recording.*

'Let's eat and try again after dinner.'

'I don't think I could eat anything.' Stephanie's stomach churned into knots.

'I don't want you going home tonight. You'll stay here, won't you?' Francine moved towards the kitchen.

A chill rushed down Steph's spine. She wouldn't sleep at all if she went back to her place tonight. If only putting trust in God was the answer. During dinner, she pushed her food around the plate, barely eating.

'Right, Lola is all settled in the cot upstairs. Now let's get you settled. How about you take a long hot shower while I make you a cup of chamomile tea.' Francine offered Steph a fresh towel.

While in the shower, Steph burst into tears. Jason was gone. She was never meant to see him again. She never wanted to see him again. Why did this have to happen?

When she returned downstairs, Francine handed her a strong cup of tea. Tom had arrived home, and looked at her with pity.

'I'll take this upstairs and try to get some sleep.' She had enough pity for herself.

As she sat on her bed, sipping the tea, she noticed a leather-bound book on the table by the window. Tabbie found comfort in reading it. Maybe now would be a good time to have another look inside. She opened the Bible and flicked to a page with handwriting in the margin. *Saved by grace through faith not by works.* She read the text on the page, then read it again before turning to another section.

She read about sin and how she was a sinner by nature and she couldn't change it. Then she read that Jesus came so she could be forgiven. Could she really be forgiven for all she'd done?

She turned a few more pages, searching for text that had been highlighted or words written in the margin.

As Christ forgave us, we must also forgive.

Forgiveness. Tabbie talked about forgiveness a lot.

She whispered the word, 'Forgiveness,' and let it hang, suspended in the air. Could she allow herself to forgive Jason? He'd hurt her beyond repair. He'd wooed her into a relationship she wasn't ready for. He'd encouraged her to drink, take drugs, and work in horrendous situations to cover rent and living expenses.

It was too much. If he was alive, she had to focus on keeping her distance. *God, if You really are out there, help me forgive but not give in. Help me through this.*

Steph rested back on her pillow and fell into a deep and peaceful sleep. Next she knew, it was daylight and the Bible lay on the bed beside her. Perhaps Tabbie had found something worthwhile after all.

At the sound of a gentle tap on her bedroom door, she sat up. 'How did you sleep?' Tabbie peeked through the slightly open door.

'Peacefully.' Steph smiled and shrugged. 'I didn't expect to get any sleep at all. And look, Lola's still in dreamland.'

'That's great.' Tabbie pushed the door open, her gaze dipped to the Bible beside Steph.

'Yeah, I read a bit last night.' She joined Tabbie in the hallway, leaving Lola to sleep. 'I'm stuck on forgiveness. I don't know how I'd ever forgive Jason for what he did. What he made me do. I know I should take some of the blame, but there were times where I said no, and he wouldn't accept it. I gave in every time.'

'You're stronger now. Forgiveness is healthy. It's like passing the burden over to God. It does more harm to you than Jason when you hold onto resentment and unforgiveness.'

'But what do I do? Let him back into my life?'

'You're overthinking it. You don't even know if it was him.'

'You're right. I should try calling the number again, shouldn't I?'

Tabbie nodded. 'To know will give you peace of mind.'

'Okay, I'll try again now. I'm not as scared today. What about the cops? Should I call them?'

'Dad already did. Someone will contact you today.' Tabbie headed downstairs.

Just as Steph grabbed her phone from the bedroom, Lola stirred. Making the phone call could wait. Francine rushed in behind her. 'Here, I'll take her. You get ready to go to the studio. It'll be good to take your mind off things for a few hours.'

In the shower, Stephanie looked to the ceiling. *God, if You're real, I really need some courage about now. I thought I was okay, but I'm scared again.* As she squeezed shampoo onto her hand, she realised she'd already shampooed. She conditioned, rinsed, shut off the water and stepped out of the shower, with one thing on her mind. She had to make the phone call.

Steph breathed in and held her breath until the ringing tone stopped. 'Hello,' the familiar male voice answered.

She leaned against the wall and slid to the floor with her knees to her chest. 'Jason. It's Steph.'

Chapter Fifty

TABBIE

TABBIE LINGERED A MOMENT. She wanted to listen in to the conversation, but she knew Steph needed privacy. So she hurried to get ready for school.

Mum came up the stairs, car keys in hand and Lola on her hip. 'Time to go.'

Steph had finished the call and was just sitting there, a surprised yet happy smile on her face. Tabbie wanted to shake her. How could the conversation have gone well?

They were driving in silence through peak hour traffic when Tabbie couldn't stand it a moment longer. 'Are you going to fill us in? He's alive?'

'Yes.' Steph nodded. 'I'm not sure if I'm in shock or relieved.'

'Are you sure you don't want to talk now?' Tabbie asked as they pulled into the studio carpark.

'It can wait.' Steph kissed Lola goodbye and climbed out.

'Call me if you need to leave early,' Mum said.

'I'll leave my phone on. Call me if you want to talk through the day.' Tabbie's stomach churned.

Steph nodded and walked away from the car.

'Do you think she's in shock?' Tabbie asked her mum.

'Maybe, love, but you need to focus on school. She'll tell us in her own time. She's with Joe and Gabriella, so it's not like she's alone.'

How was Jason actually alive? She still hadn't heard from Steph when the lunch bell rang. Was Jason nearby? What if it was him she'd sensed watching on their walk back from the lunch? Her body shuddered and a shiver ran down her spine. She needed to hand it over to God and focus on school.

STEPHANIE

It's too much. She'd managed to keep the conversation with Jason out of her mind as she focused on dancing. But being so close to Joe for the past hour as they worked on a duo routine had sent her mind into a whirl. She half-wished he'd leave her to work with the other girls. But there was something comforting about being in his arms. Feeling his breath. Hearing his heartbeat.

Maybe bouncing Jason's requests off Tabbie would make it all clearer. Right now, her head pounded like it was about to explode. At first, Jason's voice had made her feel warm again, but now she'd rather run the other way.

'Man, it's hot.' Joe pushed damp hair back off his forehead. 'Want to grab an iced chocolate before the school kids come in? My shout.'

'Yeah, okay.' She welcomed the distraction.

'You know, Steph,' Joe turned to her as the machine whizzed behind the counter. 'I've been ignoring it for a while, but after we danced together today, it's more than just a… what I'm trying to say is…'

Steph drew in a sharp breath. *Of all days. No. He wasn't going to…*

'I'd like to take you out to dinner.'

'But I have Lola…' She wanted to stick her fingers in her ears and sing lalalalala.

'Yeah, I know.' He looked to his feet for a moment.

Typical guy, only thinking of himself.

'We need to get back.' Joe grabbed their drinks, handed one to Steph and headed back to the car.

She followed, head down, watching the ground. As she opened the car door she recognised a familiar face in her peripheral vision, but as she turned, he disappeared. She slid into the front seat and slammed the door, glancing from side to side. Was it Warren? Was she imagining it?

'Hey, I didn't mean to upset you.'

Her skin prickled. She glanced at Joe. His regard was warm, caring. She couldn't tell him about her past. Not right now.

'If you want to keep our relationship purely professional, that's okay.'

She looked deep into his eyes and relaxed. He would never force her to do anything. He was attractive and comfortable to be around, but she couldn't go there.

'We'd better get back before the next class arrives.'

'Thanks for the drink.'

'Any time. Are you okay? I'm sorry I said anything about going out.'

She forced a smile but said nothing.

As soon as they returned, Steph checked the back door of the studio. It was locked. She kept her focus on the front door—the only doorway everyone came and left through. The fact that Joe avoided her for the rest of the afternoon was the least of her problems.

Warren. She tried to blink away the image of his face. Could it really be him? Wasn't he in jail? After the last class she dawdled, not wanting to walk outside alone.

'Ready when you are,' Francine texted. 'We're in the carpark.'

  Spiralling Solo

Taking in a deep breath, she grabbed her bag and braced herself at the doorway.

'Hey, Steph.'

She jumped at the sound of Joe's voice.

'I'll walk you out.'

Her shoulders relaxed.

'Can I just say, the offer still stands. I know it's hard with the baby seat, but maybe I could borrow Francine's. But if you aren't interested, that's okay.'

Steph shrugged as she blew a wisp of hair off her face, glancing around to check her surroundings.

'Or maybe Tabbie could watch Lola one night—'

'Um… I'll get back to you.' Steph rushed towards Francine's car.

Chapter Fifty-one

STEPHANIE

'Is everything okay?' Francine asked as she turned the key in the ignition.

Steph shook her head. 'I think I saw Warren, I'm still trying to process the conversation with Jason, and Joe asked me out. Nothing is okay.' Steph covered her face with her hands as a sob threatened to explode.

'Warren? Are you sure?'

'No.' Was her mind playing tricks on her?

'Tabbie wants to stay with you tonight. I think it would be good. She's at the supermarket grabbing bits and pieces for pizza.'

'Um, okay.' She didn't really want to be home alone but didn't want to stay another night with the Morays.

'What did you say to Joe?' Francine broke into her thoughts.

'That I'd get back to him. I thought he might have been interested when we first met but he seemed to lose interest when he found out I had Lola. I kind of got used to it.'

'I see.' Francine pulled into the supermarket car park.

'Yeah. The more I get to know him, the more I agree with Tabbie. He's one of the nice guys.' She looked out the window. 'I don't deserve someone like him.'

'Oh, Steph, you're wrong. You deserve nothing but a nice guy.' Francine parked the car and left the engine running.

'It's just bad timing, I guess.'

'Would you like to talk about the conversation with Jason?'

'Sorry. I should have told you straight away. Jason's been in a police protection scheme in another city—he couldn't tell me where. They've caught a few of the dealers and closed the case. But there's still lots of people in Sydney who have it in for him. He reckons they'd kill him if he moved back.'

'How do you feel knowing he's actually alive?' Francine asked.

'At first his voice brought back some of the nice memories, but now I feel horrible. I just wanted to keep it all in the past, but the past has reared its ugly head.'

'You've had a double shock today, with talking to Jason and maybe seeing Warren. I wonder if a counsellor might help you sort through your feelings.'

Steph shrugged.

'Here she comes,' Francine pointed to Tabbie.

'We are going to have a feast.' Tabbie climbed onto the back seat and dropped the grocery bags at her feet.

'Shh, Lola's sleeping,' Steph snapped.

'Sorry.' Tabbie whispered and leaned forward. 'I got pizza ingredients, lemonade, and some triple chocolate ice cream. Comfort food.'

They'd end up feeling sick, but it might ease the pain of her past trying to work its way back into her life.

'Lola fell asleep just before you came out, Steph. I hope she'll transfer to the cot and sleep right through for you,' Francine said as she parked on the kerb.

Thankfully Lola didn't stir as Steph unclasped her. Her head rolled back and forth on Steph's shoulder as she carried her inside.

She placed her in the cot and pulled the curtains. 'Tabbie, it smells amazing.' Steph breathed in the scent of pizza after her shower. 'Thanks for doing this.'

'No worries. Lola hasn't made a sound.'

'It is nice when she stays asleep.' Steph leaned against the kitchen bench. 'Jason's alive, and I think Warren is back.'

'What? No way!' Tabbie's eyes widened.

'Jason's been in police protection and doesn't think he'll come back to Sydney. But he wants to meet Lola. Wants me to fly and meet him somewhere.'

'Where?' Tabbie asked.

'He wouldn't tell me.'

'Do you want to see him?'

'I don't know. He is Lola's dad. It wouldn't be fair to not let him meet her, would it?' Steph sighed. 'I think I've started to forgive him.'

'Wow. Really?'

'He apologised. He sounded sincere. Says he's been clean for twelve months—hasn't touched any drugs, not even a drop of alcohol.' Steph sat on the couch as Tabbie pulled the pizza out of the oven. 'Wish I could say the same for myself. What if I never get past the craving?'

'I have heard some alcoholics have been healed by God. You only have to ask and see what he does.'

'Hmm.' Stephanie bit into a piece of pizza.

'Now he's told you he's a changed man, you're not thinking of going back to him, are you?'

'I don't know.' She looked away. 'I don't have a clue what to do. I was so in love with him.'

'Are you sure it was love and not just lust?'

Steph looked Tabbie in the eye. 'Love. If it was just lust, I wouldn't even be thinking about the possibility of meeting with him again.'

'Miracles do happen, but I'm not sure going back to him would be good for you. And what did you say about Warren?'

'I thought I saw him, but when I looked around, I couldn't see anyone.'

'Should we call the police, check if he's been released? Tell them you saw him?'

'I didn't think of doing that.'

'Let's call them now.'

Steph listened to Tabbie's side of the conversation.

'When was that?… So he's back this suburb?… Stephanie saw him yesterday… No, she wasn't… Okay.' Tabbie hung up.

'What?' Steph's hand shook.

'Apparently, he was released on one of those community work programs. He's meant to be staying on the other side of Sydney. They said they'd follow up and make sure he's still there. If you see him again, take a photo and send it to them.'

'Maybe I didn't see him. Maybe my mind was playing tricks.'

'Just be careful.' Tabbie shrugged. 'I can stay a few nights so you're not alone.'

Great, just what I need, a babysitter. She clenched her jaw. 'Oh, yeah. Joe asked me out on a date.' Her skin tingled as she remembered the way she'd felt when he guided her across the floor earlier that day. It was similar to how she'd felt when she'd first met Jason. The tingle was one hundred percent better than the churning fear in her stomach when she thought about Warren.

'What did you say to him?'

'That I'd get back to him. Maybe I should have said no straight away.'

Tabbie pulled a pilled fluffball off the cushion. 'I knew Joe had a thing for you.'

'You sound disappointed.'

'No, not disappointed.' Tabbie's face glowed a shade of pink. 'Just wish I wasn't sitting in this stupid limbo land of having a boyfriend missing in action.'

'Enough about me.' A lump formed in Tabbie's throat. 'Let's talk about Joe. I know you keep saying he's just good to look at, but...?' Hopefully Joe's invitation to Steph would shut down Tabbie's physical response to him. It had been so confusing having Joe around and not hearing from Danny for so long. 'Tell what's going on in your mind. Jason, Warren, Joe?'

'I don't know.' Steph sighed.

'So there's Jason,' Tabbie held one hand out and then the other. 'And there's Joe.' It was a no-brainer in Tabbie's view. She hoped Steph wouldn't trust Jason again.

'Hey, what if you date Joe to stop pining over your MIA boyfriend?'

'What? No.' Tabbie shook her head. 'Look, maybe after you get used to the fact Jason is alive, you'll have more clarity and be able to think clearly again.'

'You're right. But right now my head hurts thinking about it.' Steph went to check on Lola.

'Sleeping peacefully?'

Steph nodded and sat on the couch facing Tabbie. 'I don't have the money to take Lola to meet Jason. To tell you the truth, if I saw him today, I'd be tempted to jump straight back into a relationship with him.'

'In that case, it's a good thing you don't have the money.' In Tabbie's mind, she could see Steph and Jason with Lola and wanted to squash the idea. 'I still can't believe he's alive.'

'I know. It feels weird. I wonder if he'll want me to change Lola's last name to his? I wrote Stronge on the birth certificate because I was so angry with him at the time and didn't want her to ever know about him.'

'You never told me that.' Tabbie gaped at Steph. 'Maybe don't worry about that yet.'

'Yeah, you're right. I'm so thankful you came over tonight.' Steph smiled. 'But I still have no idea what I'll do tomorrow.'

Chapter Fifty-two

TABBIE

TABBIE LAY ON THE COUCH in darkness, staring at the ceiling. As much as she denied it, she still had a confusing attraction to Joe. Was it real, or was it just envy? And why was she feeling unfaithful? But her problems seemed trivial when she thought about Steph.

Lord, please help Steph make the right decision. Jason wasn't good for her in the past. If returning to a relationship with him isn't right for her, please help her say no and build her life here rather than with him.

Tabbie blinked away the sun streaming through the window the next morning. She rolled over and off the couch, reaching for her runners. Making the least amount of noise possible, she found front door keys, locked the door behind her, and set off for a run.

Each step hit hard on the path, pounding out her frustration. Why had Danny taken time to contact his mates but not her? She turned a corner and headed off the path. How she loved the feeling and sound of fresh grass under her shoes. She continued towards what she liked to call the forest in the city. Slowing down to walk, she breathed in the cooler air under the dense trees as thick roots massaged the soles of her feet.

At the end of the thicket, she turned to head back towards Steph's. Blinded by the sun as she left the canopy of the trees, her foot plunged into a hole. Shards of pain pierced upwards in her leg. She rocked on the grassy strip, clutching her weak ankle.

Tears ran down her cheeks as memories of past injuries came rushing back, along with the warmth of Danny's arms carrying her onto the beach. It had been eighteen months since he'd left. They'd never even gone on a date. Their relationship had been purely long distance. She wanted—no, *craved*—a present, in-the-flesh boyfriend.

She flexed her ankle back and forth. It wasn't too bad, just a slight strain. Limping back to Steph's took forever as she wiped her runny nose and teary eyes. As she reached the driveway, the hair on the back of her neck prickled. Warren was facing Steph's door.

Tabbie stepped backwards and stood close to the bushy garden where she could only just see him. Within moments, he turned and walked back down the driveway. She held her breath until he was out of sight before moving.

'Have you seen Warren again?' She kept her voice calm and locked the door behind her.

Steph shook her head.

'I saw him outside. Wish I'd had my phone on me to take a photo.'

'What?' Steph rushed to the window and looked out.

'I'll call the police and let them know.' Tabbie picked up the phone and searched for the number. When she hung up, she relayed the conversation back to Steph. 'They said to call 000 if we see him again.'

'But what if…' Steph went to check on Lola.

Tabbie's thoughts went to alcohol and her friend living alone. 'She still sleeping?'

Steph nodded.

'You realise you'll be eighteen soon?'

'Of course I realise.'

'Eighteen. You'll no longer need someone to buy you alcohol. You'll have to rely on your own self-control.'

'I know.'

'Do you reckon you'll be okay? Maybe you should go back to AA for a while.'

'Nah. I'll be fine.' Steph shook her head.

Conversation closed. 'Are you worried about Warren?'

'It mightn't have been him. He's not meant to be on this side of town. I'm fine.' Steph looked out the window again then turned back to Tabbie. 'Hey, have you been crying?'

'Just feeling crazy emotional this morning. Hit me while I was running. I guess my fantasy of Danny and a long-distance relationship working out has been shattered.'

'What's new?' Steph raised her eyebrows.

Tabbie shrugged. 'You're right. Nothing is new. It's the same drama in my head, constantly returning.'

'Oh, Tabbie.' Stephanie wrapped her arms around her. 'We make a great team, don't we. Maybe we should both make a vow to stay single and ignore all guys forever.'

'Can we?' Tabbie laughed, knowing neither of them would stick to it. 'Any more thoughts as to what you'll do if Jason contacts you again?'

'No.'

Tabbie sighed, and Lola stirred in her cot.

'I'd better get her sorted, and you'd better jump in the shower.'

Tabbie's mind wandered from Steph staying away from alcohol and Jason to whether or not Jaya was still drinking too much at parties. Tabbie pulled her school uniform on then flicked Jaya a Thinking of you text.

She grabbed her bag as Steph picked up Lola. *What if Warren's still lurking?* She opened the camera on her phone, ready to take a photo, it buzzed. Jaya.

Nice to hear from you. Everything's crap. I'm going to have to repeat or leave school. I've stuffed up. Granny's really sick. 😣

Tabbie groaned.

'What's up?' Steph asked.

'Jaya isn't doing so well.'

'Same ole, same ole,' Steph said.

Tabbie ignored Steph's comment and replied to Jaya after they climbed into her mother's car.

Tabbie hit *Send* and wondered if she should call her and talk to her rather than continuing the thread of texting.

'Wow,' Tabbie said out loud.

'Everything okay?' her mother asked.

'I'll tell you later.' Tabbie didn't want Steph to hear the details of Jaya's life.

Tabbie sent the text to Jaya then climbed out of the car, waving goodbye to Steph, Lola and her mother.

Her phone rang as she walked through the school gates.

'Hey.' Jaya's voice sounded sweeter than usual. 'I'm busy tonight. Can we chat now?'

'Only for a bit. The bell's about to ring.' Students filled the path in front of her.

'Are you staying in Sydney next year?'

'That's the plan at the moment.' *Where's Jaya going with this?*

'So you're not taking a gap year to go play missionary with Danny.'

'I told you that was a closed door. I still haven't heard from him.'

'Yeah, sorry. Forgot about that. Are you okay?'

     Spiralling Solo

Is Jaya actually thinking about someone other than herself? The bell sounded and everyone around her moved a little faster. 'It's really nice to hear your voice but I've got to get to class. Keep in touch. See ya.' She hung up, wishing she'd had more time to really check in on Jaya.

Tabbie sat in her usual window seat and found her thoughts wandering outside instead of focusing on the teacher. Steph. Jaya. Danny. Joe. Warren. Jason.

After school, everything tumbled from Tabbie's mouth as she climbed into Shelly's car.

'Hey…' Shelly passed her a pack of tissues to mop the stream of tears.

'I must be hormonal. I'm not usually so emotional.' Tabbie blew her nose.

'You're letting things you have no control over get to you.'

'But what should I say to Steph and Jaya? What if Warren turns up again? He's such a creep. And what about Jason?' Tabbie took a deep shuddering breath and put her head back to stop the tears. 'Danny—will I ever speak to him again?'

'It's almost funny how Joe wouldn't leave your side, then you twisted your ankle the minute he did. Sorry, but you have to admit it's kind of funny.' Shelly laughed, then stopped. 'Steph's a big girl. All you can do is encourage her and be there for her. If Jason is still alive, she'll probably have to go to court if he wants custody. It's something she needs to work through. You and your family are such a blessing to her, being there for her.'

'I guess so.' Tabbie nodded. She wasn't trying to make Steph's decisions for her again, was she?

'And Jaya… she's with her grandmother right now, so maybe you just be there for her to talk to. Remember to keep your boundaries. She might have changed, but it's good to be a little guarded so you don't find yourself rescuing her again.'

'Hmm, was that what I was doing?'

'I think you were.' Shelly nodded as she parked the car on a hill. 'Don't you love the view from up here?'

'Yeah.' Sydney was a pretty captivating city with the Harbour Bridge joining north and south, and magnificent buildings lining the harbour.

'You contacted the police about Warren, so hopefully they're on to it. Guess you need to be careful as well. He sounds dangerous. Is Steph safe?'

'She locks up. But she gets anxious and jumpy.'

'It's a lot for her to be going through.' Shelly paused for a moment and stared ahead.

'She shouldn't be living on her own right now.' Tabbie chewed the inside of her mouth.

'We can pray for her protection. God can work miracles.'

'Yeah, but Steph doesn't believe that.'

'So we stand in the gap for her.'

Tabbie nodded. She could do that.

'Danny… there's no need to be worried about being tied down at seventeen—'

'Nearly eighteen.'

'Sorry. Your birthday is just around the corner, hey?'

'Yep.'

'Maybe we should have a party to remind you to have fun and stop worrying about everyone else.'

Tabbie shook her head. *Is that really what I'm doing?* She felt like she was spending a lot of time worrying about herself.

'Try to live in the moment. Enjoy being you for a while. There'll be plenty of time for relationships later.'

'I know you're right. But there is something that confuses me… I seem to notice other guys a lot.'

'I recall having a similar conversation with you a while back. To notice someone for their good looks is fine. It's what you do with the thought that can be dangerous. Avoid taking the thought further. It's why God's Word tells us to take our thoughts captive.'

'I just wish I could have a conversation with Danny.'

'Yeah, that would be helpful. Until he contacts you, try living in the moment and focusing on what's going on here and now.'

That night, Tabbie sat on her bed with a churning stomach. She went over and over her conversation with Shelly. She wished she'd gone to Steph's again. Shelly, of course, had reminded her of the importance of prayer, so she grabbed her Bible and prayed.

Half an hour later, she realised Steph hadn't replied to the text she'd sent earlier.

Hey. You okay?

Tabbie tapped the *Send* button and watched her phone in anticipation.

No. I keep hearing noises outside, but I can't see anything.

Why didn't you call?

Tabbie hit *Send* and went to her parents' bedroom. 'Can one of you drive me over to Steph's? She's hearing noises outside.'

'This has to stop!' Dad swung his legs over the side of the bed. 'If she's not safe there on her own, something has to change. We've got room for her here.'

Tabbie clenched her jaw. Her father was annoyed, but got up anyway. She rushed back to her room to grab her school bag and clothes. Bold font on her computer screen grabbed her attention. She thought she'd turned it off. A new email. *Danny.*

Her floor rumbled as the garage door opened. *Argh! Why now?* She turned away and ran downstairs in case her father changed his mind before she got there.

'Sorry.'

'I know, love. And I'm sorry I snapped.'

Why hadn't she grabbed her laptop to read the email at Steph's?

'So she's hearing noises?' Dad asked as he reversed. 'Could it be a cat or something?

'Warren has been hanging around a bit. I saw him yesterday.'

'What? She's talking to him again?'

'No, no. It's like he's stalking her. We called the police. He's not meant to be on this side of town, and they said they'd follow it up. Maybe that's still worrying her.'

'Tabbie, the guy is dangerous. Why didn't you tell us earlier? I'll have a look when I get there. But I won't be leaving you there alone.'

'What, you want to share the couch with me?'

'No, we'll bring them back to our place.'

Chapter Fifty-three

STEPHANIE

STEPHANIE HUGGED HER KNEES to her chest. The television blared. Lola slept beside her, stirring with the rise and fall of the uneven volume. She knew Lola would be cranky after a disrupted sleep, but it was the only way to shut out the noises while knowing Lola was safe.

Knock. Knock.

The soft rumble on the door hit her like a punch in the stomach. Should she turn the TV off? She couldn't move from the couch. *God, if You're there. Please help me.*

Knock. Knock. Knock.

She hugged her knees tighter.

Her phone buzzed. Tabbie.

Hey.

I'm scared, Steph replied, heart thumping at triple time.

I'm outside. Can you open the door?

Steph dropped her phone, unravelled herself and opened the door.

'I've had a good look around.' Tom rubbed his forehead as he followed Tabbie inside. 'I can't see anyone lurking. Did you call the police?'

Steph shook her head. Tom reached for his phone and walked outside to make the call.

'I told you. I'm going insane.' Steph turned the lights on and flicked the TV off. 'Your dad seems angry. You didn't need to come over.'

'Don't worry. He wouldn't have come if it really bothered him.' Tabbie sat beside Lola, reaching out to stop her rolling off the couch. 'But he doesn't want you staying here scared.'

'I'll be fine now that you're here.'

'He wants us to go back home for the night.'

Lola cried. Steph picked her up. Kicking her legs, she clung to her mother.

'Do you want me to pack her bag?'

'I guess.' *Why can't I get it together on my own?*

Tom returned. 'The cops said Warren was securely on the other side of town and there's nothing for us to worry about.'

Glass smashed outside.

Steph jumped.

Tom rushed outside.

'Sorry,' she heard someone call.

Tom came back inside. 'Just one of the neighbours taking the rubbish. He didn't quite get it in the bin.'

'Can we trust the police?' Steph chewed on a fingernail.

'Look, Steph, you're all wound up,' Tom said. 'Come back to our place and we'll talk things through tomorrow.'

When Steph opened her eyes, the soft light of dawn seeped through the Morays' window and Jason entered her thoughts. The one who'd caused her pain, the one who'd taken her down paths she never thought she'd go, the one she'd fallen in love with, the one she'd thought was dead. She was so confused.

The chirp of her phone sent her heart racing. She tapped the screen to check the message.

> My shout—how about I bring dinner over for you and Lola tomorrow night? Tabbie is welcome if she's around. J

She tried to swallow away her dry throat as she double-checked the sender. *Joe.*

Thank goodness it wasn't Jason. Why did she even think it might be him when he was in another city? She climbed out of bed and pulled Lola close to her chest.

Maybe having Joe over would be a good distraction. And maybe inviting Tabbie would be a good idea. Having Tabbie there would be also be a good distraction. Plus, Tabbie would make sure she didn't do anything dumb.

*T*ABBIE

Tabbie had tossed and turned all night after reading Danny's email. Danny's one-line email. She hoped she could make more sense of it after sleeping, so she rolled over at daybreak and powered up her laptop. She gently bit down on her pointer finger and reread the one short line.

> How are you? Please wait for me.

She pushed her computer away and flung herself back onto her pillow. Didn't he understand? Of course she'd wait... if she had a reason to. But she needed more than one line. She needed to hear his voice. See his face. Be held by him.

Argh! She opened the laptop. Maybe she'd missed something. Maybe she wasn't thinking clearly. Nope. That's all he'd written. *How are you? Please wait for me.*

She could hear Lola chattering. Would Steph take up Dad's offer and move in with them?

'Morning,' Steph said as Tabbie opened her door.

'I'm worried about you.' Tabbie sat on the bed beside Steph. 'What will you do tonight? Stay here again?'

'Nah, I need to be independent.' Steph sighed. 'Anyway, Joe said he'd bring dinner tonight, so I won't be alone. Want to join us? He invited you too.'

Joe? At least Steph wouldn't be alone in her unit. But he wouldn't be staying. At least she didn't think Joe would stay.

'Maybe.' Tabbie sighed as Danny's email continued to run on endless repeat through her mind.

$\mathcal{S}$TEPHANIE

Gabriella touched Steph's shoulder as she walked into the studio. 'You've seemed a little preoccupied the last couple of days. Is everything alright?'

'Yeah.' Steph forced her mouth to smile.

'Are you sure?'

'Not really. There's something I have to sort out.' She wasn't about to spill everything to her boss.

'Try not to let it interfere with dancing, okay?' Gabriella rested her hand on her hip.

'Sure. Sorry if it has.'

'No, it hasn't. You just haven't been yourself for the last few days. I guess I've seen other dancers mope around for a little while, then their dancing goes downhill. Chin up and sort it out away from the studio and all will be fine.'

Stephanie clenched her teeth and smiled. Could she do this? She'd have to focus on dancing and work things out later when she was home.

Joe set them a task of choreographing a contemporary dance that was thick with emotion. Steph found herself doing the opposite of what Gabriella recommended and put all her emotion and turmoil into the dance she created. One heroine and two men. At the end of the dance, the heroine had to choose between the two. She chose the bad guy in the dance, but as she worked through the steps, the last thing Steph wanted was to return to the dark life of her past.

She was sure now. She didn't want to go back to Jason. She'd worked it out in the studio.

'We on for tonight?' Joe asked in a lowered tone, glancing around at Gabriella.

'Yeah, sure.' Warmth pulsed through her veins.

Steph made jokes with the kids as they filed into their after-school classes. The weighty decision had lifted from her shoulders. She bounced out of the studio, excited at the thought of having dinner with the nice guy. The *hot* nice guy.

'Hi,' Tabbie called from the car. 'Is the invite still open for dinner tonight?'

'Yes,' Steph laughed.

'Yay. I've got my things to stay the night,' Tabbie said as Steph climbed into the back seat beside Lola. 'You seem like a different person.'

Steph's phone rang.

'I forgot to ask what time Lola goes to bed, and whether I should come before or after?' Joe asked.

'She's likely to fall asleep on the way home, so come any time.'

'How does six-thirty sound?'

'Sounds great.' She glanced back towards the studio as she hung up. Her heart picked up speed when she saw him punch the air. A smile spread wider across her face than it had in a long time.

'For some crazy reason I thought I'd be on Lola duty,' Tabbie said. 'You know, because he wanted to take you on a date. But if she's sleeping… maybe I'll be in the way.'

'It'll be fine.' Steph's excitement dipped a little as she wondered how the night would pan out. 'I wasn't expecting you to be on Lola duty, but if she does wake, that would be great if you could help out.'

'Sure. That'll work.'

Steph transferred Lola from the car to her cot without a problem. When she tucked the sheet in, she paused for a moment. Lola seemed so content. Maybe there wasn't anything to worry about. Francine doted over her like a grandma would.

She left Lola sleeping, showered, flicked some make-up on and then blow-dried her hair.

'Oh, wow, thank you.' Steph glanced around her kitchen and lounge room. The place was spotless. 'I was just coming out to do that.'

'No worries.' Tabbie smiled. 'You seem much happier today. Is it the dinner, or has something else happened?'

'I choreographed a dance today.' Steph sighed with a smile. 'It was cathartic, maybe even healing.'

'Ooh, sounds interesting. Tell me about it.' Tabbie finished wiping the bench.

'It was a love story—one girl, two boys. One bad boy and one nice boy. The girl in the dance chose the bad boy, and it made me realise I didn't want the bad boy anymore.'

'That sounds huge. Tell me though…' Tabbie leaned against the kitchen bench. 'What if you do see Jason again one day and he's really changed like he says he has? What if he's not the bad boy he used to be?'

'I'll never forget the way he treated me. He was nice when I met him and then… I could never completely trust he wouldn't go back to the drugs and drinking again.'

'That's huge, Steph. You sound like you finally have clarity.'

Steph nodded. Her shoulders relaxed. Yes, she was finally clear on where Jason stood in her life. And also open to what might lie ahead with Joe.

Chapter Fifty-four

TABBIE

TABBIE GLANCED OUT THE WINDOW. Joe was about to arrive. She really needed to shut down the attraction. Though envy crept under her skin, she was happy for Steph. *Who did Danny think he was, expecting her to wait? For how long? No.*

She was finished with waiting.

Finished.

Done.

Over.

'Whoa, what's going on inside your mind? I can see steam rising from your head.' Steph said.

'I can't wait in hope any longer. I'm going to email Danny as soon as I get back to my laptop and tell him it's over.' Tabbie sank into the couch.

'Do you really want to give up hope?' Steph's shoulders flinched with the loud clatter as a neighbour dumped rubbish into the community bin.

'I'm glad I'm staying the night. You seem jumpy.'

'You noticed?' Steph locked the newly installed security screen, leaving the wooden door open.

Tabbie gasped. *Warren.* She opened her eyes wider to check she was seeing correctly.

'Steph.' He rested his palm flat on the screen door. 'I think we had a misunderstanding.'

'You're not welcome here.' Tabbie stepped towards the door but stopped, remembering he was unpredictable.

'That's up to Steph.' Warren grabbed the door handle and rattled it when it wouldn't open. 'Steph?'

More footsteps crunched on the loose pebbles outside. Scuffling and then voices echoed down the pathway. All the colour drained from Steph's face, and she swayed. Worried she was about to faint, Tabbie rushed towards her. 'Are you okay?' She grabbed Steph's arms. 'Try taking a deep breath.'

Joe's exotic cinnamony aftershave alerted her senses. She nudged Steph to sit on the couch. *Thank God. Joe's arrived.* She glanced at the door… but the person staring back at her wasn't Joe or Warren.

It was Jason.

$\mathcal{S}$TEPHANIE

Steph locked eyes with Jason and stood up, legs shaking. Her mind raced. *Warren?* Fear gripped her.

'That guy—' Stephanie pointed. Her throat constricted. 'Dangerous.'

'Looks like the local officers have that sorted,' said a well-dressed man standing beside Jason.

'Did he hurt you?' Jason clenched his jaw.

Stephanie opened the door and stepped out past Jason to see Warren getting pushed into the back of a police van. She wanted to yell at Jason. *Who are you to question if someone has hurt me?* She turned to run inside but stopped. Joe and someone else were walking towards her.

She didn't want to deal with them all at the same time.

Warren.

Jason.

Joe.

At least Warren had been taken care of.

She just wanted to close the door and gather her thoughts, but the well-dressed man spoke. 'I think you are aware Jason is in a—'

'Jason.' The name stuck in her throat like someone had punched the wind out of her.

'I couldn't tell you I was coming. They wouldn't let me.' He motioned to the man behind him. 'I only want to see you and Lola. Then I'll leave. Looks like you have company.'

Joe hung back, his face questioning, confused.

Steph's shoulders tensed. She looked from Tabbie to Joe, to the well-dressed man who appeared to have official ID clipped on his suit pants. She looked back to Jason.

'Please accept our apologies for arriving unannounced. We were unable to advise you for security reasons.' The words swirled around her ears like a tornado trying to take her down. 'I believe you have a child Jason would like to meet.'

'I know it's too much to expect you to come back to me after all I put you through.' Jason's voice softened as he stepped closer to her. She shuddered with fear watching his hand reach towards her face as if in slow motion. Her arms flung up to protect her face. 'Hey, I'm sorry.' He pulled back. 'I'm sorry. I wish I could have come back sooner to apologise. I'm not going to hurt you. I just miss you so much. I want to be your protector, but it looks like you've found a bunch of guys willing to take my place.' Jason glanced at Joe and the guy standing behind him.

Steph pulled at her fingernails, trying to stop her hands from trembling. She fixed her gaze on Jason, unnerved. Even with the police there. No, she could never trust him again.

'Is our baby here?' A smile tickled Jason's lips as he moved forward. 'I just want to see her.'

'Steph, you don't have to let him inside.' Tabbie had fire in her eyes as she moved beside Steph.

'Maybe we should come back.' Joe sounded different, unsure.

Steph's head throbbed. Did she really have a choice whether Jason saw Lola or not? They could have dinner with Joe any time. Maybe it was best if he came back. She nodded and signalled for Jason to follow her.

$\mathcal{T}$ABBIE

We? Who was with Joe? As Jason and the gentleman followed Steph to the bedroom, Tabbie edged closer to the door to gain a better view of who was outside.

Her breath caught in her chest. Her feet were suddenly heavy like she wore heavy moon boots. Her gaze locked on those familiar intense eyes. Eyes she'd dreamed of over and over and over. His skin was deeply tanned and his unruly hair even messier than she remembered. 'Man, bad timing,' Danny's voice punctuated the air. 'We'll come back another time.' They turned to walk away.

No! Don't leave! Tabbie screamed the words in her mind until they pierced her racing heart. 'Don't go…' The words were barely a whisper. He hadn't heard her.

'Please don't wake her.' Steph's voice came from behind her. 'She's in a routine. She's happier that way.'

'Can I come back when she's awake?' Jason asked.

'No.' Steph shook her head.

Tabbie blinked and somehow Joe was back at the door. 'I'll see you tomorrow, Steph,' he called from outside.

'Please… stay.' Tabbie trembled and fumbled at the door handle. The world was spinning in front of her. She could only see

Joe turning to leave. Danny? But there was no one at the door. *Did I just imagine him?*

$\mathcal{S}$TEPHANIE

Lola stirred.

'Okay, you've seen her. Now can you leave before you wake her.' Steph's voice was quiet but firm.

'But Steph—' Jason pleaded.

Lola grizzled, rolling over she opened her eyes then closed them again.

'Shh. I asked you not to wake her.' Steph moved away from the bedroom. 'Can you come out here? Please?'

'Steph, I had to disappear to keep us all safe. I'm her dad. She needs to know who I am. Because of our baby, we'll always be family.' Jason's voice was tender. He looked outside, as if glaring at someone, but no one was there. His body language didn't match his tone.

Steph cringed at Jason's comment. A pang of disappointment sat in her soul, knowing Joe had left. Perhaps it was for the best. He'd want nothing to do with her after this.

'I'm sorry, Ms Stronge.' The officer held Jason's arm and guided him outside. 'Would you prefer we come back when the baby is awake?'

'No! He asked if could see her, and he's seen her.' Steph faced Jason. 'Now leave. I don't want to talk to you again. I don't want to see you again.'

'Well, there's no mistaking she's mine.' Jason looked towards the road.

'Just go. Please.' Steph followed his gaze. Joe was still there, on the footpath, with the other guy. They hadn't left.

'Maybe we can talk when everyone else isn't around before I head back.' Jason's voice softened again.

'No. You've proved you're alive. You've seen Lola.' Her heart pounded. She rubbed the dull throb in her temples. Did he really think he could talk her round this time?

'You can't keep me out of her life.' Jason stepped forward, pointing a finger at Steph's face, his knuckles white.

Steph turned and retreated inside as the gentleman grabbed Jason's arm and pulled him away. Memories flooded back of him shoving her. He hadn't changed. He never would.

'Thank you for your cooperation, Ms Stronge,' the gentleman called over his shoulder. 'Any further communication can go through mediation, if you'd prefer.'

'Yeah, I would. Thanks.' She bit her lip. He didn't deserve any more of her tears.

Shoes scuffed the path at her door. *Joe. And his friend.*

'Are you okay?' Concern was written all over Joe's face.

'Sorry. I'm sure you didn't expect a drama when you offered to bring dinner.' Steph pressed her hand against her head.

Joe's friend held up a plastic bag filled with takeaway containers. Tabbie couldn't take her eyes off him.

'Okay, so that was Jason? Lola's dad? Who was the other guy, the one the cops dragged away?' Joe's questions held no judgement or accusation. His tone emanated warmth and his eyes somehow threw a comforting blanket over her as he waited for her to reply. Suddenly she felt safe in his presence.

'Long story. I'd rather not go into it right now.' She looked past him. 'And you are?'

'You haven't met?' Joe asked.

'Don't think so.'

'Steph, this is Danny.'

'Hi. Sorry to turn up uninvited.'

     Spiralling Solo

This wasn't a dream.

She wasn't seeing things.

She was awake.

This is real.

He is here.

Danny is here.

Right in front of me.

Her breath shortened. She wasn't sure whether to hug him or wait.

'Hi.' He lifted his hand and gestured a slight wave to Tabbie. 'Hope you like Thai.'

Tabbie closed her eyes for a moment then opened them again. *He's still here.* She curled her fingers until her fingernails indented in her palms.

Danny stepped forward and touched Tabbie's arm, sliding his hand down until his fingers linked with hers. A warm tingle darted through every cell in her body. All the anger she'd held towards him disintegrated. 'Um… ' Breathless, Tabbie tried to form words to speak.

'I could stand here and look at you all night.' He glanced from her face down to her toes and back up again.

Warm tingles ran through her spine. 'We need to talk.'

'We'll be back in a minute.' Danny glanced at the others then gripped her hand and led her outside.

'Can you leave the food?' Joe said. 'I'm kind of hungry.'

'Sure.' Danny handed over the bag. 'We'll be back soon.'

'Take as long as you like.' Joe smiled. 'No guarantees there'll be any left when you return.'

Danny waved at Joe and laughed, but his gaze remained on Tabbie.

Her whole body tingled.

'Were either of those guys friends of yours?'

Tabbie shook her head.

'Right,' he said like she'd given him good news. 'Great.'

They walked a few metres down the path when Danny stopped. He pulled Tabbie to his chest and leaned down. He gently pressed his lips to hers.

First kiss. She relaxed in his arms. His touch was long and soft until passion fired between them. Tabbie pulled away, her head spinning. She fought to catch her thoughts. How could he just turn up out of the blue and kiss her?

'Why didn't you reply to my emails?' She took a step back.

'I did. Yesterday.'

'I mean before that.' Her voice trembled as she fought to control her emotions.

'I couldn't for a long time. Then I wanted to surprise you.'

'But I thought it was over.' The lump in her throat expanded.

'Did you? I didn't have internet access, and we had to go through a computer operator. It was awkward.'

'Oh.' A computer operator? 'How long are you here?'

'A week.'

'When did you fly in?' She swallowed, clenched her teeth.

'I came straight here.' He pulled her into a hug.

'You came straight here?' Her heart turned into a gooey mess as she turned her head and rested her cheek on his chest. His heartbeat raced in sync with hers. Tears formed in her eyes until one escaped and rolled down the curve of her face.

'Well, I had a shower at Joe's first. I couldn't wait any longer. I would have loved for you to come and visit Uganda, but it's been so volatile there. You wouldn't have been safe.'

'But you're going back?' She clung to him, not wanting to let him go. *A week isn't enough time.*

'Yeah, there's more work I'd like to get done before I move back here.'

'If it's that dangerous...' She looked up as another tear escaped.

He nodded and gently wiped her tears with his thumb.

She needed more answers. It wasn't like their first long-winded conversations just after he'd moved away. She took in his face and stopped at his mouth. Words could wait. If he was only here for a week, she needed to taste his kiss again. She leaned in again and kissed him until their passion was too hot for public display.

Chapter Fifty-five

Stephanie

'How long have you known about Danny coming home?' Steph leaned back on the couch, exhausted.

'A couple of weeks.' Joe sat on the other end of the couch. 'He asked me to keep an eye on Tabbie.'

'Tabbie did mention that—'

'Yep. Until she told me to go away. I had to keep the secret, but deep down I was hoping to spend more time with you as well.'

A warm flush crept up Steph's neck.

'You know Tabbie thought it was over?' Her mind wandered to Jason. She hoped mediation would mean she didn't have to see him again.

'Wow, I didn't realise that.' Joe raised his eyebrows. 'Hopefully they're sorting it out.'

His small talk pulled Steph's thoughts back into the room. She looked at her hands. The nail polish had chipped. The need to pull at her fingernails wasn't there while she was talking to Joe. She'd

     Spiralling Solo

wanted to kick that habit for years. Steph took a minute to be aware of everything around her. She realised the mindfulness thing was coming to her without thinking about it now.

'I'm raving, and you've stopped listening.' Joe pressed his lips together with the hint of a smile.

'Sorry. I was thinking.' She let her hands fall into her lap.

'I'm sorry, too. It's been a pretty full-on night. Would you rather we left?'

'No, please stay.' She wanted to grab him. She needed a hug. Her trust in him was growing, but she held herself back.

'I'll grab some water.'

'Thanks.' *Water.* Yes, that was what she needed.

Water really was all she felt like drinking. Since she'd had the bad boy revelation while choreographing, she hadn't thought about an alcoholic drink. Not even with Jason and Warren turning up.

The crunch of pebbles outside pushed Steph back on her feet, and her stomach cramped up. She released her breath and relaxed when she saw Danny and Tabbie velcroed together, arms wrapped around each other's waists. Just them. No one else. After they'd come through the door, she locked it behind them.

'Let's eat.' Joe pulled the lids off the plastic containers. 'I'm famished.'

'So you didn't eat it all without us?' Danny shoved Joe's shoulder gently as he began to fill his plate.

'Hey, hold up.' Joe shoved him back. 'Where are your manners? Ladies first.'

Steph tensed but told herself to relax. They were just mucking around. She hoped no one noticed how jumpy she was. The scent of ginger and garlic mixed with Joe's aftershave left Steph lightheaded, almost like she was intoxicated. She drank the rest of her water then filled her plate. 'Drinks anyone? I've only got water.' She glanced outside. No one was there. The police had Jason and Warren. There was nothing for her to worry about.

'Water is fine with me,' Danny said.

Maybe Tabbie was on to a good thing with these church people who didn't need alcohol. If alcohol was available, would she be tempted? She didn't know.

TABBIE

Danny's scent continued to thrill and invade Tabbie's senses. It was even more exotic than Joe's. Or was it the same but smelt more exotic on him? His biceps stretched the fabric of his t-shirt every time he moved. She tried to steer her vision away but failed. Her insides quivered whenever he brushed against her.

Crazy. She'd gone from angry to ridiculously mushy-gushy in love in half a second. Now she'd tasted his kiss, how was she going to live without it for another year?

With dinner finished, Danny held Tabbie's hand, gazing at her.

'Why don't you drive Tabbie home then come back and pick me up?' Joe nudged Danny's arm.

That sounded like the perfect plan to Tabbie. She'd take all the time she could with Danny while he was there, except she didn't want Steph to be alone after what had just happened.

'Just behave yourselves.' Joe grinned and winked.

'Thanks, but I'm staying here for the night.' Heat rushed up Tabbie's neck and into her cheeks.

'Oh.' Danny was already standing, keys in hand. 'How about ice cream?'

Joe laughed. 'I'm in.'

'Come help me pick?' Danny asked Tabbie.

'Sure.' She didn't have to be asked twice. She nearly tripped over her feet until she fell into step with him. Her fingers entwined with his as she savoured every moment.

'I wish we could spend more time together while I'm here, but I've got to catch up with family, and my mates will be dirty at me if

I don't make time to see them.' Danny opened the car door for her.

'Oh.' She slid into the seat. Was she being brushed aside to make room for everyone else in Danny's life?

He closed the door then walked around the front of the car to the driver's seat. She watched his jaw tighten then relax. They were both silent for a few minutes. Tabbie wanted to tell him she needed to see more of him while he was in the country but didn't want to sound like a needy girlfriend.

'Maybe we could hang out on Saturday.' He glanced at her as they stopped at the traffic lights. 'Can you take a day off study?'

'The whole day?' Her heart raced at the thought. She'd drop school in a second if it meant time with Danny.

'Yep, the *whole* day.' He grinned.

'I'd love to spend the day with you.' Warmth rushed through her veins. She couldn't stop smiling as they walked through the shop to the ice cream section. She shivered when the air from the freezer hit her arms. Danny wrapped his arms around her, and she melted against him.

When they arrived back at Steph's, Danny rushed around to Tabbie's door.

'Can you come to youth group?'

'Not this time.' He cupped her cheek in his hand. 'Beautiful Tabbie.'

She leaned in as he kissed her on her forehead before brushing his lips against hers. But it was over too soon. She wanted more.

'Right.' He leaned away. 'The ice cream will melt if we stay out here too long, and I'll turn into a pumpkin if I don't get some sleep soon.'

'That could be fun.' Tabbie forced a smile. 'I'd like to see the pumpkin version of you.'

The rustle of a plastic bag outside grabbed Steph's attention. She jumped.

'Are you okay?' Joe asked.

'Did you hear that?' Steph chewed on a chipped fingernail.

'What?'

'Is someone outside?'

'I'll check.' Joe rushed to the door.

She felt like an idiot and shuddered.

'Just those two who were meant to be getting us ice cream. It might be a little defrosted by the time they come in. Are you sure you and Tabbie will be okay here tonight?'

She nodded. 'Sorry. I guess I'm being paranoid.'

'That's understandable. You thought Jason was dead, didn't you?'

'Until I heard from him a few days ago.' Steph clenched her jaw. 'I want nothing more to do with him.'

'Who would? He sounds like a complete thug.' Joe didn't take his gaze off her.

As caring and caressing as Joe's eyes were, a dull throb intensified in her head. She rubbed her temples. She needed darkness. The lights made the pain worse. 'I think I'm getting a migraine.' She stood. 'I need to go lie down for a few minutes.'

'Yeah, of course. Can I get you some painkillers or something?' Joe put his arm around her and led her to her bedroom.

'I ran out last week.' *Oh no, what's happening?* Would Joe turn out to be yet another guy trying to take advantage? She could barely open her eyes. *Tabbie. Where are you?*

'When Danny and Tabbie return, I'll go buy you some painkillers. Then we'll head off and let you rest.'

She looked at him. He really was helping her to her room. Nothing more. Joe closed her door as she pulled the doona up over her head. In the darkness, the pain began to dissipate.

Steph lay in bed with her eyes squeezed shut. Was he interested, or had dinner been all about Danny and Tabbie? It was stupid to think anything would ever eventuate. Why would he want to date a girl who carried so much baggage? How did she go from everything being fine after the police left to panicking and getting a migraine? Maybe she should go back out to Joe. A cup of tea might help.

Somewhere between deciding to go back out and rolling over, she must have fallen asleep.

The low-pitched rumble of the electric jug woke her. She blinked in the fully lit room. *Tabbie?* Steph rolled over sending dust flecks into the rays of sun streaming through her window. Thankfully the pounding in her head hadn't stayed to see the daylight.

'Mum, mum,' Lola called.

Steph swung her legs over the edge of the bed, planted her feet on the floor and walked out of her bedroom to a content smiling face. How long had Lola been awake?

'Pooh, you smell, let's get you changed.' Steph reached down to pick up Lola.

'Yeah, sorry.' A male voice made her jump.

Steph spun around to see Joe in the kitchen.

'I could smell it, but I've never changed a baby before and didn't want to wake you.'

'Oh.' Steph scooped Lola into her arms, her heart still racing after hearing Joe's voice.

Why is he here? What have I missed? Did he sleep over? She took Lola into her room to change her and tried to recall what happened last night. The migraine. Going to bed. No alcohol, so she couldn't blame a blackout.

'Why are you here?' she called as she reached for another wipe.

'I was worried about you and had a chat to Tabbie. I thought I'd let her and Danny spend a bit more time together, so I decided to stay.'

'Oh.' He'd stayed the whole night. Where had he slept? She swallowed then closed her eyes until Lola squirmed on the change mat. How deep a sleep had she actually been in? Why hadn't she heard anything?

After she'd changed Lola, she grabbed her phone and sent Tabbie a text.

Why did you let Joe stay? Arghghghgh!!! What did you tell him?

Nothing you wouldn't want him to know.

Y is he still here?

He's still there? I don't know. Ask him if he's there. LOL

'Hey, Steph,' Joe called.

Steph returned to the lounge to find Joe folding Tabbie's blanket. She glared at him.

'Are you annoyed that I stayed?'

She shook her head. Shrugged. She was confused. Too many questions whirled around in her mind.

'How about I run home and have a shower, then come back and give you a lift into the studio?'

'That's okay. Francine will be here soon, and she has the baby seat. You didn't need to stay.' Steph suddenly felt like she'd just had a one-night stand, only the guy hadn't touched her other than help her to bed.

Lola squealed and pointed towards her toys on the floor. Steph put her down to let her play.

'I don't think you realise how strong you are. It blew me away last night to see how well you coped. I know this is bad timing after last night, but I want to see you… more than just at the studio. That was the whole reason for us coming over for dinner. I'm enjoying getting to know you.'

'But what about… my past?' Steph faced him. Feet planted where she stood. How much of her past did he know?

'It's exactly that, in the past. You can leave it there.'

'But Jason has dangerous friends.'

'It sounds like the cops have it under control.'

Steph clenched her teeth. She wasn't convinced they did.

'I'm not after an all-in serious relationship. I just want to get to know you outside of work. How does that sound?'

   Spiralling Solo

'But what about Lola?' Could she really trust him?

'She's a cutie. You'll have to teach me how to change a nappy. Then I can help out.'

Do I have a say in this? It's too complicated. Too messy. Too much to think about.

'I'd better get going.'

Steph nodded and looked into his eyes. Her heart warmed. As he walked towards her, she didn't know what he was about to do. Her body tingled all over as he wrapped his arms around her. She felt his breath on her head.

He pulled away and looked down at her. 'Is that okay? If we spend more time together?'

'Um, I guess.' Something about Joe made her feel safe.

'Mum, mum,' Lola pulled on her leg.

Steph picked her baby up. Lola smiled at Joe.

'Maybe she likes the idea.' Joe grinned and headed towards the door. 'Maybe I could get a baby seat and pick you up in the mornings.'

A siren grabbed her attention, reminding her of Jason. No, if she was going to date Joe, it would be on her terms. 'I'd rather Francine pick me up.'

'No worries.' He shrugged but lingered at the door.

'Think I'll be Gabriella's offsider today.' Why did she tell him that?

'Why's that? She hasn't mentioned anything to me.'

'She gave me a warning yesterday.' Steph wanted to pull the words back.

'I'll have a chat to her.'

'No, it's okay. I'll work it out with her.'

The last thing she wanted was to cause tension between Joe and Gabriella. She'd noticed Gabriella's tummy had grown somewhat, and so had her shortness with Steph and the students.

Joe's phone buzzed. 'Danny's out the front. I'd better run. See you at the studio.' He beamed his adorable smile, sending her heart to mush.

Chapter Fifty-six

GABRIELLA TOOK THE FULL-TIME CLASS and worked them hard. Then she expected Steph to learn every routine for the classes she was assisting with in the afternoon, all before the girls arrived. Joe invited her out for a cold drink, but she had to say no. He returned with two large cups, breaking her concentration.

Later in the afternoon, she was grateful she'd spent the time learning the routines. Otherwise, the sassy girls would have crucified her. Joe entered in the middle of one class. She lost her train of thought, lost where they were in the dance and one of the more confident girls came to the front and took over as half of the class snickered and giggled. She tried to gain their attention when Gabriella appeared in her peripheral vision.

'I shouldn't have left you alone.' Gabriella stormed over to stop the music.

'Gabby, can we have a word?' Joe asked.

'Can it wait? Obviously I have to stay here, or these girls won't learn anything.' She turned back to the class.

Steph felt Joe's gaze on her but couldn't bear to look up.

'Positions, girls! Let's start from the top.' Gabriella glared at Stephanie and started the music again.

Steph left the room to get a drink of water. As she swigged from her bottle she checked her phone.

Francine had texted hours ago, followed by another—

That wasn't going to work. Tabbie had given her keys back. She was texting Francine when Gabriella called her. 'Sorry, I just have to send a text.'

'Surely it can wait.'

'It can't. I have to organise Lola.'

'If you can't organise your life, maybe this isn't the right position for you.'

She wasn't going to cry in front of Gabriella. She wasn't. She wasn't. Steph clenched her teeth, swallowed and looked up at the ceiling. Her lip quivered.

Gabriella went back to the class. Steph knew she had to push her emotions aside.

she messaged.

She hit *Send* and jumped when someone tapped her shoulder.

'Sorry. Didn't mean to startle you. Everything okay?' Joe asked.

'Actually, I just got a message from Francine. She can't pick me up today—'

'Too easy. I'll drop you home.' Joe's smile melted her insides.

Her anxiety disappeared. Something about Joe calmed her.

Steph stayed out of Gabriella's way, grateful to see the back of her as she left for a doctor's appointment. Moments later, Tabbie stuck her head in the door. 'Just running in to grab the keys. Can Joe drop you home? Or are you catching a bus?'

'Joe can.' Steph smiled. 'Do you want to hang round till I'm finished?'

'I could, but Mum's outside ready to drop me at yours. Plus, it'll be easier to look after Lola there.'

'I'll walk you out.'

'Have you left Joe inside on his own?' Gabriella met them in the doorway.

'Give Lola a cuddle for me. I have to go back inside.'

Gabriella glared at Steph. Then she left again, holding a piece of paper in her hand.

Was this how working with Gabriella was always going to be? What was it with her? Was she jealous?

Steph pushed it out of her mind and enjoyed the rest of the afternoon, working alongside Joe. They closed up together in a sweet peacefulness while Gabriella wasn't there. He opened the car door for her. She could get used to that. He offered to put her bag into the back seat. She could get used to his help as well. 'Thanks.' She handed it to him then smiled, realising she wasn't flirting. She was simply happy.

'What?'

'Nothing.' She laughed at herself and climbed into the car.

The fact that sex hadn't even come up allowed her to enjoy the moment rather than thinking about what was coming. Yes, she could get used to dating Joe.

When they pulled up outside her block of units, Joe jumped out of the car and ran around to open her door. 'I'll walk you in.'

'You don't have to. Tabbie's waiting for me.'

'I won't come in. I'd just like to walk you there.'

She didn't protest further. It was sweet, and she enjoyed his old-fashioned gentlemanly ways.

A police car pulled in behind Joe's car. Steph's breath caught in her throat. *Now what?* The car took off again with the siren blasting.

'You okay?' Joe watched the police car turn at the end of the street.

Steph nodded. Hopefully one day she wouldn't fear every police car. She reminded herself she had no reason to avoid the cops. They approached her front door, and she knew she didn't want the moment to end. 'Would you like to come in?'

'Sure,' he said.

She smiled and opened the door. 'Tabbie, we're home.'

The moment wasn't quite what she was expecting. Tabbie handed Lola to her, poo running down her leg.

'I'll run her a bath,' Tabbie said. 'Can you deal with that mess?

'Nappies don't always catch it all.' Steph rolled her eyes, not ready for Joe to leave.

'I'll see you tomorrow,' he said.

'Thanks for the ride,' was all Steph could manage to get out.

*T*ABBIE

Tabbie dried her hair and applied a light coat of mascara and lip gloss. She checked her hair and the time. Nearly nine. Danny would be there soon, and she couldn't wait.

She struggled not to be annoyed he couldn't find more time to be with her. Why couldn't he stay more than a week? He hadn't told her where they were going. Would jeans and a t-shirt work? She hoped so.

'Tabbie,' Steph called. 'I hear footsteps.'

She glanced out the window. He wore shorts and a singlet.

'Hey,' she said as he arrived at the door. 'Should I get changed?'

'You look amazing. What you're wearing is fine.' He took a moment to say hello to Steph and Lola before taking her hand and leading her to the car.

'Your hand's sweaty,' Tabbie said, not wanting to let go but feeling awkward.

'I thought it was coming from your hand.' He laughed and dropped her hand to wipe his palm on his shorts before opening the car door. 'I guess today is special, our first real date.'

They sat in the car and Danny took a loud, deep breath. 'Maybe we should pray for God's blessing over today.' He took her hand and began to pray.

Tabbie knew she should be listening and agreeing with his prayer, but all that came to mind was…

It's here and now

He's here and now

The moment I've waited for

for more than a year

Is here right now

It's freaking me out

Contain the fear

Hold the excitement

I can't even talk

Overwhelmed in the moment.

'It's going to be a great day.' Danny started the car.

She tried to slow her racing heart, taking long breaths as she watched the streets whizz by. Danny turned the music up. She'd never heard it before. He must have sensed her wonder.

'Do you like it?'

She nodded.

'It's a band a friend in Uganda introduced me to.'

'They're Christian.' She realised as she listened to the lyrics and watched his fingers tap the steering wheel in time with the bass. 'You still play?'

'I learnt acoustic guitar and drums while I was away.'

'Did you take your bass with you?'

'Nah. I knew I wouldn't have access to electricity in some places.'

'Tell me more about life over there.'

Spiralling Solo

'It's pretty amazing. The people… they have such joy for the simple things. Their lives are so hard compared to ours. It's incredible they have such peace when they could be living in fear every day. Where my parents are now is dangerous. People go missing all the time.'

'Are you worried about them?'

'God will protect them. I have to trust that.'

'And you're going back?'

'Yeah. I've been helping develop education and sporting programs for the kids. With more education and knowledge, chances are they won't be trafficked. But without education, many of them are simply unaware, and that leaves them vulnerable.'

'The sport?'

'The games draw them in.'

'I hate that there's still slavery in the world. It needs to be wiped off the face of the earth.' Goosebumps ran through her body. What he was doing was huge, and she wanted to be part of it. 'I'd love to do missionary work, but…' *But what?* She only wanted to do it with him. *Does that disqualify me?*

'Maybe go somewhere less dangerous for your first trip.'

'What if I was with you?'

'It's really dangerous—especially for beautiful young girls like you, travelling alone would be… just no.'

'I could come back with you…' She glanced at him out of the corner of her eye. Her heart pounded as he smiled.

'Could you get your visa and flights organised in three days?'

'Probably not.'

'It won't be long, and I'll be back.'

'I hope it's not as long as this time.'

Chapter Fifty-seven

*T*ABBIE

'THE BEACH?' SHE ASKED when he pulled into the beachside carpark. 'But I haven't got my swimmers.'

'That's okay, we'll just go for a walk.' He turned the car off and faced her. 'You still running?'

'Um, about that—'

'Did you sprain your ankle again?'

'Not quite. Just rolled it.'

He laughed.

She sighed. She flexed her foot, wondering if she should start running again. She missed it.

Next minute, he was opening her door, drawing her into his arms. She tingled all over at the closeness of their bodies. He let go and reached for her hand. 'Ah, no longer sweaty.'

'Neither is yours.' She laughed. 'I think I like being with you. You're easy to talk to.'

'I think I like being with you too. And I am sorry I didn't keep in touch more often while I was gone.'

'You're going back too soon.' A lump formed in her throat at the thought of having to say goodbye.

'I am. Let's just enjoy today. We've got six whole hours together.'

She rolled up the bottom of her jeans, wishing she'd changed into a pair of shorts.

'How's your ankle feel? Not strong enough to walk on the sand?' He bent down and swooped his arm under her legs, lifting her off the ground.

'What are you doing?' she asked, laughing.

'Remember the time you hurt your ankle and I carried you?'

'But my ankle is fine.' Fire burned through her body with his strength.

'You're beautiful, you know that?'

She shrugged, blushing. 'But I'm capable of walking.'

He laughed again and carried her until they reached the water's edge where he gently lowered her onto the sand.

They walked the entire length of the beach, letting the wash of the waves lap their feet. No subject was left untouched. No conversation felt awkward. He'd been her best friend over the internet for months until he'd gone silent, and now he was here, in the flesh. The exact same person she'd typed hundreds of messages to.

'Are you getting hungry?' Danny stopped and pulled her into his arms.

She nodded as he kissed her. Though now they were kissing, food was the furthest thing from her mind. He let go, stepped back, and began to draw in the wet sand with his foot.

She read the words as he drew.

I

LOVE

YOU

TABBIE

WILL YOU … no way
MARRY … he wasn't, was he?
ME
WHEN I RETURN

Tears prickled as a lump formed in her throat. He scratched out a giant question mark then returned to her and dropped down onto both knees.

A wave crashed behind her, splashing cool water up to her knees, washing away half Danny's sand art.

Danny jumped up, laughing.

Was he joking or serious? Just as she went to ask, he raised his eyebrows, questioning.

She'd spent the last few months trying to get over him. She had to be honest. 'You realise I thought we were over?'

'I'm sorry I couldn't keep in touch.'

'I feel like we're just getting to know each other.'

'Really? I thought we knew everything about each other.'

He was right. They'd talked about everything. 'All that time I couldn't keep in touch, I was planning this. What I was hoping would be a perfect day. But I've missed the mark by an ocean, huh?'

'But… I'm not even eighteen yet. I don't think Mum and Dad would be okay with this.'

'Yeah, I thought of that.' He took a step closer to her. 'I wanted to be here for your birthday, but I couldn't time it right with the flights and everything.'

'Really?'

Tabbie's thoughts drifted back to the emails. Yeah, they were sweet but nothing had prepared her for a marriage proposal. She'd imagined this day would be like she'd watched in the movies. She'd imagined herself a little older. She'd imagined anticipating it coming. Never ever had she expected it to come out of the blue like this.

They were too young, weren't they? Plus, he'd be leaving again soon. Would he wait for her if she put him off today? If she said no,

Spiralling Solo

would the proposal be washed away forever like the waves washed away the words in the sand?

'I've spoken to your parents. We have their blessing—if we work in their preferred timeframe.' He took both of her hands as another wave crashed against their legs, saturating her jeans.

'When did you talk to them?' *Why didn't they say something?* Goosebumps broke out over her skin as he glanced from her eyes to her mouth then back to her eyes. Warmth rushed through her as he led her away from the waves. He raised his eyebrows. A curl of hair fell forward. Her heart thumped in her chest, betraying her. He was just so darn hot!

'Why didn't they tell me?' She reached out to push his distracting curl from his eyes.

'I wanted to surprise you. You've kind of left me hanging. Do you need to think about it?'

'But we're so young. Can't we live a little first?'

'It would be exciting to do things together.'

She shrugged. Her whole body trembled. How long would they be engaged?

'We wouldn't be getting married straight away. I'd like my parents to be here for the wedding.'

A confused nervous laugh bubbled inside until it ruptured the air. 'It's like you read my mind.'

He bent down and kissed her. Yeah, she could live with that kiss for the rest of her life.

'You're the only girl I want to kiss. You're the one I want to wake up beside every morning. You're the one I want to do life with. And if God leads us, the one I want to travel to the mission field with.'

She found herself nodding.

'So you feel the same?' he asked.

'Yeah.'

'Tabbie Moray, will you marry me?'

'Yes! Yes, I'd love to.'

He lifted her up and twirled her around.

She clasped her hands around his neck and kissed him over and over until she was completely out of breath.

'Let's go ring shopping.'

'Okay.' A stream of tears fell down her cheeks. Were they tears of joy, fear, or panic?

'I didn't want to presume you'd say yes.'

'You don't have much money.'

'You're right, I don't. That's why I chose the free proposal. I hope you're okay with that.'

She was. He could have taken her up in a hot air balloon and proposed. He could have taken her on a chopper ride. He could have taken her to a fancy five-star restaurant or even hired a limo and paid for a private dinner at a spot overlooking the city or the ocean. But he drew in the sand with his foot, and it was perfect.

She shivered.

'You have goosebumps.' He laughed as he rubbed her goose-pimpled arm.

Love. Yes, she loved him. She just wished this wasn't so rushed. She'd dreamed of marrying him and it wasn't like they were getting married tomorrow. She'd have time to process all her fears. Wouldn't she?

'You'd better keep in touch this time!'

He smiled. 'As often as I can, yes. Promise.'

Chapter Fifty-eight

Tabbie

'Can everyone make it?' Mum asked Tabbie.

'Joe and Steph will be late.' Tabbie counted on her fingers as she thought through everyone she'd invited. 'Jaya can't leave her granny.'

'Did you tell her the real reason for the party?'

'No, I haven't told anyone. I kind of wanted it to be a surprise. I thought an early eighteenth celebration would be enough to get them here *if* they really wanted to.' Truth was she felt awkward telling people about the engagement. She wasn't looking forward to everyone's reaction.

'Sure, love. It will be a wonderful surprise for everyone.' Her mother opened the oven to check on the roast, then lifted the lid off the white box on the bench. 'Come look at this.'

'Wow!' Tabbie said as she read the words on the decorated cake.

Priscilla and Shelly arrived first. Then a few of Danny's friends, and finally Danny.

'So should we tell them?' He reached into his pocket.

'Let's wait until Joe and Steph arrive.' She took a deep breath in and held it. She was stalling. *Fear.* She released the breath and forced a smile.

'Happy birthday!' Steph screamed as she swung the door open, Joe following her. 'Sorry we're a bit late.'

'Mumma,' Lola squealed from the highchair.

The door rattled, and everyone turned.

'What have we missed?' Pete walked through with Phoebe on his arm.

Tabbie went to welcome Pete, but Danny gently pulled her back, the small velvet box now open in his hand. He slipped the diamond solitaire ring out and pushed it onto Tabbie's ring finger.

'No way!' Steph dropped her bag and rushed to give Tabbie a hug.

Danny's friends looked shocked, but Joe had a huge smile on his face. Tabbie guessed he already knew. Pete whooped, and Dad tapped his glass with his knife to grab everyone's attention.

'Welcome to Danny's farewell, Tabbie's eighteenth, and Danny and Tabbie's engagement dinner.'

Everyone cheered.

Tabbie smiled. Nervous, excited, but now a little unsure.

$\mathcal{S}$TEPHANIE

While everyone was distracted, Steph grabbed Tabbie and took her into the kitchen. 'Are you sure about this?'

'No! I'm scared as anything.'

'Do you love him?'

'I thought I did. And when I didn't hear from him, I thought I didn't. And then when I saw him again… But right now? I'm just confused.'

'You're scared.'

'Was I stupid saying yes?'

'Maybe.' Steph shrugged. 'But, maybe getting married young is right for you two. Heaps of people have, and it's worked out fine.'

'But heaps of others have got divorced.'

'Is there anything you don't love about him?'

Tabbie thought for a moment. 'Only that he didn't keep in touch.'

'What is it that you love about him?'

'I don't really know how to pinpoint it. Every time we're together, I can't imagine not being near him.'

'If that's the case, maybe you've made the right decision.'

Tabbie took a deep breath and nodded.

'I can't believe you didn't tell me he'd asked you to marry him!' Steph threw her arms around Tabbie, hugging her. 'We could have had this conversation before tonight.'

'You're right. I'm sorry.'

'Have you set a date?'

'No. He doesn't know when his parents will be back. It'll be more than a year.'

'So you have a year to get used to the idea. If you're still unsure, opt out. Go enjoy him while he's still here.'

'You're right.' Tabbie rushed back to Danny's side.

The crowd moved in to sit around the extended table. Joe jumped into the seat beside Steph and reached for her hand. A warm tingle rushed around her body. Phoebe sat on her other side. Maybe she could get to know her now that she was well and truly over her crush.

'The cops rang today,' she said so only Joe would hear. 'I didn't want to talk about it at the studio. They've assured me Jason won't return. They've served him restraining orders and told me to contact them if I hear from him.'

'That's great. Did they say anything about Warren?'

'Yes, he's been given five years in prison.' She smiled. 'So, I guess there's no need for anyone to stay over anymore.'

'Are you sure?' He winked.

'There might be exceptions.' She felt heat rush up her neck as she spoke. He nodded, smiled then they both tuned back to the conversation around the table.

'We won't set a date until my parents can return.'

Tabbie's smile didn't exude joy, but she seemed content.

Steph leaned back in her chair letting her arm rest against Joe. Things were going to work out for Tabbie and Danny after all, and the guy sitting beside her was the sweetest gentleman she could ever hope for. She'd stopped resisting and relaxed against Joe's shoulder, knowing she'd fallen for the tall, handsome dancer.

Maybe, just maybe everything was going to work out for her as well.

Spiralling Solo

You were never designed to slip into depression
or have days of darkness.
Feeling down or depressed is not a weakness,
but a reality in our world.
Beyond Blue and Black Dog Institute
both have an abundance of
information and guidance
on their websites.
I urge you to seek help.
There is a way out of the darkness,
tomorrow is a new day and may just be the day
you turn a corner.

Beyond Blue **beyondblue.org.au**
Black Dog Institute **blackdoginstitute.org.au**

       Spiralling Solo

Keep in Touch...

Visit
MichelleDennisEvans.com
to connect with Michelle on social media

If you've enjoyed reading this book,
please leave a review on Amazon and Goodreads!

Thank You...

To my daughters, my son and my husband—
you bring joy and laughter into every day. I am so
thankful we are family. I am also thankful to my parents
who first recognised my gift for writing back in my early
primary years when I chose to write dialogue for my
spelling sentences. Thank you to Roald Dahl who ignited
my passion for reading.

A huge thank-you to all of my critique partners and beta readers.
Some stayed with me right through the novel and some helped
with just a few pages. You are all appreciated, and I am scared
if I start naming you, I'll miss someone.
I mustn't forget my local cheer squad and my online friends —
your support is welcomed and appreciated.

And above all I am thankful to my Creator, the giver of life,
the one who showers me with crazy favour and ridiculous grace.

Cause...

I am passionate about seeing girls and women pick up the pieces and move forward in life after major upheaval. One of my favourite local organisations that help to facilitate this is **Yahweh House.**

A portion of sales from *Spiralling Solo* will go towards supporting organisations that help women and girls.

Also by Michelle

Spiralling
Out of Control

Book 1 in the Spiralling Series

Print book available at online
bookstores, and
MichelleDennisEvans.com

Spiralling
Out of the Shadow

Book 2 in the Spiralling Series

Print book available at online
bookstores, and
MichelleDennisEvans.com

Sink, Drift, or Swim

A young adult novel in free verse

Print book available at online bookstores, and MichelleDennisEvans.com

Life Inspired

A beautiful collection of poems

eBook available at MichelleDennisEvans.com or Amazon

www.ingramcontent.com/pod-product-compliance
Lightning Source LLC
Chambersburg PA
CBHW071726190726
48292CB00003B/625